The Invasion of Britain

August - September 1941

A Misfit Squadron Novel

Simon Brading

First published 2025

This edition published 2025

ISBN: 978-1-917470-10-0

PROLOGUE

21st August 1941

This was what he lived for. This moment, just before, when his heart was pumping and his every sense was heightened in anticipation of what was to come. When he was sure that he had done everything he could to be prepared and all that was left to do was to was complete the job - when his lines were learned and the rehearsal was done, when he stepped on stage at the award ceremony, when the silk dress dropped to the floor in front of him, when his finger curled on the trigger and applied pressure...

It was the best feeling in the world and he couldn't help but have a wide smile in place as he waited the final few seconds until he was sure that everything was perfectly in place and ready.

He rolled his shoulders, clenching and unclenching his hands to release any tension that might have built up while he'd been waiting, then took a deep breath and nodded.

The door of the aircraft opened at the flight attendant's push and there was a roar as the hero of the Prussian people, Hans Gruber, stepped out into bright sunshine and onto the small platform at the top of the steps that had been rolled into place for him. Even though he was half blind from the transition from darkness into light he lifted his hand to wave, flashing his perfect teeth as cameras clicked and whirled, basking in the adoration that was rightfully his. He didn't need to see the crowd to imagine the women, and undoubtedly a few men, swooning as he turned his eyes their way, but, unfortunately, he was expected at the palace, so there was no time to linger and find out whether anyone in the crowd was worthy of his further attention.

He wiped away a few imaginary tears, pretending to be overcome with emotion to be back home and to have been welcomed so warmly, while in reality he was taking the opportunity to give his eyes a quick rub to hasten their adjustment to the brightness of the summer sun. The large black blob on the taxiway next to the aircraft now resolved itself into an extremely large open-topped Imperial autocar and he gave a last wave to the crowd that had gathered to greet him at Tempelhof Airport, then trotted down the steps to it and leapt in athletically. The sirens of the motorcycle police escort sounded as they pulled away and he turned his brilliant smile to the cameras one last time as the autocar smoothly followed them out of the airport's gates and onto the wide boulevard that ran through the new centre of Berlin, between the monumental white marble buildings. There were cheering crowds lining the route as well and his arm soon ached from waving, but he kept it up, his smile still plastered in place; being popular with the people had brought him far and no harm would come from remaining so. Quite the opposite.

He had no idea why he'd been called to Berlin so urgently, but it couldn't be anything bad, otherwise he'd have been rushed in and out in secret and not have his arrival made into such a spectacle. There were rumours of troops being moved around in secret in huge numbers in preparation for a big push, so perhaps he was being given a new command, perhaps even overall command of the attack, but it might only be another medal - an excuse to get him to Berlin so that he could do more public relations work. Whatever it was, he would smile, accept the accolades, film whatever they wanted him to film, take photographs however and with whoever they wanted and shake whatever hands were held out to him, all while getting some well-earned rest and relaxation in the nightclubs and luxury hotels.

Never let it be said that Hans Gruber didn't do his utmost for the Prussian Empire.

There were quite a few new propaganda posters hanging from the lamp posts and on the walls, alongside the old ones, with slogans he hadn't read before, like "Peace is Just Around the Corner!" and "Youth serves the Kaiser!", but, disappointingly, his face wasn't on any of them. Instead, there was a stylised and very flattering version of the Kaiser on some, which he thought was acceptable, but what looked like pictures of ordinary peasants on the rest, which he didn't.

He was careful not to let his disapproval show, though; that wouldn't fit with his public persona.

Even though the cavalcade went slowly to allow the people plenty of time to see their returning hero, it didn't take long to drive the two-kilometre length of the boulevard, from Tempelhof airport to the grand white marble palace that sat in the middle of the city on top of a small artificial hill. Gratifyingly, the Kaiser's personal secretary, a small and rather slimy man with round glasses and slicked back black hair, was waiting for him at the main entrance, flanked by an honour guard of ceremonially-dressed palace guardsmen and the man gave Gruber a curt bow as he stepped from the autocar.

'Herr Gruber. Welcome to Berlin.'

'Adolf.' Gruber replied, barely nodding in reply. 'Why am I here?'

The man smiled. 'All will become apparent in good time.' He held out his hand. 'This way, please.'

The secretary led the group into the palace, through the reception hall, up a wide staircase and into the main throne room. As large as a hangar, it had a massive domed roof high up overhead, a confection of glass and glowing white marble from which hung a dozen huge chandeliers. The walls were covered with gigantic red-painted wood panels, framed with gold leaf and covered in enormous paintings, the works of hundreds of years of masters, plundered from the galleries of the conquered nations of Europe. The focal point of the whole room, though, and what the eye couldn't help but wander towards, despite the wonders displayed on the walls and on plinths throughout the room, was the grand golden throne at the far end. It was on a wide platform, illuminated both by light focussed from the dome overhead and its own chandelier, and was raised about two metres above the floor so that it could be seen from everywhere in the room, even over the heads of a crowd, and so that its occupant could see everything and everyone in turn.

It was vacant at that moment, though, because the man who had sparked the conflict that was slowly and inexorably spreading to every corner of the globe was walking towards Gruber, the smile on his face as ostentatious and overlarge as the architecture he'd commissioned. He looked far older than his fifty-nine years, with his hair almost gone, deep lines furrowed in his forehead and large bags under his eyes, but there was an undeniable energy about him and a charisma to match Gruber's own.

'Hans!' Kaiser Wilhelm III called out as he approached. '*Wunderbar!* I'm glad you could make it!'

Gruber bowed smartly, clicking his heels together.

The Kaiser put both hands on Gruber's shoulders, slapping them down companionably and then shaking him gently. He locked eyes with him for the briefest of moments, then, keeping one hand where it was, he turned to address his other guests.

'The hero of the Prussian Empire! The hero of the Prussian people!'

There were at least five hundred people in the room, but the space had been designed to fit thousands, not hundreds, and the sound of their applause was lost in it. The vast majority of them were wearing normal, everyday clothes, like suits, dresses and a few quaint local costumes - the Kaiser liked to surround himself with what he called "common people" like architects, scientists, engineers and businessmen and preferred to keep the men of his armed forces where they were needed, consequently there were only a few military uniforms scattered here and there, most of whom would likely be men on leave. The Kaiser himself was dressed in a severe black three-piece suit and he too looked like the kind of person who would be at home in a bank or a courtroom rather than ruling almost half of the world.

Gruber barely had time to acknowledge the crowd's approval before the Kaiser was holding up his hand for silence.

'The list of well-deserved accolades that we have already heaped upon our beloved son is long and we seem to be running out of new ones to give him.' He paused and smiled indulgently as the people laughed. 'However,' he continued when it died down, 'there is one honour that I have been reluctant to bestow upon him as I have been afraid that it might bring upon him the burden of being unfairly compared to another aviator, an *incomparable* hero from the last war - that of the rank and privileges of a Baron. That changes today!'

He lifted his hands and two attendants stepped forwards. The Kaiser took a black silk sash from the box that one of them held open for him and placed it on Gruber, then the other attendant hung a fur-lined red velvet cloak around his shoulders.

'Congratulations, Baron Gruber.' The Kaiser announced to the room as he stepped back and led the applause.

Gruber smiled and looked out at the crowd of people. He gave them the barest of bows before turning to thank the Kaiser, but the man had already gone and he only just managed to catch a glimpse of him going through a door at the side of the room.

Rather than being disappointed, or feeling snubbed, Gruber's smile only widened further; with the Kaiser gone he was now the undisputed star of the show. There was nobody else at the party who would take any of the spotlight from him. Which was as it should be; this was the one accolade he'd been missing, the one he'd been angling for since the beginning of the war, dropping hints in as many ears as he could that he was the natural heir of von Richthofen and should be ranked accordingly.

Over the next half an hour, Gruber moved around the room from one group to another, not out of any desire to give as many people as possible the chance to meet him - he wasn't the Kaiser's pet to be put on display for the gratification of his sycophants - but rather because that was the best way to find a willing body to share his bed while he was in Berlin. The pickings in Spain had been meagre to say the least and it wasn't as if things had been much better in Italy, France, Belgium, Norway, or any of the other countries he had made his way through in the last couple of years. They were a far cry from Hollywoodland, where he had been spoilt for choice with so many beautiful people.

Unfortunately, there were very few likely-looking prospects. Almost none, in fact. Anyone even remotely interesting seemed to be married, which he didn't mind, of course, but they'd all brought their husbands with them, which didn't allow him much room to manoeuvre.

He was about to give up and start drinking in earnest - the Kaiser's schnapps was the finest in the world and would be a fairly adequate consolation prize - when he caught sight of a pair of bright blue eyes watching him from the side of the room. The eyes were shaded by long lashes and set in a face that wouldn't have looked out of place next to his on the silver screen, with luscious bright red lips standing out starkly on creamy skin and framed by golden hair that fell to her shoulders - that was usually a little too short for his liking, but on her it seemed right.

He smiled at her, giving her one of those movie star smiles that let her know that he'd seen her and liked what he saw, but then he turned back to the group he'd been talking to.

She would come to him.

They always came to him.

She didn't come, though, and the next time he managed to shoot an unobtrusive glance her way he, annoyingly, found her gone.

He extracted himself from the conversation he'd been in as soon as he could without being rude and wandered in a roundabout way towards where he'd seen her, searching for her in the groups he passed as he went, while trying not to make it too obvious that that was what he was doing.

There was no sign of her anywhere and he had resigned himself to returning to his original plan of getting drunk and passing the night that way when he turned and, instead of a servant with a tray of drinks, found himself looking into blue eyes.

'Herr Gruber,' she said in greeting, with a smile, 'or should I say, *Baron* Gruber.'

Gruber inclined his head graciously, a gesture he'd practised over and over for one of his more romantic roles where he played a humble post office pilot. 'Thank you, Frau...?'

'Fraulein. Fraulein Reitsch.'

'Pleased to meet you.'

'Likewise.'

She held out a hand and he took it, but when he started to bend over it she shook his sharply, then withdrew it.

He raised an eyebrow, but didn't comment and just straightened, as if he had intended just to bow.

'Are you a regular visitor to the palace, Fraulein Reitsch?'

'Only recently.'

He nodded and waited for her to elaborate or tell him how much he liked his flyvies or say how much she admired his work for the war effort or start gushing over how much of an honour it was for her or say one of the other things that anyone who ever met him couldn't wait to say, but she remained silent, just looking at him with those eyes and smiling faintly, as if she were amused by something.

'And what do you do?' he asked eventually. 'I mean,' he went on, waving his hand vaguely to encompass the people in the room, feeling the need to say more when her only reply was to raise an eyebrow slightly. 'Wilhelm enjoys surrounding himself with people who are useful, so I assume you are too, but in what field?'

'I work in aviation.'

'Really?' Gruber smiled, relieved that he would have something to talk about with her while he was charming her. While he could talk about himself for hours, something that most of the people he came across were more than happy for him to do, if she'd told him she was an accountant or an architect and ended up wanting some actual conversation he would have been lost for anything even remotely interesting to say. He leaned in to her and dropped his voice conspiratorially, 'what a coincidence! Because, believe it or not, so do I.'

The woman laughed softly, a wonderfully melodic laugh like the ones he was used to hearing in Hollywoodland, not the braying that many Prussian women passed off as laughter.

Gruber laughed with her, then leaned just a little closer, intending to capitalise on the success of his opening gambit, however, before he could, an annoyingly familiar voice sounded in his ear.

'Baron Gruber.'

Gruber pulled back and turned to find the Kaiser's private secretary standing uncomfortably close beside him.

'What is it?'

'The Kaiser would like to see you. This way, please.'

The man gestured to the door at the side of the room, through which the Kaiser had disappeared earlier, but Gruber deliberately turned his back to him and smiled at the woman.

'Duty calls, I'm afraid. Would you do me the honour of a dance after dinner?'

She smiled. 'Don't worry, I'm not going anywhere.'

Gruber gave her one of his very best smiles in return, along with a bow, then turned smartly and strode away, forcing the smaller man to trot to catch up.

Beyond the door was a small reception room - small by the standards of the palace, at least. It was a stateroom where the Kaiser and his family could go to rest for a while, away from the prying eyes of visitors, or where special dignitaries could be taken to have a private word with the Kaiser in comfort. Gruber had been there several times when he'd been called to consult with the Kaiser and each time he'd come the furniture had been arranged differently - in winter there tended to be a group of armchairs arranged around the open fire at the side of the room, while in summer the armchairs were set in the middle of the room around a coffee table, a large rotating fan high overhead keeping the temperature in the room comfortable. Today, though, it was set out in a way that he had never seen before: empty aside for a single armchair in the centre of the room, placed as if it were a throne and occupied by the Kaiser, and the only sign of refreshments was the single glass of water placed at the Kaiser's right hand on a small wooden table. Also, unlike every other time, there was nobody else in the room. It was just him and the Kaiser, there were no guards and the secretary had remained on the other side of the door.

The Kaiser watched as Gruber strode across the room towards him. His expression was cool, cold even, and Gruber found his confidence waning rapidly. His smile was getting harder to maintain so he allowed it to drop and instead took on a more professional, more military demeanour, sensing that the social side of his visit had finished and he was about to find out the real reason for his summoning.

He came to a halt in front of the Kaiser and bowed.

'Baron Gruber.'

Gruber smiled. It did have a very nice ring to it, especially coming from the Kaiser.

'Do you know why I have raised you to the rank of Baron?'

'Because I...'

'Because of the people.' The Kaiser said, cutting him off abruptly. 'For a long time the people have asked for you to be given the honour and so I have finally acquiesced to it, despite your not doing anything to deserve it.'

'Thank you, sir, I...' Gruber came to a halt and frowned as what the Kaiser had said eventually sunk in. 'Sir?'

'The fiasco in Gibraltar is only the latest in a long line of embarrassing failures that we have had to keep from the people, but it was by far the most costly. Thankfully, the war is going well enough for us that we have been able to bury your mistakes deep enough in victories that they will never see the light of day, but I will not permit you to continue act like a fool and throw away my assets, just so you can satisfy your ego.'

During his speech, the Kaiser was getting more and more worked up and now he pushed himself to his feet and advanced on Gruber, who found himself falling back involuntarily.

'You will no longer have access to unlimited funds, only those sufficient for the running of your squadron. You will be assigned to a proper airfield and billeted in accommodations in accordance with your rank as an officer. You will no longer get to pick and choose your assignments, you will carry out the ones that your superior officers give you. And, as for the monstrosity you left rotting on Sicily, I have already ordered it salvaged for parts and metal; there is no need or use for such a ridiculous vehicle in modern warfare.'

'But, sir...!'

The Kaiser cut him off again, thrusting a finger in his face for emphasis. 'If you hadn't wasted an entire mechanised division on your personal feud, then there might have been money and resources to repair it, but right now I need armoured vehicles more than you need your toy.'

'Very well, sir.'

Gruber gritted his teeth. He stared at the far wall, not daring to move as the Kaiser began to walk around him.

'I'm not finished.' The Kaiser warned, coming back around in front of him. 'I don't trust you to behave yourself and not shirk your duty or charge after the Misfits as soon as you can, so I'm sending someone to keep an eye on you.'

He looked over Gruber's shoulder. 'Adolf!' he bellowed.

Gruber winced at the sheer volume of the man's voice and turned to look as the secretary came in.

'Him?' he asked incredulously. 'You're sending *him* to keep an eye on *me*?' he scoffed. 'He doesn't know the first thing about flying. Or war.'

'No, he doesn't,' the Kaiser said. 'But she does.'

The secretary stepped to the side to allow the person following him to enter the room - the woman Gruber had been talking to before.

'Fraulein Reitsch! What a pleasant surprise!' Gruber called out, smiling widely; perhaps this wouldn't be a complete loss after all.

The woman didn't smile back at him, though, she just stared at him coldly as she came to stand with them.

'You two have met, then?' the Kaiser asked.

'Yes,' Gruber answered.

'Not really.' The woman said, dismissing Gruber with a disdainful look.

The Kaiser chuckled. 'I see Fraulein Reitsch has been playing one of her little games.' He walked back to his chair and sat down. 'Baron Gruber, meet Melitta Reitsch, chief test pilot for the Muhlenberg company and one of the principal members of the design team responsible for the MU9 and MU10, among others.'

'The front line is no place for a civilian.' Gruber said, completely soured on the woman.

'No place for a woman, you mean?' Reitsch said, looking down her nose at him.

'Fraulein Reitsch is not a civilian.' The Kaiser said before Gruber could come up with a suitable retort. 'I have awarded her a commission in the Fliegertruppe.'

'As long as she stays out of my way and out of my sight.'

'It seems that you still don't understand.' The Kaiser said wearily. 'Fraulein Reitsch will be joining your squadron as your new second in command and will be flying missions with you.'

'That's...!'

The Kaiser cut him off again. 'And before you even *think* about ordering her into any questionable situations, be aware that she holds the same rank as you and has my authority to countermand or change your orders if necessary. She also reports directly back to me and I will not hesitate to have you stripped of command and brought home in disgrace if you do anything even remotely as stupid as you have done up till now!'

The Kaiser was panting by the end of his tirade, his voice having risen to a roar that had filled the large room as if it were a broom closet.

'Do you understand?' he hissed.

'Yes, sir.' Gruber said quietly.

'Then get out! There is an autocar waiting to take you back to Tempelhof. You report for duty in France tomorrow morning. Adolf has your orders.'

'Sir!'

Gruber turned and stalked out as well as he could on shaking legs that barely supported him. The secretary opened the door for him and he snatched the brown envelope that he held out as he went past. As soon as he heard the door close behind him, he grabbed a passing servant by the collar, making the man squeak. Gruber ignored his protests and kept hold of him as he downed the glasses of schnapps on his tray one after the other until it was empty, then grabbed the bottle and stomped towards the exit.

The Kaiser waited until the door had closed, then looked at Reitsch.

'Last chance to back out.'

She shook her head. 'Never. This is the way I can best serve you and the Prussian Empire, now that my talents are no longer needed at Muhlenberg.'

Wilhelm nodded. 'You are clear on your instructions?'

'Yes, sir.'

'And you have no problem with them? This is your last chance to express any doubts you might have about them or your ability to carry them out.'

Reitsch smiled coldly. 'Having spoken to the man, I am absolutely positive that I will have no hesitation in carrying out your instructions, should the need arise.'

'Good. Good.' The Kaiser stared at the door and snarled. 'That man has brought me to the limit of my patience. One more mistake and I want him out of my hair for good.'

'Understood, sir.' Reitsch nodded. 'But, if I may ask, sir - if it is your intention to have me kill him, why did you make him a Baron?'

The Kaiser smiled slowly. 'Because the higher I raise him in the eyes of the people, the more worth he will have when he is martyred.'

.

CHAPTER 1

22nd August 1941

'Thank you for coming at such short notice. Don't worry; I know you all have a lot to do, so I'll keep this brief.'

Sir Douglas Pewtall, Commander of the Royal Aviator Corps, held up a copy of that day's edition of *The Times*, the headline "TRAITOR" blazoned across its front page. The details of the War Minister's treason and the extent to which the rot had spread within his government had finally been released to the public that morning, fully three days after his arrest on the morning of 19th.

'We now know why the invasion hasn't yet come.' He tossed the newspaper onto the table in front of him and looked around.

Every seat at the large oval table that filled the small briefing room at RAC Bentley Priory was filled by one high-ranking member of the RAC or other. All of the regional commanders were there, as were a few of the key squadron commanders. One face in particular stood out from the crowd, that of Group Commander Dame Abigail Lennox, and he gave her a nod before continuing to address the group.

'Now that the War Minister is gone we don't expect them to hold back much longer, and, indeed, reconnaissance flights are bringing back pictures showing more movement than ever. Thanks to the Misfits and the good people still holding Gibraltar, we have almost an entire mechanised division less to worry about, but that still leaves the Prussians with an overwhelming force already lined up against us and we believe they have reinforcements on their way - our allies in Muscovy have reported a diminishing of pressure over the last few days and it's not as if they need to worry so much about the Mediterranean anymore.'

He turned and nodded at his aide, who was standing behind him at the ready, and the woman went to the corkboards and pulled away the cloths covering them.

'As far as we can tell, this is the current situation. We have Prussian troops and ships to the south, east and north east, but we expect the Prussians to try to take control of the air first, like they did last year, before sending any kind of invasion fleet. The main concentration of aircraft is along the south and south east, much as it was last summer, and that is where we can expect most of the attacks to come from.'

He gave the men and women around the table a few moments to look at the boards. Enough time to absorb the information, but not enough for them to start to despair at the enormity of the task ahead of them,

'Right now,' he said quietly, drawing every eye back to him, 'my opposite numbers in the army and navy are briefing their people on what is expected of them, but essentially the plan is the same as it has always been - shoot down as many of their aircraft as possible, sink their ships and, Darwin forbid any of them set foot on British soil, but, if they do, then shoot the bastards.'

There were a few chuckles at that, but they were subdued and short lived. Which was as he'd expected.

'When the Prussians tried it on last summer they hadn't consolidated their hold on Europe and they were fighting on several fronts. Even so, we weren't prepared for them and nearly lost. This time they've had a whole year to gather strength, using the plundered resources and manufacturing capabilities of most of Europe. However, they're starting later in the year this time round, so they don't have long until the weather turns and their invasion fleet can't come and will have to cut corners with whatever plan they have in mind. We're also more ready for them than we were last time round - even though we've taken losses abroad, we've been quietly building up our strength here at home and have more than five times as many aircraft and pilots as we did in August last year.'

He smiled now, for the first time. 'So, we can afford to change our tactics slightly from last summer. Instead of being purely reactive and just running round trying to intercept the raids as radar detects them we're going to be a bit more flexible. We have enough aircraft and pilots to adapt to the attacks as they come in, sharing resources between fighter groups so that the Prussians can't drag us around and pull us apart like they did before and none of the groups gets swamped.'

'What about us?' asked Sky Vice-Marshal Isombard Levy, the bomber group leader. 'Are you going to let us do anything this time?'

'I was just getting to you, Isombard.' Pewtall said. 'Even if we do manage to beat back the Fleas and retain control of our skies, they may just decide to send their boats over and hope for the best before the summer ends. So we want to thin their forces as much as we can before they can even think about sending them across the channel. You'll keep up your usual night raids, but you'll also be kept on standby during the day and if they ever commit too many fighters to protecting a raid we'll take advantage and send over our own counter raids. Your people are already causing the Prussians a fair bit of bother in the dark. I'm looking forward to seeing what they can do when they can see their targets.'

'We'll give them what for, sir!' Levy said, banging his fist on the table and making the water glasses shake.

'I'm sure you will!' Pewtall smiled at him, then looked around the group. 'And that's about it. I have a few tricks up my sleeve for if things start going too badly for us, but I'm hoping it won't come to that. At least not too soon.'

'And the Misfits? Where do *they* fit in with this plan of yours?'

There was obvious disdain in the voice and Pewtall wasn't surprised when he looked down the table and found Sky Vice-Marshal Spark, commander of 10th Group, lounging rather insolently in his chair, staring back at him. Spark had been one of those officers who had opposed the formation of Misfit Squadron from the very start and it was rumoured that he had been the originator of the "Abbess" nickname that Abby Lennox had been lumped with. There were also rumours that he had been one of the War Minister's co-conspirators. However, while Pewtall could well believe that the first rumour were true, the second was patently false; the man might be bigoted, chauvinistic, prejudiced and quite a few other frankly intolerable adjectives, but he was no traitor and had fought as hard as anyone to keep the RAC in the air last summer.

'The Misfits will act as a wild card and will go to where they are most needed.'

'And who decides where they are needed?' Spark asked.

'The *circumstances* will dictate it.' Pewtall answered coldly. 'Now,' he said, cutting the man off before he could continue his pestering, 'you all know what needs to be done, so I suggest you get out there and do it.'

He stood and made his way straight out of the room.

As soon as Pewtall had gone, Abby joined the general movement towards the door. Unlike them, she didn't have entire fighter and bomber groups to brief, but she was still in a hurry to get back. However, Pewtall's aide intercepted her and pulled her aside before she could even get around the table.

'Sir Douglas would like to have a word with you, ma'am.'

Abby nodded, then followed her out and along the corridor. A few of the other officers were still hanging around and they gave her a look as she went past, curious as to why she should have been singled out, but they knew better than to ask and just gave her a smile and a friendly nod, which she returned.

Pewtall looked up from a pile of papers on his desk as she entered.

He smiled at the aide. 'Thank you, Janet,'

'Sir.' She nodded, then slipped back out, closing the door behind her.

'Take a seat, Abby, I won't be a moment.'

Pewtall went back to reading whatever it was he'd been reading and Abby moved towards the chairs in front of his desk. She didn't sit down, though, but took the opportunity to look around his office - it was the first time she'd been in it and she was curious as to what someone with such a long and distinguished career would chose to display.

The obligatory portrait of the king was on the wall behind him, but above it, in pride of place, was a large, very old-fashioned, single-bladed wooden propeller covered with signatures, most of which had faded beyond legibility. There was a single photograph on Pewtall's desk, facing him, which she assumed was of his family, but there were dozens more photographs scattered about the room, on the walls and on the shelves. Many of them were the typical squadron photographs, posed in front of aircraft, but there were also quite a few more candid ones of him with men and women, most of whom she recognised, many of whom were dead. There was even one of him with the Misfits, signed by all of them, from the time he had visited Badger Base. Half the pilots in that photograph were dead as well, the aircraft they were standing in front of destroyed and the base they were on bombed out. She grimaced; it was tragic, but that was the nature of war.

'One of my prized possessions.' Pewtall said quietly, seeing the direction of her gaze. 'But I didn't ask you to come to reminisce about better times.' He leaned forwards, propping himself up on his elbows and looked at her. 'What is your status?'

Abby slipped into one of the chairs with a sigh. 'At the moment I have five proven pilots, one unproven pilot, who I think will do very well, two unproven pilots I'm not yet sure about and one sabotage specialist. If I'm lucky, three more of my pilots will get back from gallivanting all around the world sometime soon, but they are likely to be out of practise, so it may take them a few days to get back into the swing of things.' She shrugged. 'All of which means that right now I can put up one combat-ready flight and another that should do well, but that I can't depend on. However, when I get my pilots back I'll be able to put up two good flights plus most of a spare, which means the Misfits will be back to about the same strength as they were last summer. If not slightly stronger'

'Hmm.' Pewtall frowned as he drummed his fingers on the desk. It took a few seconds for him to absorb the information that Abby had thrown at him so rapidly, but then he nodded. 'I got word this morning that Arrowsmith is due to arrive in Plymouth tomorrow, but I don't know when Stone and Wright will arrive; they're necessarily maintaining radio silence, so nobody knows precisely where they are. If they stay on the rough schedule the Japanese transmitted then it should be within a week.'

Abby nodded. 'That's good to know, thank you.'

'As for the Misfits. Well...'

He trailed off and sat back in his chair.

Abby, though, sat up a little straighter; she could tell when a superior officer was about to give her bad news.

'What I said in there is true,' he began slowly, reluctantly. 'We *do* have enough fighters to cover any raid that comes over. Obviously, the more aircraft we can throw at the Prussians the better, but four, or even eight aircraft more or less isn't going to make much of a difference, even if they are Misfits. Certainly not like the difference you made last year, when we could barely field a full eleven, let alone have a twelfth man left over to run the scoreboard. What *would* make a difference, though, and *not* in our favour, is if you were seen to do badly - if, for example, one of your new recruits were to buy it straight off the bat. The effect on our morale would be disastrous and would be a very unwelcome boost to theirs.'

Abby nodded. Aside from the questionable cricket metaphors, what he was saying made sense and what he was so tactfully asking wasn't as bad as it could have been. Or as bad as she'd been expecting, to tell the truth.

'I understand, sir, and I certainly wouldn't put my new people in any position that I wouldn't be confident they could get out of. Having said that, they do need to get experience and mollycoddling them will do them no favours.'

'Of course! Of course!' Pewtall nodded enthusiastically. 'I wouldn't have it any other way. Just, you know, be careful. Don't let them go tilting at the Barons as soon as they see them. Things like that.'

'Is there anything else, sir?'

'No, no! That's all.'

Abby stood to go, but he called out to her before she got to the door.

'Happy hunting, Abby.'

She turned and smiled. 'Thank you, sir.'

RAC Bentley Priory was not an operational base, it was an administrative one and, as such, despite its importance as RAC headquarters, it had no airfield. That suited most visitors fine as it seemed to be below their dignity as senior officers to fly to appointments with the commander, but Abby had somewhere to be and very little time to get there. She'd known things were going to be tight and had borrowed one of Lord Bagshot's incredibly fast spring-powered sports autocars, but, after her unexpected meeting with Pewtall, she was far later than she'd thought she would be. She jumped into the autocar and roared off of the base and onto the, thankfully mostly empty, roads. She drove like the clappers, got to the gates of Bagshot Hall in less than half an hour and skidded to a halt in front of the manor just as the clocks were striking ten. However, the people she had wanted to be there to greet had, as usually happened in these kind of situations, arrived early and their bus was sitting off to one side, its driver sitting on the grass with a group of off-duty servicemen and women, a mug in her hand. They straightened up as she approached and she singled out the driver.

'Are they inside?'

'Yes, ma'am,' the woman said. 'With his lordship.'

'Thank you.'

Abby nodded her thanks, then ran up the steps and into the manor. She was met in the hallway by a servant, who pointed her towards one of the sitting rooms.

She'd only met her new recruits a few days before, up in Scotland, and had had just a single day to fly with them. That had been enough to get their measure, though, and she had jokingly commented to Penny and Scarlet in her quarters afterwards that they were "a definite, a probable and a possible".

The woman, Eleanor Perkins, was by far the best of the three. She was all instinct, flying as if the aircraft were a part of her, like *she* was a part of *it*, her technique perfect, not because she had worked to refine it, but because she just knew the right thing to do. She was the very definition of what Abby had always looked for in a Misfit - someone to whom flying was a part of their very being.

Unfortunately, the two men weren't quite as impressive and, while she had made Perkins a full member of the squadron, they would only be provisional members and would have to prove themselves.

Robert Sherborne, her "probable", was a bit rough around the edges and only recently reconciled to actually *being* a pilot, but he had the makings of an excellent pilot, if he were given the time to grow into his talent. Unfortunately, if Sir Pewtall was right, he might not get that time. The other, the Honourable Benedict Charles Something Something Wilberforce - she couldn't remember his full name, despite having read his file several times - was the "possible" and the one she was most doubtful about. He was the polar opposite of Perkins - all technique and almost no instincts, except on those rare occasions that he let himself go. He was learning to do that more often, according to Derek Niven, who had been his instructor at Galath, but, like Sherborne, she wasn't sure he would have time to fully mature as a pilot.

Under normal circumstances she wouldn't have taken either of the men, wouldn't have even gone to take a look at them, in fact; she would have let them go to a regular RAC squadron and perhaps taken another look at them in a few months. But these weren't normal circumstances, not by a long shot, and something Drake had said when he'd told her about them had sparked her interest, something they had that she thought might give them the edge over other candidates - each other.

The reports of their instructors, a dozen or so independently written reports with little to no cross contamination, had all spoken of something special, something *remarkable*, even - their recruit group would be progressing like any other group of recruits, with some coping better than others with the tough training, but then suddenly, inexplicably, overnight, the ones being left behind would catch up and then the entire group would leap ahead of the curve.

No group *ever* did something like that, it was unheard of, but theirs did and their instructors had been at a loss to explain it, beyond attributing it to a "group spirit", or to Perkins' remarkable flying ability, or even, in one memorable case, a group loathing of Wilberforce. Whatever the reason, she was hopeful that something of that ilk would happen again and quickly bring Wilberforce and Sherborne up to speed, although it might be unlikely, seeing as the group had split up on completion of the accelerated program at Gwynedd and one of their most promising members, Tyler Oakley had died.

Reports and observations in the air could only tell her so much about whether they would fit in with the Misfits, though, and she took a few moments to observe them from the doorway before someone spotted her; how they dealt with the eccentric Lord Bagshot would tell her a lot about their personality and suitability.

Biffy was regaling them with a story. An anecdotes from his racing days, she assumed. Wilberforce, who was used to being in the presence of the aristocracy, was sitting comfortably in an armchair, dunking a biscuit in a cup of tea. He was laughing when it was appropriate to do so, but she could tell he was just humouring Biffy and was more interested in the biscuits than the story. Perkins and Sherborne, on the other hand, were wide-eyed, completely absorbed in the story. They were far from comfortable, though, both of them perched on the edge of their seats, as if they were sitting to attention, their backs ramrod straight and knuckles white on the cups and saucers they held, forgotten, on their laps. This was probably the first time they'd been in the company of someone like Biffy. Wilberforce was titled, of course, but he didn't count, especially not to them, and if you didn't know Drake was a Lord then you wouldn't be able to tell. Biffy, though, Biffy absolutely *screamed* aristocracy, from his way of speaking to his manner of dress. It also didn't help that he was one of the most famous racing drivers that Britain had ever had and, even now, years after his retirement, he was still a hero to many.

The tale concluded with a bang and a crash, as many of Biffy's racing stories did, and it was as if a spell had been broken. Almost in unison, Perkins and Sherborne blinked, then lifted their cups to their mouths, while Wilberforce gave a somewhat belated chuckle, without lifting his eyes from his cup, before stuffing another biscuit in his mouth.

Biffy lifted his head to look at her and Abby chuckled; most likely he'd been aware of her the whole time.

'Ah, there you are, Abby!' he called out 'I was beginning to think you'd pranged my car!'

'Of course, not,' Abby said, walking across the room to them, 'it's far too slow for me to get into any kind of trouble.'

'Ouch!' Biffy said, wincing theatrically, even as he grinned.

The three young officers hurriedly put down their refreshments and leapt to their feet.

'As you were,' she said, slipping into a spare armchair. The servant had followed her in and she smiled a thank you at him when he placed a cup of tea and a plate of biscuits in front of her.

Lord Bagshot pushed himself to his feet. 'Well, I'll leave you to it.' He gave Wilberforce a cool look, but then smiled warmly at the other two pilots. 'I hope you'll be comfortable in my humble home. See you at dinner!' He gave Abby a courtier's bow. 'I hope you will grace us with your presence this evening, Dame Lennox.'

'I would be delighted, Lord Bagshot,' she nodded back, haughtily.

He laughed and limped from the room.

Abby turned back to her three recruits and was amused and not a little gratified to see that all three were now perched nervously on the edge of their seats and not just the two nice ones. That wouldn't do, though; they couldn't be nervous around their commander, it would be detrimentally in more ways than she could count.

'Oh, relax, would you? I don't bite.'

She slouched down in the armchair, twisting herself sideways and putting one trousered leg up on the arm, which allowed her to comfortably reach the plate and her cup on the low table in front of her. She stuffed an entire biscuit in her mouth, then grinned at them.

She waited patiently while they looked at her, then looked at each other, then looked back at her when she reached to take another biscuit, then finally started to relax a little when they realised she wasn't testing them or anything.

'Did you have a good trip down?' she asked.

The two boys nodded silently, but the girl, Ellie, smiled. 'Yes, thank you, ma'am. The train was delayed slightly for an air raid on Liverpool, but apart from that we made good time.'

'I see that!' Abby said, chuckling. 'I was hoping to be here to welcome you, but Sir Douglas had other plans.' She brushed her hands over the now empty plate and picked up her tea. She gestured at them with the cup. 'Finish up your tea, grab any biscuits or sandwiches you want and let's go take a look at the airfield, shall we?'

The bus was still outside and Abby approached the driver. 'Would you mind giving us a lift down to the airfield?'

'Not at all, ma'am.' The woman handed her now empty mug off to one of the group and led them to the bus. She opened the door for them, then settled herself in the driver's seat.

Abby waved the three to seats in the middle of the bus, took note of the fact that Wilberforce made sure that he sat on his own by sitting next to the aisle, then sat in the row in front of them.

'Bagshot Hall has been Penny's home since she married Lord Bagshot,' she began as they pulled away from the mansion. 'She persuaded him to build her an airfield on the grounds, with a workshop and a design shed so that she could design and build her own aircraft. The airfield has been expanded considerably since the start of the war to the point where it's now a fully fledged base. This isn't the first time we've been stationed here - after Badger Base was destroyed we came here temporarily before we shipped out to Muscovy - but it's going to be rather more permanent this time, so we're going to construct a few more barrack buildings, another mess, and a few other things to make it more of a home and so that we don't have to keep bothering Lord Bagshot in his. Although, as you've already seen, he quite enjoys the attention.'

She pointed out the window. They had just passed the thick line of trees that separated the grounds of the manor from the airfield and it was now in full view. She grinned as the young pilots gasped and craned their necks to look out of the windows - she'd asked Alasdair Patterson, Penny's fitter and the man who had run her airfield until it had become the Misfits' home, to have the doors of the hangar thrown completely open that morning and the aircraft within were in full view from the road. As welcomes went, it was far better than any that she or Biffy could possibly give them.

The driver was having to go fairly slowly on the gravel, so they had plenty of time to get a good look and Abby took advantage of that to point out the individual aircraft.

'From left to right, in case you didn't already know what they are, you've got Gwen Stone's *Excalibur*, my *Dragon*, Drake's *Lion*, Tanya's

Wolf and Derek's *Kite*. You can just about make out Bruce Walker's *Wraith*, which he's kindly let us have, in the shadows behind that, and last, but not least, three slightly modified Spitsteams.'

There was a sudden buzzing noise and the recruits ducked involuntarily as it reached a deafening crescendo and a shadow passed directly over them.

'And, right on cue,' Abby said, shaking her head in exasperation, 'that's Scarlet's *Hummingbird*.'

They watched as the camouflage-patterned gyrodyne did a snap roll, then pulled its nose up sharply. The three recruits held their breath as it lost speed rapidly, expecting the aircraft to stall and fall from the sky, but it didn't, it just righted itself and settled gently to the ground on the track right in front of the hangar, scattering the half a dozen or so people who'd been sitting on the grass verge, enjoying the sun.

The Irishwoman jumped out before the rotors had even stopped turning and waved to the bus before stomping away to meet the group of fitters rushing to take care of her aircraft.

'Are the Spits for us?' Ellie asked timidly.

Abby smiled at her. 'We don't have the time or money to make new aircraft for you, so I'm afraid you're going to have to make do with them. Don't worry, the latest Spitsteam marks are already incredible aircraft and we've made a few modifications to make them even better, so you shouldn't have any trouble keeping up with the other aircraft. Except, maybe, for Excalibur and Dragon.'

She looked around the group. 'I hope you've done the homework I gave you.'

They nodded smiling at her.

'Good.' The bus pulled up next to Hummingbird in front of the hangars and Abby made her way down the aisle to the door.

'Thank you,' she said to the driver in passing.

'You're welcome, ma'am.'

They followed Abby towards the hangar, but, before they had taken more than a few steps, there was an ear-piercing squeal and they turned to find a tall woman in a dark grey flightsuit charging towards them, her blonde hair streaming behind her with the speed she was going.

'Ellie!' the woman screamed in glee as she approached.

Ellie recoiled a step, holding her hands out in panic, sure that the woman was going to barrel into her, but somehow she managed to pull up short and wrapped her arms around Ellie.

'I'm so glad you joined us!'

'So am I.' Ellie squeaked, barely able to breathe.

Tanya stepped back, grinning, but kept hold of Ellie's hands.

'I'm happy to see you too,' said Drake, who had followed the Muscovite at a rather more sensible pace, 'all of you.'

'Drake, Tanya.' Abby nodded a greeting at them. 'Is Derek here too?'

'In the ready room.' Drake said, hooking a thumb over his shoulder. 'He got this month's Ornithology whatsit magazine this morning and has forgotten there's a war on.'

Abby snorted. 'Well, he has less than an hour before we all go up. Let him know he has to be ready, please.'

'Will do.'

'And Tanya, please let Ellie go. You can catch up later.'

Tanya winked at Ellie. 'See you in the sky. We can take up from where we left off.' The Muscovite let Ellie's hands drop and skipped away after Drake.

Abby rolled her eyes. 'And I was worried about squadron morale...' She waved at the recruits. 'Come on, then, let's take a look at your Spits.'

The three Spitsteams were half of a batch of six aircraft that had come straight from the factory the week before. The fitters had begun modifying them immediately, but had only gotten one finished before receiving Abby's message two days previously that three would be needed. They had worked night and day since then and had been able to get two more ready, but only just. They had been left grey, with only a coat of primer to protect them from the elements.

'These are the same mark of Spits that you've been flying at DART,' Abby said, reaching up to pat the side of one of them, 'but you'll soon find that their performance is rather different. They have the latest Ozzy spring, which is about ten percent more powerful than the one that's currently in production, and a slightly bigger airscrew to take advantage of the extra power.' She grinned. 'There's so much extra power, in fact, that we had to strengthen the airframe slightly to cope with it.'

'You've clipped the wings?' Rob asked, frowning at the squared off ends of the wings.

'I was just getting round to that,' Abby said, 'but yes, we took off a foot or so. That will give these birds a faster roll rate than they had before, which we reckon will allow them to turn tighter than an MU9 and hopefully match an HH190.'

Rob nodded in understanding - he'd found a book on aeronautical engineering in the DART library and had found it mostly incomprehensible, but fascinating nonetheless. Some of the things he'd read had stuck, though.

'So,' Abby said, rubbing her hands together. 'About that homework I gave you.' She looked at Rob.

'I'll have mine painted green, please, if that's alright?'

Abby nodded. 'Of course it is.' She gestured towards one of the groups of fitters that had wandered over when the pilots had appeared. 'Aviator Sergeant Pratt is the chief fitter on your aircraft. When we get down this afternoon you can speak with him and find the right shade of green.'

'Yes, ma'am.' Rob smiled at his fitters and gave them a wave. They smiled at him proudly.

'Next. Wilberforce.'

'Purple. And I'll call it Predator.'

'That's a very ambitious name,' Abby said, mildly amused, 'but you'll have to keep it to yourself for now; the Spits don't get names, just a nice paint job so that we know where you are. Understood?'

Benedict pouted, but nodded. 'Yes, ma'am.'

'Good. Your aircraft is looked after by Sergeant Cotter over there.'

The leader of the next group raised a hand and Benedict gave her the smallest of nods, but then immediately turned his gaze back to the Spitsteam they were standing next to.

Abby stared at him for a moment, but said nothing and turned to Ellie.

To minimise the work the fitters had to do if they failed to make the grade she was only allowing Wilberforce and Sherborne to paint their aircraft a single colour. Perkins, though, was a full member and she had told her she could ask for any colour scheme she wanted.

'Ellie?'

'Um... I'd like blue on the bottom and light brown on the top, please,' she said, looking towards the last group of fitters.

Abby grinned. 'Those are good choices, surprisingly sensible for a Misfit. Sergeant Tonbridge will take care of things for you.'

Ellie smiled warmly at her fitters. 'I look forward to working with them.'

'Obviously there's no time to paint your aircraft now,' Abby said, addressing all three of them, 'but, knowing the men and women we work with, I'm sure your teams will find some time to do it before tomorrow's flights.'

She gave the fitters a knowing look and they grinned at her, some of them looking a bit sheepish.

'Come on, let's go to the ready room and leave them to do final checks before we go up.'

Abby wandered away towards the small building where Tanya and Drake had gone.

Benedict rushed to catch up with her, but Rob and Ellie hung back slightly.

'Green?' Ellie asked quietly. 'Like Tayler's aircraft? *Finch* was it?'

'That's right.' Rob nodded. 'And you? Blue and light brown?'

'Eyes and hair. Something to remember him by.'

They slipped their hands into each other's and squeezed, drawing comfort from the other, but then had to let go when they got to the building and stepped inside.

Half a dozen worn, but comfortable-looking Chesterfield sofas were pushed up against the walls of the ready room, with a couple of armchairs scattered amongst them along with a few mismatched coffee tables. A round wooden table that was far too small for the eight or nine chairs around it sat in the centre of the room and there was a small buffet table against the wall to one side with a tea urn and plates of food on it. Photographs, framed newspaper articles and a couple of paintings of aircraft were on three of the walls, but the fourth was almost completely covered by a large blackboard and a few maps. The room was small and crowded, with barely enough room to move between the furniture, but it was cosy and they could well imagine resting there in comfort between sorties.

Derek, Tanya and Drake were there, the couple sitting close on one of the sofas and Derek in an armchair on the other side of the room to them, underneath a window. Derek, as they'd already been informed, was engrossed in a birdwatching magazine and looked up just long enough to nod a greeting before returning to it, but Tanya and Drake had obviously been waiting for them and stood when they came in.

'Derek...' Abby called out gently, when he showed no sign of stopping reading. 'Would you mind dragging yourself away from your birds and joining us for a moment? There is still a war on, you know.'

It took Derek a moment to realise he was being spoken to and a further couple of seconds to figure out what she had said to him, but eventually he smiled sheepishly and put the magazine to the side.

'Oh, right. Yes. Sorry,' he said, standing and coming over to them.

Abby smiled indulgently, then perched on the edge of the table in the middle of the room and looked around the group. 'Well, it looks like the invasion is finally coming. There is movement on the continent that points towards it coming very soon, perhaps in the next couple of days and I want us to be ready for it. When Penny gets here there will be eight of us, so we'll be able to divide into two full flights of fighters.'

She went over to the chalkboard on the wall where flying assignments and aircraft readiness were written. It hadn't been used since they'd last been there, in the weeks leading up to their mission in Muscovy, and the rude drawing that Bruce had done was still there. It had faded and become barely recognisable, but if you looked hard enough you could still just about make out the caricatures of the Kaiser and Hans Gruber and the compromising position the Australian had put them in.

Abby took a moment to appreciate it one last time, then sighed and wiped it off.

'A flight,' she said as she wrote, 'will be myself as lead, Penny as my wingmate, Tanya as Three and Ellie as Four.'

She turned and looked directly at Ellie. 'You are Tanya's wingmate, you are to stick to her like glue, even if it means you have to bend your airframe when she starts doing those things she does. You are not to go off on your own. Do you think you can do that?'

Ellie nodded. 'I can keep up with her; I know her tricks.'

'Not all of them, you don't,' Tanya said, grinning at her.

Abby shook her head and looked at Drake. 'Why do I think I'm making a mistake putting those two together?'

Drake grinned at her. 'More of a mistake than putting the squadron together in the first place?'

'You've got a point.' Abby conceded, matching his grin for a moment, before looking at Rob and Benedict. 'B flight will be led by Drake as Five, with Rob on his wing as Six. The other pair will be Derek as Seven and Benedict as Eight.'

'Sausage Boy.' Tanya said under her breath, covering her mouth with her hand.

'Now now,' Abby said, pointing a finger at her warningly. 'Any nicknames that were earned before joining the squadron are null and void unless the person wishes to keep up their use. However appropriate they might be.' She looked at Benedict, trying hard to keep a straight face. 'Benedict. Would you like to be known as Sausage Boy?'

'No, I would not.' Benedict said sourly.

'How about Cleaner Boy?' Rob asked innocently.

Benedict just glared at him in response.

'Anyway,' Abby said, pointing at the board behind her, 'those are the assignments. However,' she added abruptly, 'until further notice B flight will not be engaging the enemy unless they have a clear position of superiority.' She looked at Rob and Benedict again, 'I've already talked to Drake and Derek about this and they've agreed to hold back for a while until you've had a chance to settle in and get up to speed. Disobey orders or go charging off on your own and you'll be out of here quicker than Scarlet can down a drink.'

'Oi! I heard that!' Scarlet came bouncing in through the door. 'What are you implying, Abby?'

'Not a thing, darling.' Abby said with a smile.

Scarlet winked at the recruits and they grinned back at the extremely likeable woman. They knew full well what Abby was implying because they'd watched her drink the group of pilots they'd gone up to Scotland with under the table both nights they'd been there. Then keep drinking for another hour or so before striding off to bed looking none the worse for wear.

'Yes, well,' Abby said, 'we don't want to waste any more time if we want to be ready for the Prussians, so let's get you three to your quarters so you can change into your flight gear, shall we? Wheels up in...' she consulted her chronograph, 'thirty-five minutes.'

The rooms in the officer's barracks were excellent, better than anything the new recruits had ever had before, with decent furniture, a sink, thick walls and enough room to actually move around without stubbing their toes. Their bags had already been delivered and unpacked for them, but there were leather cases, a little smaller than a suitcase, lying on Rob and Ellie's beds.

Ellie ran her hand over the deep red leather of the case and took in the name embossed on it - her own. There was an envelope on top of it made of expensive, thick, creamy paper and it too had her name on it. She opened it curiously and found a single sheet of paper inside. The paper had Lord Drake's crest on it in red wax and a short note in his handwriting saying "Welcome to the Misfits. I'm sure you will make good use of this." Underneath, in a script that was so flowery it was barely legible, Tanya had written "I picked the colour.

Men have no idea; he was going to get black! Looking forward to flying with you again!"

Ellie smiled, but then set the note aside eagerly and flipped the catches on the case.

'Oh, my!' she breathed at the sight of what was inside.

Ellie came out of her room just as Rob was coming out of his, saving her the trouble of having to go and thump on his door.

'You have one too?' she squealed excitedly at the sight of him.

'Yes!' Rob said, equally excited, holding his arms out to the side and looking down at the brand new tailored leather flightsuit that had been in his room. It was black, shiny and extremely comfortable.

'And it's got green seams!' Ellie said, admiring him. 'To go with Finch.'

'They can't possibly have known I'd chose green for Finch, but it's a good coincidence, yes!'

'It really suits you, and it looks like it fits perfectly.'

'It does! I reckon Tanya had a hand in that.'

Ellie nodded. 'She chose the colour of mine for me.'

Rob looked at her appreciatively. 'That dark red is a lovely colour, it looks great on you. And it looks like they got your size right too, it fits... uh...' he blushed suddenly and looked away. 'It...'

Ellie blushed as well; she'd seen how tight and form-fitting the flightsuit was in the mirror in her room and had a moment of doubt as to whether she would be able to wear it in front of other people.

She'd considered putting her greatcoat over the top of the flightsuit, even though she would boil, but quickly discarded the idea as ridiculous and unworthy of her new status. After all, what did it matter what she looked like? The flightsuit looked like it did because that was how it helped her to do her job better. Yes, there *were* some people who made more of pictures of the Misfits than they should, but it wasn't as if she was that good looking, especially compared to Tanya, Scarlet, Gwen Stone, or Kitty Wright. Nobody would be looking at her anyway.

Even as she blushed, she laughed and reached out to take his arm. 'I don't mind you looking, Rob; I'm fully covered. And it's not as if you didn't see more every time we ran in the rain in Wales.

Rob smiled at her, but before he could say anything Benedict came out of his room. The boy stopped at the sight of them and gave their flightsuits a sour look, but then turned and stalked away from them towards the exit.

Rob and Ellie grinned at each other.

'Time to fly!' she said and, hand in hand, they ran down the corridor after him.

The aircraft were parked on the edge of the airfield in front of the hangars by the time they got back and the other pilots were already there waiting for them.

Abby nodded at the sight of them. 'Well, you certainly look the part now.'

'Thanks to Lord Drake.' Rob said, nodding at Drake.

'Yes, thank you!' Ellie added effusively, smiling at him. 'It's wonderful! And you chose such a lovely colour!'

Ellie winked at Tanya, who laughed.

'You're very welcome, both of you,' Drake said, 'but from now on you have to call me Drake, or Rudy if you really want; there's no "sir" and definitely no "Lord" here in the Misfits.'

'We'll have time for all the social niceties later,' Abby said, 'let's get up; we're wasting daylight.'

The aircraft were lined up in their flights and pairs and Tanya walked with Ellie towards theirs.

'You look gorgeous in that.' Tanya said, putting her arm around Ellie's shoulders and hugging her to her. 'Really sexy!'

'Stop!' Ellie said, blushing again. 'I'm trying *not* to think about how much I'm on display!'

Tanya laughed. 'You *should* think about it!' she dropped her voice and leaned in closer. 'You do know that Rob was looking at your bum when you turned up, right?'

'No!' Ellie hissed, mortified. Then, slowly, she smiled. 'Was he? Really?'

CHAPTER 2

'Now that we are finally all here, perhaps we can get on with this invasion? If that is, you don't mind, Generalleutnant Gruber? Oh, beg your pardon, I mean - *Baron* Gruber?'

Gruber glared sulkily at the man standing at the end of the table and slumped further down in his chair.

Generalfeldmarschall Schmidt, who had been given overall command of the invasion force by the Kaiser, stared at Gruber for a moment more to get his point across, then looked around the large table.

A thin man in his early sixties with no hair to speak of, Generalfeldmarschall Schmidt was one of the most experienced officers in the Prussian armed forces. He had fought in the trenches of the first Great War, helped Kaiser Wilhelm II rebuild the army in preparation for the Second Great War, won acclaim and promotion in the Iberian conflict, devised the lightning attack tactics that had won them most of Europe and most recently forced the British out of Greece and Cyprus. He had never suffered a defeat while in command and was often compared to historical commanders like Alexander and Napoleon. No Prussian was more highly regarded or capable and he was the natural choice to lead the attack that would spell the beginning of the end of the war.

Schmidt's eyes slowly moved from one officer at the large table to another, seeing familiar faces everywhere he looked. Reichsflotte, Fliegertruppe, Reichsheer, the commanders of the invasion fleets, the army divisions that would go to Britain, the bomber and fighter wings, it didn't matter who they were; he'd commanded them all and requested them all for this. Except for Gruber, of course. That man had been under his command once, but he hadn't requested him and never would have done - the Kaiser had forced him on him for some inexplicable reason.

There was, however, one unfamiliar face at the table - a woman, Melitta Reitsch, and his eyes settled on her last of all. It was the first time a woman had ever been at one of his command briefings and he couldn't say he was comfortable with her being there, but, again, it was at the Kaiser's request, so there was nothing he could do about it.

He cleared his throat and looked down the length of the table at Generalfeldmarschall Weissman, the commander of the Fliegertruppe; he was on safer ground with his eyes on him, even though he detested the fat sweaty man, than looking at the woman, or that damn Gruber.

'The offensive begins tomorrow at first light,' he announced and smiled at the stir it caused. 'As always, the Fliegertruppe will lead the way.'

He picked up a long wooden pointer and strode over to the huge map on the wall showing Britain and the conquered countries surrounding it.

'The key to victory over Britain is, and always has been, control of the air. However, we are slowly beginning to learn that that is not an absolute truth. We do not need to utterly destroy the Royal Aviator Corps to have enough control to launch the invasion. That was where my predecessor erred last summer; the British air force was so weak that we could have just walked into London, but he refused to commit while there were still aircraft in the sky and we lost the opportunity.'

He struck the wooden pointer loudly against the map, making many of the men around the table jump, Gruber among them, and Schmidt grinned as the despicable man groaned and put his head in his hands, evidently the victim of too much drink. The woman didn't even flinch, though, she just continued to watch him with those unnervingly cold eyes.

'We now know that the success the British had in intercepting our raids, both by night and day, was not due to their love of carrots, or the giant ear trumpets on their coastlines that their press widely publicised. Instead, it was due to a network of crude radio direction finders spread out along their coastline.' He moved the pointer over the map, pointing out the dozens of red dots marked on it. 'These will be our first targets. We believe we know where all of them are, but, even if we don't and we do not completely destroy them, we should be able to knock out enough of them to create large gaps in their early warning system. This will delay their response to us and allow our bombers to reach their targets with far fewer problems.'

He slapped the pointer against the map again, deliberately making as much noise as he could, then walked back to the table.

'We have modified as many of our fighters as we can to take two hundred and fifty kilogramme bombs and our entire force of MU9s, MU10s and HH190s will take off just before first light tomorrow. They will race across the sea, staying as low as they can to avoid detection for as long as possible, bomb and strafe every single one of those sites, then race home before the British can react. They will rewind and rearm as quickly as possible and then accompany our fleet of bombers to their targets - the bases of the Royal Aviator Corps and the factories that supply them.'

There was murmuring at that and he slapped the pointer down onto the table.

'We will no longer be bombing British cities!' he bellowed. 'The Kaiser's tactic of attacking the citizens of Britain was a valid one when we were trying to scare them into surrendering, but he agrees with me that it is no longer necessary. With the number of bombers we are able to commit to these raids and the progress we've made in the efficiency of our ground crews to turn them around I fully expect the British air force to be weakened enough in the first week for us to be able to launch our invasion fleet.'

He leaned forwards, putting his hands on the back of his chair and looking around at the officers. 'There is nothing to stop us from our objective. As long as we remain focussed and you do the jobs I have picked you to do, then the prize is ours. I have every confidence in you. However,' he said, glaring at them warningly, 'fail me even once and you will find yourself in Berlin, explaining to the Kaiser why you have delayed his triumphal march into London. I'm sure he will be very forgiving.'

He met the eyes of the officers one by one, deliberately avoiding those of the woman, who he was fairly sure was hiding a smirk behind her hand.

'Dismissed!' he shouted, unable to resist making them jump one last time.

As they scrambled to their feet and started hurrying out he turned back to the map. He studied it for the hundredth, maybe the thousandth time, looking for anything he'd missed, any way to improve the deceptively simple plan that he'd already revised over and over to make as perfect as it could be. There was nothing, though. Everything that could have been done had been done, the pieces had been put on the board and all that remained was to make sure they did what they'd been told to do. Then maybe, just maybe, he would accomplish something that nobody had been able to accomplish in almost nine hundred years - the conquest of Britain.

The door to the briefing room closed behind the last of the men, cutting off their muttered complaints and comments along with the jangling of the numerous medals on their chests, most of which had been earned off the back of *his* hard work. Finally, he had the peace and quiet he needed to go through his final preparations and write his final orders.

He turned to go back to the table and his notes, but stumbled to a halt, almost tripping over his own feet when he found the woman still in her seat, still staring at him.

'Yes, Generalleutnant?' He asked, fighting to control his voice and slow his racing heart.

The woman stood, slowly, languidly unfolding from the chair, then came towards him. Her movements reminded him of a snake and he shuddered involuntarily.

'I just wanted to make sure that you are clear on the Kaiser's instructions, Herr Generalfeldmarschall.'

The woman stopped in front of him, uncomfortably close, and stared into his eyes. She was tall, taller than him, even, and he found himself looking slightly upwards to meet her gaze.

'Of course I am. The Kaiser was perfectly clear in his orders on both your role here and what is required of me.'

'Good.'

The woman smiled and for some reason he found that worse than her normal expressionless countenance. She maintained the smile, remaining almost unnaturally motionless for a few seconds, then suddenly turned and stalked away.

He held his breath, forcing himself to stay still and upright until she was gone and the door had closed firmly behind her and only then allowed himself to let out a sigh of relief. He flopped down into the closest chair, put his shaking hands in his lap and bent over them. When he was a bit more in control of himself he fumbled in his pockets until he found a handkerchief and used it to mop the sweat from his face.

Damn her. There was no place for a woman in his briefings, no matter what rank she held. He couldn't keep her away, though, couldn't stop her from doing anything, in fact, because the latest packet of orders from Berlin had included not only an explanation for why she was there, but also an official document with the Kaiser's seal on it. That document gave her the power to act in his name in any way she saw fit, with no recrimination or consequence.

That made *her* the most powerful person at the briefing that morning, not him. The most powerful person in the world, after the Kaiser himself.

And he dreaded to think how she might use that power if he somehow, inadvertently or not, got in her way.

Gruber struggled out of the back of his staff autocar and staggered up the steps to the door of the chateau that served as headquarters for the Crimson Barons. The painkillers he'd took had barely taken the edge off his headache and he was looking forward to having an early lunch then going back to bed.

He was brought up short just inside the door, though, when he saw that all his pilots were gathered in the drawing room, the woman with them.

'What's going on?' he asked, stumbling into the room, his headache suddenly much worse.

'We were waiting for you,' Reitsch said.

'What for?'

'The briefing.'

'What briefing?'

'The one I scheduled for you.'

She smiled sweetly, batting her eyelids, and he couldn't help be impressed; she didn't look anything like the cold-hearted bitch he knew she was.

'Thank you,' he replied after a moment, straightening up and smiling charmingly back at her - two could play at that game and he had shared the screen with much worse than her. 'This briefing will just be for pilots, though, so please leave.'

She laughed. 'Baron Gruber, you forget! I am one of your pilots now.'

'I'm afraid we don't have an aircraft for you, you'll have to wait until...'

'Oh, no need to worry about that; I brought my own.'

'Even so,' he persisted, 'the squadron is full. We only need twelve pilots, so I'm afraid...'

'Herr Fleisch!' she called out without taking her eyes off of Gruber.

A pilot, one of the youngest and newest arrivals, shot to his feet. 'Ma'am!'

'Your services are no longer needed. Report to Fliegertruppe headquarters immediately for reassignment.

'Yes, ma'am! Thank you, ma'am!'

The young man ran from the room, chased by the envious looks of many of the other pilots.

'There!' the woman said. 'Twelve pilots!'

Gruber laughed, but inside he was seething as he stalked to the front of the room where the squadron's copy of the map that had been in Schmidt's briefing room was pinned.

CHAPTER 3

'Shortjack control, this is Badger Leader. Badger Squadron is on a training flight. Do you have any business for us to steer clear of, over?'

'Badger Leader, this is Shortjack control. The skies are clear. Have fun. Over.'

'Thank you, Shortjack. Let us know if the situation changes, please.'

'Roger, Badger Leader. Shortjack out.'

'Right then, Badgers.' Abby said once the local air traffic control had signed off. 'We haven't flown together for a while and we have three new aircraft to get used to, so we'll take things easy this flight.'

Taking things easy for the Misfits wasn't the same as taking things easy for anyone else. After doing some formation flying as a squadron, then as individual flights, they had split up into their pairs and played follow-my-leader. If Ellie had thought Tanya had been throwing them around the sky before at DART, she had a rather rude awakening when the Muscovite started using the full capabilities of her custom-built aircraft, Wolf. However, the performance of the modified Spitsteam was much higher than that of a standard Spit and she managed to keep up, only straying from her wing a couple of times, which she was rather pleased about. She wasn't sure if she would have been able to do so without her new flightsuit, though. She had filled the pockets in the legs and abdomen from the bottle of distilled water that had been left in her room and it made a real difference, making withstanding the extreme forces of the strenuous manoeuvres far easier. Even so, she was still on the edge of exhaustion when they landed, but she took some consolation in the fact that both Benedict and Rob looked in just as bad shape as her, if not worse.

They left their aircraft in the more than capable hands of their fitters and trooped into the ready room. Scarlet was laying on a sofa, leafing through Derek's magazine while she munched on a sandwich from a plate resting on her belly.

'Comfortable, Scarlet?' Abby asked as they came in.

'Yes, thanks!' the Irishwoman said with a grin, 'although I haven't had time to raid Biffy's drinks cabinet yet... anyone got anything stashed nearby?'

'Please,' Abby said, huffing and shaking her head, 'don't scandalise the children yet. At least let them settle in first.'

'And then can I try to corrupt them?'

'Yes, of course you can.'

'Yay!' Scarlet grinned at the new recruits, but then buried her head back in the magazine.

'Grab what you want and sit down, everyone. Let's debrief.' She looked at Ellie, Rob and Benedict in turn. 'And yes, we are going to talk about you in front of you.'

While Rob and Ellie went to pour teas for everyone from the urns, Benedict helped Derek and Tanya distribute plates and when everyone was ready they found places around the table in the middle of the room.

Abby squirmed uncomfortably, sandwiched between Derek and Drake.

'We really need to build a bigger ready room,' she muttered. 'It's going to get very crowded in here when everyone gets back.'

She took a big bite of a sandwich, then pointed at Derek. 'You start,' she mumbled around the food.

'I'm afraid it has been a rather disappointing morning.' Derek began. 'Officer Wilberforce failed to remain on my wing on numerous occasions even though I did not push Kite to her limit during the entire flight.'

'Because my Spit isn't as good as Kite.' Benedict grumbled, half under his breath.

'Ellie had no trouble keeping up with me.' Tanya said, casually, without looking up from her plate or pausing in stuffing sandwiches in her mouth.

'Alright,' Abby said, raising her voice slightly to forestall any further comments and prevent the morale of one of her newest pilots being destroyed instead of just a bit bent. 'We will accept that there is a learning curve when a pilot steps into a new aircraft and that the learning curve might be a little different for each pilot.' She looked at Benedict. 'You need to pull your finger out, Officer Wilberforce, otherwise one of two things will happen - either I will ship you off to another squadron or the Prussians will solve my problem for me before I can. Understood?'

'Yes, ma'am.' Benedict said, a little grumpily.

'Good.' Abby pointed at Drake. 'Next.'

'Rob has risen to the challenge admirably this morning.' Drake said confidently. 'He still needs to fully explore his aircraft's capabilities, but I'm sure that won't take him too long.'

'Excellent.' Abby said, smiling at Rob. 'Tanya?'

'Ellie is good.' Tanya said, without looking up.

The other pilots looked at her expectantly, but apparently that was all she was going to say and they chuckled.

'A glowing recommendation.' Abby said eventually. She looked at Ellie. 'What is your assessment of the modified Spitsteams?'

Ellie blinked at her a moment and swallowed when everyone around the table looked at her. She caught movement out of the corner of her eye and turned her head to find that even Scarlet had stopped what she was doing and sat up to listen.

'Me?' she asked looking back to Abby hurriedly when the Irishwoman poked her tongue out at her.

'You.' Abby said. 'From what I saw you had the best handle on the capabilities of your aircraft and you're a Misfit now, so I expect you to speak up whenever you have something to contribute.'

'Oh... alright...' Ellie said, 'uh...' she stared at the table, blocking out her audience, took a deep breath to steady herself, then began, her words coming out slowly at first, then in a rush. 'Generally, the overall performance of the aircraft is much improved over that of a standard Spitsteam. It accelerates faster and the roll rate is a *lot* higher. It still has many of the drawbacks of a Spitsteam, though,' she gestured at Tanya, 'for example, the two times I lost my wing leader were after pushing the nose forward into a dive.'

'That's...' Abby began when Ellie paused to take a breath.

Ellie hadn't finished, though, and didn't even register that the commander of the Misfits had spoken.

'The rate of climb was lower than a standard Spitsteam, though, noticeably so, probably because of the decreased surface area of the wings creating less lift, so we'd need to be aware of that if we were climbing to intercept. And I'm fairly sure I noticed as significant reduction in performance when we climbed higher, which might cause a problem if we're tangling with bomber escorts flying at high level, but I'll have to test that a bit more to be sure.' She thought quickly. 'Uh... that's it.'

She lifted her eyes and found everyone staring at her. She grimaced. 'Sorry, I'll try to do better next time.'

'Yes, make sure you do.' Tanya said, rolling her eyes before returning to her seemingly unending supply of sandwiches.

Abby laughed and shared a look with Derek and Drake who nodded at her.

'That was more than sufficient, thank you, Ellie.' She looked around the table. 'Does anyone have anything they'd like to add? No? Does anyone need anything?' she pointed a finger at Scarlet when the Irishwoman drew breath to speak, 'apart from a drink!'

When nobody spoke up she nodded. 'Well, the Prussians seem to be giving us the day to enjoy the sunshine, so let's take advantage of it. We'll take off again as soon as the fitters have finished rewinding - I want to get in at least three more flights today.'

A further three flights was all they had time for, even skipping a proper lunch and making do with sandwiches. When they came down the final time, just as it was starting to get dark, they found Penny waiting for them by the hangars with Scarlet, who was lounging in a deck chair with a glass in hand and a bottle on the grass beside her. She walked over to them, a slightly odd rhythm to her stride the only thing betraying the fact that her legs were artificial.

The pilots went to greet her and Abby gave her a hug. 'Is everything sorted?'

Penny nodded. 'Yes. All the tedious paperwork has been done and I've left the base in capable hands.' She nodded a greeting at the rest of the pilots. 'But you don't want to hear about that and I really don't want to have to think about it anymore.' She turned and started leading them towards the ready room. 'Oh!' she said, turning back and smiling widely. 'I almost forgot. I brought you a present from Scotland.'

'Hello, everyone,' Gwen Stone said, stepping out of the shadows of the ready room.

'Miss us?' asked Kitty Wright from beside her.

'Wait!' Penny called out, holding up her hands to stop Abby, Derek, Drake and Tanya as they leapt forwards to greet them. 'Yes, we know you want to hear all about what they've been doing the last couple of months, but we rushed to get down here and haven't had a decent meal today. So, go and get changed and you can interrogate them over dinner up at the house!'

'Yes, ma'am!' Abby said with a grin before turning to her pilots. 'You heard Lady Penelope! Dismissed!'

The pilots said a hasty hello and goodbye to Gwen and Kitty, then rushed off to shower and change.

In less than half an hour the pilots were in their dress uniforms and they drove up to the manor house in a pair of the drab green base autocars.

Over dinner with Biffy, Gwen and Kitty regaled them with tales of assassination attempts and failed negotiations, American snubs and Japanese welcomes, of meeting emperors and presidents and of reinforcements that were on their way, but might not come in time. They were only able to scratch the surface of everything that had happened to them, though, because, all too soon, it was time to call it a night and they returned to the base and retired to their rooms.

Gwen placed her top hat carefully into its box, then hung her dress uniform inside the wardrobe before doing the same for Kitty, who had just dumped her clothes on a chair and gone straight to the pile of post on the writing desk. She didn't blame her; the letters had been delivered to them by one of Algernon Billingsworth's people right as they were leaving to go to dinner and they hadn't had a chance to look at them, beyond to see that the vast majority were for Kitty. She had a large family and it looked like every one of them had written to her. Several times.

Gwen finished making sure the uniforms were taking care of then got changed into her pyjamas and joined Kitty.

'Anything for me?' she asked.

'I don't think so,' Kitty said without taking her nose out of a letter. 'Have a look.'

Kitty pushed the stack of letters towards her and Gwen picked them up and flipped through them. Aside from the couple of dozen or more letters with American postmarks on them there were a few official letters for both of them with the stamps of various government departments on them and one letter from her parents, which reminded her that she needed to contact them about Tesla's cereal boxes. There was also a telegram addressed to them both.

'What's this?' she asked, showing it to Kitty.

The American barely glanced at it before going back to her letter. 'No idea. Can you open it? One of my cousins just got engaged and she's telling me about her fiancé.'

Gwen slit open the brown envelope with the letter opener and pulled out the flimsy telegram slip. She frowned.

'It's from an E. Balsells. Who's...?'

'Eulalia!' Kitty cried out, snatching the paper from Gwen and scanning it rapidly. 'She's coming to England!'

'When?'

'On the next available transport! That means she could be here in a week or two!' Kitty shot out of the chair and ran for the door. 'I've got to tell Algie; he can start the ball rolling on her paperwork!'

'Um...' Gwen started, lifting her hand to stop Kitty, but the American didn't notice and ran out of the door, not giving her the chance to tell her that she was only in her underwear. She grinned; she hoped Algie Billingsworth was in his room down the corridor otherwise quite a few people were going to be in for a treat when Kitty started looking for him.

She opened the letter from her parents and went and laid down on the bed with it. She didn't start reading straight away, though, instead she looked around the room, at all her and Kitty's things that had been brought out of storage and that they'd placed around the room while they'd been waiting for the squadron to come down. The things that made the room a home, rather than just something temporary. She hoped it lasted; she was very tired of moving around all the time.

Abby threw her hat and jacket onto the armchair in the corner in passing then sat wearily on the bed and put her head in her hands. She was tired, dead tired, but not because of the exertions of the day.

'When did they get so young?' she asked herself.

She lifted her eyes to the two photographs on her bedside table. The first was of her and James on holiday in Great Yarmouth, eating ice creams on the pier, and she trailed her fingers over it, but it was the second one that she picked up. Taken in France in April of 1940, before the Prussian invasion, it predated the one in Sir Douglas Pewtall's office by a few months and showed the squadron as it had been originally. Her sister, Cece, was next to her in the middle, her arms crossed over her chest and legs spread wider than decorum dictated, as always rather unhappy with having her picture taken. The others were gathered around them, laughter in their eyes and a few arms on shoulders - a close group of friends, united by a cause and with a common interest to bind them tightly together.

The three new pilots were barely eighteen, less than a year older than her son James, *Jimmy*, who, even though he thought himself so grown up, was still just a child. The Misfits had never been that young, though. The faces that looked back at her from the photograph, the smiling, confident faces, had all *lived* before they'd gone to war. None of them was younger than twenty-five, several of them were married or had been at some point and all of them had known exactly what they had been getting themselves into when she had recruited them, what most likely awaited them. She wasn't entirely sure the new recruits did.

She dropped the photograph onto the bed next to her and put her head back into her hands. Last summer she'd been thankful that she hadn't been one of those squadron commanders who had been forced to watch as one far too young pilot after another was killed as soon as they arrived and she prayed to anyone or anything that was listening that she wasn't going to have to do that now.

CHAPTER 4

23rd August 1941

Gruber's autocar was waiting outside the chateau to take him to the airfield and he slipped in and got himself comfortable, then wrapped his hands around the mug of coffee that Lang, his servant, handed him. There was a plate of croissants already on the seat and he grabbed one and stuffed most of it into his mouth as the vehicle pulled away smoothly. It was a very short trip to the hangars and he barely had time to chew, swallow and grab another pastry before they were turning onto the apron and driving behind the line of aircraft.

He smiled at the sight of *Hölle* and the ten *Blutsaugers*, all glowing red in the light spilling out from the hangars, but then frowned when he saw the unfamiliar aircraft at the far end, beyond his. It was black, with a thick red stripe on the back of the fuselage and was one of the ugliest aircraft he had ever seen, as if the worst bits of an MU9 had been cobbled together with the bad bits of an HH190. Those weren't the best looking aircraft, but there was a beauty in their severity and functionality, this, on the other hand, was just a mess and it spoiled the perfect image he wanted his squadron to present.

Hopefully, it flew as bad as it looked; the sooner she got shot down over Britain, the sooner she would be out of his hair.

He grabbed a third pastry as the autocar rolled to a stop behind Hölle and he got out and strode towards it.

He could feel the eyes of his pilots on him, but he ignored them and just walked around his aircraft, carrying out his checks quickly and efficiently. He couldn't resist a glance towards the black aircraft when his checks meant he was looking in that direction, though, and was mildly annoyed to see the woman was already in her cockpit, but was concentrating on something in her lap and not watching him.

He finished quickly and tossed the last bit of croissant away, the mug with it, before climbing up to the cockpit to do the last few checks.

Orders had been delivered the night before with the coordinates of their target. They had included a precise time they had to take off and a precise cruising speed, so that all of the fighter squadrons arrived at their targets at the exact same time, just after first light.

He looked at his chronograph and shrugged. 'Close enough,' he muttered, then motioned to his fitter to release Hölle's spring.

'Star squadron, prepare for takeoff,' he announced, glancing down the line of aircraft to make sure that everyone was in their cockpit.

'Star Leader, this is Two.'

Gruber hissed in irritation as the woman's voice filled his ears instead of the acknowledgements he'd been expecting. 'What is it, Two?'

'There are eight minutes and twenty-three seconds remaining until the takeoff time specified in our orders, Leader.'

'I'm aware of that, Two,' Gruber said between clenched teeth, turning to glare at the woman. 'But I thought we could taxi into position so as to be ready when the time comes.'

'Roger that, Leader.'

Gruber didn't say anything else or give any more commands, he just waved away his fitters and pushed the throttle forwards. He bounced towards the men holding torches to direct them to the downwind end of the airfield, leaving the rest of his squadron to follow as best they could.

When he reached the edge of the field he turned to face into the wind and glanced at his chronograph again.

Still five minutes to go.

He watched the other aircraft feeling their way across the dark airfield. They were moving slower and far more cautiously than he had, but eventually they were lined up and ready to take off.

Four minutes.

He peered up into the sky. The weather reports had promised clear weather for the next few days at least and the stars were bright overhead, but there was a touch of mist low to the ground. It would burn off as soon as the sun came up, though.

He checked his chronograph one more time.

Three minutes.

He growled. He'd waited long enough. It was *his* squadron. *He* decided when they took off, not some general sitting behind a desk a hundred miles from the fight. What difference could it possibly make if he turned up on target three minutes early? It wasn't as if the British could pack up their radio direction finding stations and move them in that time. It wasn't even enough time for enemy pilots to get to their aircraft, let alone get in the air to intercept.

'Star squadron,' he began decisively, but then his voice caught in his throat and he hesitated. 'Er... Check in.' Damn it. He couldn't do it. Couldn't risk the woman telling tales about him to the Kaiser. He had to play nice. At least for now.

'Take off in flights,' he ordered as soon as the last man had checked in, then pushed the throttle fully forward, deliberately not looking at the time. He was fully aware that it had likely been a couple of minutes since he had last, though.

Hölle leapt into the air, leaving the other aircraft behind and he turned onto the assigned heading and settled at two hundred feet off the ground. The Barons had been assigned a prime site for their base, near Calais and the narrowest part of the channel, and in less than a minute the port and the massed vessels of the invasion fleet flashed below him and then open water was stretching out in front of him.

The sky was brightening to the east, sending colours shooting into the sky and he smiled faintly; this had always been his favourite time of the day to fly, when there wasn't enough light to shoot or dogfight, when he could just enjoy the sensation of being free in the air and when he could pretend he was on his own, even if he wasn't.

He tore his gaze from the horizon and glanced around to make sure that his squadron was formed up properly around him and only then realised that he actually was on his own. He clicked the button to transmit, but before he could say anything the woman's voice filled his ears.

'Star Leader, this is Two. Our orders specified a speed of three hundred kilometres per hour for the flight.'

Gruber snarled, sure that he detected a hint of laughter and more than a little mockery in her voice.

He put Hölle on its wing and pulled into a hard turn so that he could search the sky behind him and immediately spotted his squadron, formed up neatly on the interloper's aircraft. He completed the turn, putting the aircraft back onto its original heading, then throttled back to let them catch up. As soon as they appeared behind his wings he pushed the throttle carefully back forwards until Hölle was doing exactly three hundred kilometres per hour. He gave himself the small satisfaction of placing himself directly in front of Reitsch's aircraft, forcing her to manoeuvre around him to form up on his wing. It was petty, he knew that, but he didn't care.

'I hope you can shoot as well as you can tell the time, Two,' he said, glaring across at her, 'because I have no place for bad pilots in my squadron.'

She looked back at him and smiled. 'Wait and see, Leader. One minute to target.'

Douglas Pewtall was just being served his first cup of tea of the day in his quarters at RAC Bentley Priory when his aide burst in.

'Sir! The control room needs you right away!'

'If there are raids forming up they know what to do. They don't need me.' Pewtall said, sipping calmly. 'I'll be there in a few minutes'

'It's not bombers, sir, it's fighters and they've hit our radar stations.'

'Which ones?' Pewtall asked, setting his tea aside and standing.

'All of them, sir.'

Pewtall blanched, but nodded confidently. 'I was expecting this.'

He strode to the sideboard and grabbed a pen and some note paper. 'I'll be right there. Tell them I want a report on the operational status of the stations and in the meantime have this signal sent.'

The aide glanced at the paper. '*Illuminate*, sir?'

'That's right.'

'Yes, sir.'

The young woman ran from the room and Pewtall shook his head, smiling wryly. 'So excitable.'

He walked back to the table and sat down. He hadn't been lying - he *had* expected this from the Prussians and the boys and girls in the control room *didn't* need him to tell them what to do. Everything was already in place to respond, it had just needed his say so.

He picked up his knife and fork and began tucking in to his breakfast. He had a while before they would need him and it might be his only chance to get a decent meal that day. He wasn't going to waste it.

Gruber tossed his helmet and gloves to Lang and stalked towards the black aircraft that was only just coming to a halt next to his.

He waved her fitters away and leapt up onto the wing.

'Don't you ever show me up like that in front of my men again,' he told her quietly, leaning over her, drawing on years of experience playing villains to heap as much menace as he could on her.

She didn't wilt under his gaze, though, but met it unflinchingly as she stood, forcing him to move back to avoid a collision. She stepped out of the cockpit, onto the wing, forcing him even further back, and confronted him coldly.

'Obey your orders and don't make it necessary for me to do so again, then.'

Gruber glared at her, but she didn't look away or back down and eventually he huffed and shook his head.

'Go powder your nose or something,' he said, waving his hand dismissively, 'just make sure you're ready for the next flight. I hope you and this monstrosity are up to the challenge, because we're not just going to be shooting at buildings this time.'

'She's called Vixen, and we are, don't you worry.'

'*She?*' Gruber rolled his eyes. 'You're one of *those*, are you?'

He jumped down from the wing and stalked away, but then turned and looked back at the ugly aircraft. 'That thing suits you very well.'

'We're as good as blind, sir,' Squadron Leader Diana Fisher, the coordinator of the control room buried deep under Bentley Priory said, motioning at the map table below. 'We have no long range information and no way of telling whether there is anything building up or not.'

Pewtall peered down into "the pit" from his desk in the semi-circular gallery. The map table below, showing the British isles and the surrounding portions of Europe, was almost completely empty, The men and women who pushed the markers around standing silently at their posts, waiting for something to happen. Unaccustomed to such inactivity, most of them were stifling yawns.

'What's the damage, Dee?' he asked quietly.

'They hit every radar station on the south and east coasts apart from three. They didn't seem to know about the one in Arundel Castle, or the one in Bembridge...'

'That's the one they built into a windmill, isn't it?'

'Yes, sir.'

Pewtall shrugged. 'Seemed like a bloody silly idea at the time, but now who's laughing? And the third?'

'RAC High Road.'

'That's in Darsham, correct? Suffolk?'

'Yes, sir. High Road was, in fact, targeted, but the Fleas apparently mistook a local amateur enthusiast's radio mast for theirs and destroyed it instead, along with the poor woman's shed and outhouse.'

Pewtall huffed. 'We'll send them the seat as a trophy.'

'Yes, sir,' the woman said. She wasn't known for having much of a sense of humour and Pewtall couldn't blame her at that moment.

'You said south and east coasts. What about the northern stations? They didn't hit those?'

'No, sir, they didn't hit anything north of the Scottish border.'

'Did we get any of them on the way out?'

'No, sir,' Fisher said, 'we scrambled the four squadrons we had on standby and our standing patrols dived on them as soon as they were alerted to the ongoing attacks, but they were already heading home by then and the decision was made to recall them rather than chase.'

'Good. Correct decision.' Pewtall said. 'How long until the stations are operation again?'

'Repair estimates are still coming in, but most stations are talking about needing weeks to rebuild, if they are given the time and the resources and aren't hit again. The upshot is that we have very little radar coverage right now and there are wide swathes of Europe which we just cannot see.'

Pewtall nodded. 'Understood, thank you. Now, I have an exercise for you to carry out: I want you to imagine you could place eight radar towers on that map down there. Anywhere you want and pointing in any direction you want. Where would you put them to gain the maximum coverage?'

'Sir?'

He smiled at her puzzled expression. 'Humour me, please.'

'Yes, sir.'

'And humour me quickly, please.' He looked up at the clock, high on the wall opposite his desk. 'Preferably in the next five minutes.'

'Yes, sir.'

The woman hurried away and Pewtall picked up the telephone and pressed the button on it to talk to the man at the far end of the gallery to his left.

'Squadron ops.' The man picked up the phone without looking, then saw who it was and looked over to Pewtall with a surprised expression. 'Sir?'

'Terry, how many fighter squadrons do we have up in Scotland?'

'Twelve, sir, not including the operational training squadron.'

'Right.' Pewtall said, gazing down at the map table. 'I want you to reassign four of them. Bring them south of the border and spread them out along the major Prussian attack routes.'

'That will leave our factories in Scotland dangerously under protected, sir!' the man protested.

'I am aware of that,' Pewtall said with a smile. 'But I don't believe they will be coming under very much pressure in the next few weeks. Get it done, please. As quickly as possible.'

'Yes, sir.'

Pewtall set the telephone receiver down and looked down at the map, placing the remaining radar stations on it in his mind, picturing the arcs that they swept. On their own they were totally inadequate, but they were something that could be built on and more than he'd thought the Prussians would leave them.

'Sir?'

He turned to find Dee Fisher hovering behind him, slightly unsteady on her wooden leg.

'Got it, Dee?'

'Yes, sir.' She brandished a sheet of paper.

'Thank you.' He took another scrap of paper from his breast pocket. 'Have the information transmitted blind on this frequency, please. Make sure the operator sends the recognition code first.'

She read it and frowned. '*Sheepish*, sir?'

'That's right. Thank you, Dee. Oh, and once you've done that, bring channel fourteen up on the main speakers, please.'

'Yes, sir.' She gave him a quizzical look, but didn't say anything and just hobbled away.

Pewtall glanced up at the clock again, then looked back down at the map. From the sheer number of attacks the Fleas had carried out, they must have used most, if not all of their fighters, so they would have nothing to escort their bombers with until they'd rewound. Assuming they took, on average, half an hour to get home, another twenty minutes to rewind every single one of the aircraft, then ten minutes to scramble them again, then the raids could be on their way across the water an hour after the radar stations went down. It had been forty minutes since the towers had been hit. They still had some time, but would it be enough?

A steward set a cup of tea and plate of biscuits on his table and he nodded his thanks absently, but didn't touch it, or take his eyes off the still empty map table.

If there was no signal soon he was going to have to decide whether he was going to commit his fighters blind, hoping that the enemy raids came over while they still had enough spring tension to properly intercept them, or wait for the three remaining radar stations to pick them up.

He picked up the phone, about to call the radio operator to make sure the main speakers were tuned to the correct frequency when there was a brief crackle, making him wince, then a voice sounded around the room.

'Home control, this is Sheepish Leader. Come in, please.'

Pewtall pushed his chair back and leapt to his feet. He rushed to the back of the room where the radio operator was just answering.

'Sheepish Leader, this is Home control. We read you, over.'

'Sheepish squadron reports on station with telemetry coming in. Screens are clear. Will report any changes. Over.'

Unsure how to reply, the operator looked up at Pewtall, who bent over and spoke into the microphone himself.

'Thank you, Sheepish Leader, happy hunting.'

'Thank you, control. Sheepish Leader out.'

Pewtall smiled and straightened up. Unsurprisingly, every eye in the semi-circle was on him.

Perhaps it was time to tell them about Owen Llewellyn and the aircraft he'd been secretly building.

The sky was black with bombers and Gruber took a moment to appreciate the sight as he climbed towards them, the rest of his squadron at his back. There were hundreds of the large aircraft in the sky over northern France, banking and turning as they struggled to find their place before it was time to head across the channel towards Britain. It was awe inspiring and it made it easy to believe that an ultimate Prussian victory was close at hand, especially seeing as this was only one of four raids building up.

As was stated in their orders, the Barons flew through one of the few gaps and kept climbing into the sky, looking for a height advantage over any British fighters that came up to intercept the bombers. Gruber was of the opinion that it was an unnecessary precaution, though, that the British response was going to be haphazard at best. With their radio direction finding system utterly destroyed the British were blind and they had no way of knowing that Schmidt had deliberately delayed this raid by an hour. They had probably panicked and sent everything up after the attack, thinking that the bombing raids would be following closely behind. They would have hung around as long as they could, conserving spring tension, but then be forced to go back down and would only now be beginning the process of rewinding, unable to take off to intercept. They would be lined up on their airfields, sitting ducks, and in one raid the Fliegertruppe might well cut the British defensive force in half.

Finally, the Barons were on station, surrounded by dozens of squadrons of fighters. Schmidt had wanted them to be seen so they were the last to arrive and, as soon as Gruber had reported in, the order came to turn north-west towards the airfields of Britain.

Sir Douglas rested his chin in his hand and watched the markers being put onto the map table as more and more enemy aircraft were detected.

Four raids. Each with more than a thousand aircraft in them. Fully eight times what they had sent over for their biggest raid on September 15th last year.

It was hard to believe that the Prussians were able to put so many aircraft into the air, or that they would need to commit so many to take Britain. It was also extremely hard to believe that Britain could possibly hope to resist for very long.

They would, though.

He lifted his eyes to the light board on the wall. Last year there had been far fewer lights and many of them had gone dark over the summer. Right now it was ablaze, as every available fighter clawed for height, making ready to give Britain's response to Prussia's arrogance.

Gwen nervously glanced out of her cockpit.

The sky around and below her was filled with squadron after squadron of Harridans and Spitsteams and the Prussians were on their way in greater numbers than had ever been seen in the sky before. In any sky.

A lot of the British pilots wouldn't survive. It didn't matter if they were experienced or not, it was just a fact; the odds were just stacked too heavily against them. They had to fight even so and they had to prevail, otherwise the enemy would be able to cross the thin blue line that stretched from horizon to horizon in front of her in greater numbers than the men and women of the army could withstand.

That wasn't what had her worried, though, because she was absolutely positive that the men and women of the RAC were up to the task and would give the Prussians the hiding they deserved. No, it was the grey aircraft on her wing that concerned her, or, more specifically, the woman piloting it.

Neither she nor Kitty had flown properly since they'd left America - the couple of short jaunts they'd had in the Japanese fighter, the *Raijin*, didn't really count and buzzing around in an *Akitsu* certainly didn't. For pilots of their experience calibre that wouldn't usually mean much and indeed everything had come rushing back to her as soon as she'd pulled back the stick and *Excalibur* had leapt into the air. However, Kitty wasn't just out of practice, she was also in a completely unfamiliar aircraft. *Hawk*, her previous aircraft, had been destroyed on Malta and there hadn't been time to design her a new one before the king had sent the two of them to America, so Abby had put her in *Wraith*, Bruce's aircraft. That made sense, because Wraith's design was based on Excalibur's and her performance was very similar, but Kitty wouldn't know how to best use her and might get caught out by a Flea who understood their aircraft better. This flight would be more than enough for her to learn the capabilities of her aircraft, but she needed to survive it first.

Thankfully, in keeping with Sir Douglas Pewtall's instructions about not risking the Misfits and keeping up morale, Abby had given her discretion over which targets she and Kitty attacked, if any. And Gwen fully intended to stay out of the thick of things and only intervene where they could safely make a difference.

'Shortjack control to all aircraft. Enemy is closing. They should reach the shore in one minute. Happy hunting.'

Gwen looked over at Kitty and found the American smiling back at her. She lifted a hand and chuckled when Kitty winked cheekily, but then turned away to make her final preparations for combat.

Gruber frowned at the dark cloud racing to meet them. Quite apart from the fact that they were supposed to be on the ground rewinding, the British weren't supposed to have so many fighters to put in the air in the first place. Not only that, but the enemy weren't climbing desperately to reach the bombers, like they'd had to for most of last summer, they were already at the same height. Or worse, he saw as he peered up into the bright sky, *higher* than them, where they would have the advantage to start the engagement.

Something had gone dreadfully wrong, both with the plan and the intelligence that they were relying on, and Gruber allowed himself a very brief smile. For once he wasn't the one in charge and this failure couldn't be blamed on him - it could only make him look good in the long run, in fact. The only trouble was he was still the one who was going to have to pay the consequences, because he was the one looking down the barrel of the machine guns and cannons of the enemy Spitsteams and Harridans and not sitting behind a desk with a glass of schnapps, listening to men dying.

When he got down he would certainly send a very strongly worded complaint to headquarters, with a copy going to the Kaiser.

'Badger Eight to Badger Leader, some of the Prussian fighters have started climbing. So far they're heading towards our main force and none are coming towards us.'

'Roger that, Eight. Keep an eye on them, please, let me know if that changes.'

'Roger, Leader.'

Even as Ellie listened to the brief exchange between Benedict and Abby she was scanning ahead, trying to spot the splinter group of enemy fighters. She swore under her breath as she selected the wrong lens and almost dazzled herself with the low-light filter - one flight wasn't enough time to get used to the variety and choice she now had thanks to the new goggles that had come with the flightsuit and she was starting to regret not wearing the old ones until she'd had time to play. Eventually, she got the right one and brought them into focus.

'Leader,' she said, 'this is Four. I'm seeing red aircraft leading the climbing group.'

Abby chuckled. 'Looks like we picked the right group to reinforce today. Turning towards them.'

The Misfits swung slowly around to point towards the Prussian fighters. They had been hovering somewhat apart from the main force of British fighters, off to one side and a few thousand feet higher, where they could get a good view of how the fight progressed and intervene where they were most needed, but with the Crimson Barons on the playing field it was obvious where that would be.

'If we can shoot a couple of those down it'll do wonders for morale, Leader,' Drake said.

'It would, Five,' Abby answered, 'but we can't get so caught up in chasing them that we neglect our fellows or allow ourselves to be surprised by other Fleas.'

'Keep our eyes open and our wits about us, you mean, Leader?' Penny asked.

'Eyes, yes. Wits? I'm not sure how many of those most of you have, Two.'

'Oh, how I've missed this.'

Ellie saw Penny and Abby glance at each other and grin and couldn't help smiling as well at the camaraderie and banter.

'Me too, Two. Me too.'

There was a slight pause, but then Abby's voice came back, more authoritatively this time. 'A and B flight, we'll continue on this course and we'll join in when the initial chaos has died down a bit. C flight, climb two thousand feet and orbit the fight. Look for your chance to pick a few stragglers off.'

'Roger that, Leader.'

Ellie watched as the two aircraft comprising C flight, piloted by Gwen Stone and Kitty Wright, pulled up sharply and climbed incredibly rapidly.

'Are you ready for this, Ellie?'

Tanya's voice in her ears, loud on their private channel, made Ellie start and she blushed as she realised that she had been staring up into the sky like a novice pilot. Knowing that she *was* a novice pilot didn't help; she was also a Misfit and should know better.

'Yes. Yes, I am,' she replied, giving Tanya a reassuring smile.

'Good!'

The Muscovite grinned back, then turned away, going back to her scan of the sky, even though they knew the Prussians were all below them.

Ellie watched her for a moment, then looked down at the fast approaching Prussians and swallowed as her mouth suddenly went dry.

The thing was, she *wasn't* ready.

While everyone else in the squadron seemed to be eager to get into the fight, she really wasn't. Not because she was frightened, because she wasn't really, not as much as she thought she would be, but because she wasn't sure she could do what she needed to do when the time came. She was fairly sure she'd be able to outfly most of the enemy pilots, she'd been told as much by Tanya and Abby, and she also had a better aircraft than they did, but she still wasn't sure whether she'd be able to knowingly take a life.

She was only too aware that it was the whole point of what she had been working towards for the last couple of months and that if she couldn't then there was no point in her being a Misfit, or in the cockpit of a fighter. She was also aware that an enemy pilot she spared might go on to kill British pilots, maybe a Misfit, or even one of her friends. But none of that did anything to take away from the fact that, with every press of the button on the spade grip, she would be ending the life of someone who probably wasn't very much older than her, who had their hopes and dream, who might be just like Rob, or Benedict, who would have a family to mourn them, friends who would miss them, a lover who would...

She took a shuddering breath as a sudden realisation hit her - it was the thought of Tay that was stopping her.

She'd thought she'd gotten over his death, that she had moved on, like a pilot at war had to do, but she hadn't. Deep down she was still feeling the hurt of losing him.

It wasn't that she had doubts about the act of shooting down an enemy itself, because she knew perfectly well that that was a fact of war and necessary to save lives and her country, but rather it was the thought of inflicting the pain she'd felt, that she *still* felt, on the people left behind that she couldn't cope with.

So, no. She wasn't ready. But she'd know if she could kill someone soon enough, seeing as the Prussians were going to be within range in a matter of seconds.

'Star Leader, this is Two. Bandits. Ten o'clock high.'

Gruber tore his eyes from the approaching fighters and gazed up into the sky, concerned about the possibility of getting jumped.

He shook his head and brought his eyes back down; it was only one squadron. Nothing to worry about...

His eyes shot back up as his brain belatedly processed the information his eyes had given it and urgently informed him that the silhouettes of the aircraft hovering high overhead didn't match those of Spitsteams and Harridans.

'It's the Misfits,' he said, 'looks like you're going to get a baptism of fire, Two.'

He frowned, puzzled. *What are they doing up there? They're usually at the very heart of the fight. Is this a trap?*

He had no time to worry about that, though, and he brought his eyes back down to the British fighters. He picked out a Spitsteam almost dead ahead of him and adjusted course minutely towards it.

Wait for it... wait for it...

Now!

He pulled back sharply on the stick, then rolled Hölle onto its back. Tracer rounds flashed past below him, but he ignored them and instead centred his sights back on the enemy aircraft.

He opened fire and roared in triumph as it broke apart with the impact of his cannon shells.

His first kill of the day.

He rolled Hölle again and banked hard, searching for the next.

This is not how I thought it would be, Reitsch thought as she took a potshot at a Harridan that banked in front of her. Pieces flew from its tail, but then it was gone as she continued her turn, sticking with Gruber, doing her job as his wingman. She smiled. *It's better.*

Gruber rolled, avoiding the fire from a Harridan, not caring, or even seeing, that it hit the Blutsauger trying its best to stay with him and blew it apart. He turned onto the tail of a Spitsteam that was itself on the tail of an HH190, but then frowned - that had been the fourth Harridan that had come his way.

He disengaged from the fight momentarily, rolling onto his back and pulling the stick into his lap to take him below the main group of fighters.

He found the bombers immediately; it was hard to miss them, even now that they had split up into groups, each one with their own RAC base or aircraft factory to target. It looked like every single one of them was surrounded by a black cloud of intense anti-aircraft fire.

The British ack-ack wouldn't fire at the bombers if there were British fighters attacking them... which meant they were none there - they were ignoring them and had instead been sent to engage the fighters.

As he got to the bottom of the split S he peered up at the melee and what he saw chilled him to the bone. For the first time ever that he could remember, the Fliegertruppe did not outnumber the enemy. For the first time ever the battle would come down to who had the better aircraft, who could use them best and which side could better coordinate with their wingmen and squadrons. None of which he was confident the Fliegertruppe were better at.

It was going to be a slaughter.

He picked a group of British aircraft out of the cloud and pointed his guns at them. He began spraying them, uncaring as to whether he scored any hits or not and in less than ten seconds he had expended the entirety of his remaining ammunition.

'I'm out of ammunition,' he said over the radio to anyone who was listening. 'Heading home.'

Even as he spoke he was reversing his heading and diving for the deck, building up as much speed as he could to put as much distance between himself and danger as possible as quickly as possible.

'Alright, I've had enough of this. A and B flight, split into pairs and attack in your own time. Happy hunting, Misfits.'

Even as Abby gave the order, Dragon was rolling onto her back and she dived away, followed closely by Kingfisher. The other Misfits, taken slightly by surprise, took a moment to respond, but, predictably, Tanya was next to go and Rob watched Ellie dive away after her.

'Happy hunting, Ellie,' he whispered as she disappeared beneath his wing.

The Misfits had been circling over the melee like vultures, watching as the two sides clashed, seeing aircraft after aircraft falling from the sky for a minute or so. It had left a bad taste in his mouth and the urge to dive and do *something* had quickly become overwhelming. Abby's order was very welcome, therefore, but at the same time he'd been dreading it; the sheer chaos of the fight below, the seemingly arbitrary way in which aircraft suddenly came apart or spun away out of control, was terrifying, as if the Dark Scythesman was reaching out at random and plucking men and women from the sky.

How could he possibly dive into that?

'Let's go, Six.' Drake said and, without thinking, Rob gave him a split second to pull away slightly before matching his manoeuvre. Only when he was racing at more than four hundred miles an hour towards uncertain death did he realise what he'd just done.

Abby and Penny were barely away before Tanya rolled Wolf onto her back and pulled into a steep dive. Ellie had known the Muscovite wouldn't hesitate to follow them and had been ready for the sudden manoeuvre, but even so she was a good twenty yards behind when she settled onto her tail. The Muscovite deployed flaps and throttled back, though, instead of screaming from the sky at top speed like the others, allowing Ellie to pull up beside her.

Ellie glanced over at her quizzically, wondering what she was doing and found Tanya looking back at her.

'If we go down at top speed we only get a chance for a quick pass and have to waste time turning around and coming back,' the Muscovite explained. 'This way we can get stuck straight in. It's much more fun!'

'Oh. Alright. Wonderful!'

Ellie gave her a smile, but her heart wasn't in it and Tanya threw her head back and laughed.

'Don't worry, Ellie! There's no way any of these Prussians are good enough to kill you. Just enjoy yourself and shoot down as many of them as you can. Make them afraid to come back.'

There was no chance for Ellie to answer as the fight was suddenly upon them.

If things had seemed chaotic from a few thousand feet above, up close it was utter madness, with dozens upon dozens of aircraft all apparently trying to occupy the same space. It was all Ellie could do to keep up with Tanya when the skies were empty, but in the middle of all of that it was an almost impossible task and she expected to be separated from her at any moment. Somehow, though, whenever she looked back from craning her head to see if there was anyone sneaking up behind them, the woman was still there.

She lost count of the number of times she had to call out that there was a Prussian angling for them, lost count of the number of aircraft that fell away from Tanya's relentless attacks, lost count of the number of times she snapped a quick burst at an enemy fighter as it crept deceptively lazily across her nose. Once or twice she caught sight of a flash of red, or the bright colours of one of the other Misfits, but they were gone in a flash, lost in a sea of grey and green aircraft.

There seemed to be no end to the enemies, but then suddenly they were in clean air

'Where did they go?' she asked, peering around. 'Did we get them all?'

Tanya laughed. 'Not even close!'

The Muscovite banked them round to head back the way they'd come and Ellie saw flashes of gunfire far below and miles away as the Prussians dived for home, pursued by a few British fighters.

'Shall we chase?' Ellie asked.

'No, Four.' Abby's voice broke in on the channel. 'All Badgers, this is Leader, return to base.'

Tanya turned them on a heading for Bagshot Hall. After a minute or so they joined up with Abby and Penny, then caught sight of the entirety of B flight off their port side, about half a dozen miles away. It wasn't until they were orbiting the airfield that Gwen and Kitty joined them, though, and everyone heaved a sigh of relief; the Misfits had come through their first battle unscathed. Relatively unscathed, anyway; when they visually checked each other before landing they found a neat row of small machine gun holes in Excalibur's wing and a big gaping one in Ellie's tail.

Ellie hadn't even realised she'd been hit and, as she flew a holding pattern around the airfield, making sure that everything was working fine and hadn't been affected in any way, she found herself shaking slightly. Now that the fight was over and there was no need to fling her aircraft around or try to see everything going on in a crowded sky she could feel her energy seeping away and her eyelids beginning to get heavy. She was completely and utterly exhausted, mentally and physically, more than she'd been since the first days at DART.

She finished her checks and was relieved not to find anything that would prevent her landing safely. However, there was one thing that puzzled her for a moment, but then cheered her up no end - somehow she'd spent almost all of her ammunition without hesitating even once.

'Well, they're nothing if not predictable,' Sir Douglas Pewtall said as he read the list of airfield the Prussians had hit that morning. 'But this is why we've spent so much time and money preparing reserve airfields.' He handed the list back to Dee Fisher. 'Before you get damage estimates, make sure our pilots know whether they need to divert and where they're going please. Double check that for me; we'll need them back up in the air soon enough and I don't want any confusion. Oh, and tell Sheepish Squadron "job well done and thank you", please.'

'Yes, sir.'

Pewtall waited for Dee Fisher to go, then slumped down in his chair. He rubbed his eyes and released the breath it felt like he'd been holding for an hour.

A steward placed a fresh cup of tea in front of him, simultaneously whisking away the one he hadn't touched, and he picked it up and sipped at it gratefully while he waited for more reports to come in.

Telling the fighters to ignore the bombers and concentrate on the fighters was risky. If they lost they would be letting the bombers have a free go at their targets for nothing, for less than nothing, actually, as they would be handing them air superiority on a plate.

If it worked, though...

If it worked, then those bombers would no longer be able to come because the Prussians would be left without fighter coverage and that would effectively stop the invasion in one fell swoop.

The Prussians' arrogance in sending everything they could to Britain at once, thinking they would be unopposed, had allowed him to throw the currently accepted response out of the window, but, unless their commander was a relic from the First Great War, one of those generals who threw men into the enemy guns over and over again, expecting different results, they wouldn't try it again. The question was, what would they try? How patient would they be? And what possible response could he give.

Speaking of risky tactics - the wonderful boys and girls in their Spits and Harrys weren't the only way that they were going to hit the Fliegertruppe today and he picked up the telephone and pressed the button to connect him with Sky Vice-Marshal Levy.

'Bomber command here.'

'Time to go, Izzy. Happy hunting.'

'Thank you, sir.'

Time to see how the Prussians liked a dose of their own medicine.

Gruber was in his private dining room, tucking into the lunch the French chef he'd appropriated had prepared for him when the air raid siren sounded. He didn't react at first, except to shoot an irritated glance out of the window at the man cranking the machine and creating the noise disturbing him, but when the first of the anti-aircraft guns defending the airfield opened up he shot to his feet and raced for the door.

He ran through the chateau, pushing anyone he encountered out of his way, and went out onto the lawn outside the back door. He peered up into the sky and his jaw dropped at the sight of dozens of British bombers.

It was only when the first bombs dropped whistling from the sky that he finally came to his senses and sprinted for the nearest shelter.

This was not how things were supposed to go.

Sixty-five fighters and twenty bombers lost in the air. Another ten fighters and fifty bombers lost on the ground. Almost one hundred and fifty aircraft destroyed and countless others needing repairs before they could safely fly again. In just one morning.

Schmidt threw the report down on his desk and covered his eyes.

This was not how things were supposed to go.

But then again, what did he expect would happen? If the Kaiser's spies had spent more time investigating the strength of Britain's forces instead of trying to stage a coup, then maybe he could have anticipated the scale of their response.

However, even if the number of fighters the British had at their disposal hadn't been grossly underestimated, he still didn't understand how they could have been up waiting for them. Had it been a lucky guess that they would come when they did? Or did they have some RDF stations that they didn't know about?

In the end, none of that really mattered. The forces at his disposal were still far greater than the world had ever seen and they would sweep the British from their own island.

And then maybe the Kaiser wouldn't be upset about losing five percent of the entire Fliegertruppe in the space of two hours.

He pulled a sheet of paper towards him and considered briefly, then began to write out new orders.

CHAPTER 5

'I can't believe we have to do that all over again soon,' Ellie said as she flopped into one of the chairs at the big table reserved for the Misfits in the officers' mess. Only Rob and Benedict were there, though; the other Misfits hadn't turned up yet.

She grabbed the glass of water from the table and downed it in one swallow. A steward appeared to refill it for her and she emptied it again, then smiled up at him apologetically when he did so once more.

Rob nodded his agreement. 'It doesn't seem possible that anyone could keep doing that over and over, day after day, but I guess if there's no other option you just do it.' He frowned at her. 'Why are you so tired, though? The fight only lasted about fifteen minutes, but Tanya usually drags you around the sky for an hour or more. What happened?'

Ellie thought back to the fight, but most of it was a blur. There were actually very few specific things she could recall, just flashes of aircraft that were only in her vision for a moment. 'We dived straight into the middle of the fight where it was thickest. It was like going through the Loop back in Wales, but the turns come every two seconds and the walls are moving and trying to hit you. There was no time to rest, or think, just to react and act.'

She rolled her neck to work out a kink that was making itself known now that the excitement was all over.

'Was it like that for you?' she asked, looking from Rob to Benedict and back.

Benedict had his head cradled in his hand and was staring down at the table, toying with his napkin ring, and didn't look up, but Rob shook his head.

'No, not at all. I mean, yes, there were aircraft everywhere, going every which way and it looked like we might collide with them at any point if we made the wrong move, but we barely seemed to be throwing our aircraft around much at all. We were just weaving calmly in and out of the aircraft, lazily almost, and everywhere we turned there seemed to be an enemy to shoot at, but at the same time none of them seemed to be shooting back at us. It was incredible! It was as if Drake knew exactly where we needed to be all the time.'

'That's so different to how Tanya works.' Ellie said.

'It's also extremely boring.'

They looked up to find Tanya wandering over to them, Drake arm in arm with her.

Drake rolled his eyes at Tanya. 'And now you know why we don't fly together anymore.'

The two pilots sat down and Tanya immediately pulled the bread basket towards her. She took a huge bite of a piece, then pointed the rest at Ellie. 'You're tired because you do too much, not because you're with me. You need to calm down. You don't need to be so nervous and you don't need to keep jumping at shadows.' She pantomimed looking around frightened, like an actress in a horror movie, then rolled her eyes. 'You look,' she did a quick scan of an imaginary sky, 'then you process the information while you're doing what you're doing, then take another look a second or two later. If you just keep swinging your head around you don't see anything more, you just make yourself dizzy and tired.'

'Everyone has their own way of coping in combat,' Drake said, 'you just need to find the way that works for you.'

'Hopefully before you get killed.' Tanya added, pointing the bread at Ellie again.

'Yes...' Drake said, shaking his head. 'The one thing you can't do is worry too much about what is going on; you'll just burn out like that. There is no way you can see everything, especially in a fight as big as the one this morning and trying to will get you killed just easily as not watching your six.'

'You're a good pilot.' Tanya said around another big mouthful. 'Trust yourself and trust me.'

Ellie nodded. 'I will, thank you.'

'And you, Benedict?' Drake said turning to the young man who'd been silent until then. 'How did your flight go?'

When Benedict still didn't look up, Tanya, who was in the chair next to him, poked him in the ribs.

'What?' Benedict asked, blinking at the people around the table while absently rubbing his side.

'I asked how your flight went, Benedict.' Drake repeated, frowning faintly. 'I take it not well.'

'No, sir,' Benedict said, shaking his head and looking down again. 'I kept losing Squadron Leader Niven every time I turned to check our six.'

'Oh,' Drake said, 'well, that's not...'

He trailed off and looked up as Derek, Abby and Penny came in. Derek was waving his hands in the air, explaining something to them, but they couldn't hear what it was and he stopped when they approached the table.

Derek looked down at Benedict and the people seated around the table collectively held their breath. 'Wilberforce,' he began. 'I was just telling Abby about your performance this morning and,' he looked at Abby, 'we've agreed...'

'I understand, sir. I'll start packing.' Benedict pushed back his chair.

'What on earth for?' Derek asked.

'Sit down, Officer Wilberforce,' Abby ordered as Benedict started to stand. 'I think you've misunderstood. You're not being thrown out.'

'But I wasn't able to stay on Squadron Leader Niven's wing.'

'That is true,' Derek said, 'but that isn't the only mark of a good pilot, or the only measure of one that is worthy of being a Misfit. Your situational awareness is first class and you kept us both from being in trouble on several occasions. There were even a couple of times that you saw that enemies were going to attack us before it happened.'

'*That* is far more useful than just being able to stay on someone's wing,' Abby said, 'and *that* makes you worthy of being a Misfit. Which is why I am happy to confirm you as a full member. Effective immediately. Congratulations.'

Benedict smiled as the other Misfits echoed Abby's congratulations, but when they quietened down and started to apply themselves to the soup course that was just arriving he shot Rob a snooty, superior look. He was shocked and almost did a nosedive into his soup when Tanya's hand struck him on the back. Extremely hard.

'Well done, Sausage Boy!' she said, 'I knew you had to be good for something.'

There were sniggers from around the table and Benedict flushed.

'Actually, Abby,' Drake said when they had quietened down again. 'Rob was excellent this morning and I'd like to propose that he become a full member as well.'

'Seconded.' Gwen Stone said, arriving hand in hand with Kitty. 'We had a chance to watch you all in action before we joined in and it was clear that Abby has found some excellent replacements for us.'

She smiled at Rob and Ellie. '*Excellent* replacements.'

'Very well,' Abby said. 'It seems that further congratulations are in order.'

The celebrations were slightly louder this time, mostly because Tanya was rather more enthusiastic about them this time than she had been before, and then the Misfits settled down to eat. They knew that time was likely to be limited, so conversation was kept to a minimum as everyone tried to get through the meal with a minimum of fuss and time wasted. It was only when tea and cake had been served that Abby called everyone's attention back to herself.

'I think we're all agreed that this morning went fairly well.'

Gwen nodded. 'I certainly saw more Prussian aircraft falling than British.'

'I concur,' Penny said, 'but I estimate that the Prussians had at least double the number of fighters that we had, so for every aircraft we lose we need to shoot down two of theirs, if not three. Otherwise we'll lose.'

'We're not going to do that sitting out of half the fight.' Drake pointed out.

'No, we will not.' Abby said emphatically. She looked around the group. 'I don't know about you, but I didn't like having to hold back. So we're not going to. We're going to take the fight to the Fleas and knock them about before they can knock our boys and girls about. Any objections?'

Nobody said anything, but their smiles spoke volumes so she nodded. 'Good. Now, is everyone good with their assignments? Do we need to swap anyone around to optimise the pairings?'

She looked at Derek, Drake and Tanya in turn and each shook their heads.

'Right then,' Abby said, consulting her chronograph. 'I want everyone in the ready room in half an hour. I'm sure Sir Douglas will have business for us soon enough.'

Gruber stepped from his autocar and frowned at the line of aircraft.

'Why is your aircraft all the way over there?' he asked Melitta Reitsch, who had wandered over to meet him.

'That's what I was coming to tell you,' she said. 'I'm not going to fly on your wing anymore, I'm going to lead Alberich flight, and I've reorganised the squadron appropriately.'

'You've...' Gruber snatched the clipboard that she held out to him and glanced at the names. None of them meant anything to him because he hadn't bothered to learn any of them, but he pretended to read it anyway before handing it back.

'That looks fine. Are you sure you can handle a flight, though? Wouldn't you rather lead my second element?'

'I'm sure I'll be fine.' Reitsch said, handing the clipboard off to the aide she seemed to have acquired at some point. 'I have your wonderful example from our last flight to inspire me.'

Gruber gave her a scathing look, but she was already walking away and he watched her go. Just because she was cold and heartless didn't mean he couldn't still appreciate the sight of her in a flightsuit and it wasn't as if some of the actresses he'd bedded in Hollywoodland hadn't been just as ill-mannered and badly behaved. It often made the nights more interesting.

His view of Reitsch was cut off when she went behind her aircraft and he snatched his helmet and gloves from Lang and stalked towards Hölle.

No chance of anything like that with her, though, he thought; she was the Kaiser's. And besides, she probably wouldn't survive the day.

The bell on the outside wall of the ready room rang and the Misfits left off what they were doing and ran for the door. There was a bit of confusion because Scarlet was trying to come in while everyone was going out, but in the end Tanya just picked her up and placed her to one side, opening the way.

The Muscovite fell in beside Ellie and they ran towards their aircraft together.

Ellie glanced sideways at her and huffed. The long limbed woman was running easily, like a fox, or, she supposed, a wolf, seemingly completely unhampered by the weight and stiffness of the liquid pockets in her flightsuit, while she herself was stomping along like an elephant.

'Did you see what I did this morning?' the woman asked.

'What do you mean?'

'How I dealt with the fight.'

'I suppose.' Ellie thought back as best she could. 'You didn't fix on any one target, you just snapped shots at whatever you could and kept moving.'

Tanya grinned. 'Exactly. When everyone is in a big ball like that you can't fly like you would in a one on one dogfight. If you chase a target for more than a couple of seconds all you do is allow someone to get behind you.'

'I understand.'

'Good! Just as well; because you're taking the lead this flight.'

'What?!?' Ellie stumbled to a halt and stared at her in shock.

The Muscovite didn't answer, she just laughed and kept running to her aircraft.

'Sheepish Leader to Badger Leader. Bandits at twenty miles on your one o'clock low.'

'Thank you, Sheepish Leader. Come for dinner sometime - it'd be good to catch up with you two.'

'Thank you, Badger Leader, will do. Sheepish Leader out.'

'Well, you heard the man,' Abby said. 'Keep your eyes peeled, we should see them in...'

'Bandits, one o'clock low. On course for Felixstowe.'

The Misfits laughed as Benedict immediately interrupted her.

'Thank you, Eight.' Abby said as soon as she could. 'I see them. Adjusting course to starboard.'

This was the only raid approaching the shores of Britain at that moment, but Owen had told them that there were three more on his screens, in various stages of building up. It seemed that the Prussians were attempting to pull them apart by coming over one at a time in quick succession, undoubtedly still under the belief that they had blinded their enemy with their attacks on the radar stations.

The Misfits rapidly began to make out details of the Prussian raid as they closed the distance to them.

'They're all grouped up.' Penny said. 'Fighters and bombers all together. I can't see any top cover.'

'Neither can I, Two,' Abby answered. 'Anyone?'

Nobody answered.

'Well, that's new.' Abby said, her amusement clear in her voice. 'And it's going to make our plan a lot more effective. Four, have you still got eyes on our boys and girls?'

'Yes, Leader,' Ellie answered. 'They're in position and turning towards the enemy now.'

'Good,' Abby said. 'Time for us to spoil the Prussians' party.'

The Prussian force was almost at the Suffolk coastline now. The raid didn't look quite as big as the ones that had come over that morning, but it was hard to tell seeing as they were all grouped up like a swarm of bees, rather than spread around the sky. They still vastly outnumbered the British fighters sent to meet them, though.

'Diving in three... two... one...'

The Misfits followed Abby as she put Dragon into a sixty degree dive, spreading out into a long line on either side of her as they went.

Taking a leaf from the Prussians' book, they dived down on their prey with the sun behind them.

Oberstleutnant Klein shifted uneasily in his seat as he peered forward through his windshield at the British fighters waiting for them over the port of Felixstowe. He wasn't nervous because there were a lot of them, or because he didn't think that he could outfly their machines in his new model HH190, it was the fact that his orders had him sitting here, chained to the slow-moving pigs that were Hoffmans and Funkels, instead of searching for an advantage in height and speed. He understood the need to draw the British in close to neutralise the tactics they had employed that morning, but he couldn't help but think that they were taking away one advantage only to hand them another.

At least once the fight was joined he would be free to engage them as he pleased, but it just wasn't natural for...

'Achtung! Misfits! Nine o'clock...!'

Oberstleutnant Klein never heard the end of his wingman's warning.

Line up the target, squeeze the trigger, one thousand, two thousand, right rudder to line up the next in line, squeeze the trigger, one thousand, two thousand, pull up slightly, touch of left rudder, squeeze the trigger, one thousand, two thousand...

Ellie found herself surprisingly calm as she dived through the packed Prussian formation, sometimes only yards from collision and certain death, picking out fighter after fighter for her machine guns and cannons to rip apart. The almost arbitrary nature of how she was spreading death among the Prussians was shocking, her choice of whether to use her left or right rudder pedal the only thing dictating whether one of them ended up in her sights or another. It didn't affect her, though; she was well beyond feeling any pity for them after she'd heard the results of the morning's raid.

A fourth fighter, a fifth, and then a sixth entered her sights. She gave them all equal measures of lead, but didn't stop to see if she had actually hit or destroyed any of them, she just kept going until she found herself in clean air.

She pulled up and levelled off, then craned her head to see behind her. The Prussians were only now reacting to the Misfits, a few of the fighters turning to chase them, but they were all too slow - they'd been flying at the speed of the bombers and that meant she had a two or perhaps three-hundred mile per hour advantage over them after her dive and they would never catch up with her before she could turn around and engage them.

That wasn't the plan, though, and, even as she watched, the rest of the British fighters slammed into the formation that the Misfits had torn apart for them, causing far more damage than they would have otherwise and taking far less in return.

'Ready to go back, Ellie?'

Tanya had come up onto her wing while she'd been watching and Ellie smiled at her. 'Oh, yes!'

Tanya laughed. 'Well, what are you waiting for? You're still leading.'

Ellie immediately put her aircraft into a maximum rate turn and headed back towards the fight.

Gwen squeezed off a one second burst at a bomber that had had the bad luck of coming between her and the MU10 she was chasing. She was not one to waste an opportunity, but didn't want to waste any time or too much ammunition on it. The Prussian fighter appeared on the other side of the bomber and she adjusted her aim and gave it a full two seconds. MU10s were notoriously hard to knock out of the sky, but she must have hit this one in a vital spot because it came apart in her sights. She instantly reversed her turn and hopped over the bomber she'd taken a potshot at, putting it between her and the pair of HH190s she'd spotted swinging towards her. She found herself in a pocket of calm momentarily and she glanced over her right shoulder. She sighed in relief as she saw that the grey aircraft was still there, then pulled hard back the way she'd come, looking to surprise the Hock-Hunds.

Abby and Penny spun and weaved through the Prussian force, criss-crossing the bomber formation, picking off targets whenever they presented themselves. They swapped the lead whenever either of them had the advantage over the enemy, changing positions seamlessly and effortlessly with an understanding born of familiarity, sliding easily back into patterns that they had worked on with the other Misfits back when they had first formed the squadron.

Abby did it all with half an eye on the tension indicator on her instrument panel, though; they'd had to fly half way across the country at full unwind, climbing hard the entire time, to get into position to meet this raid. They had already been low on tension when they'd engaged and after less than five minutes she reluctantly opened a squadron-wide channel.

'Badger Leader to all Badgers, withdraw and return to base.'

She then switched to the general channel. 'Badger Leader to all squadrons, it's been a pleasure, but I'm afraid we have to go and ruin the day for some other Fleas. Thank you for having us and we'll see you again soon!'

She gave a passing MU9 one last burst, then inverted Dragon and pulled the stick into her lap, diving to gain as much speed as she could before racing for home.

The Misfits had springs to spare so, instead of waiting for the aircraft to be painstakingly rewound by the machines, the fitters just swapped the used ones for new. They were ready to take off again in a record fifteen minutes, but, even so, that was too late for them to get into position to intercept the next Prussian raid, or the one after that, however, they did manage to get into position for the fourth, and what would prove to be the final, raid of the day.

This raid was targeting the airfields of Kent, which was much closer to home than the one they'd intercepted before, so they didn't need to use quite so much tension to get to it and could linger much longer in the fight.

Once again, the Prussians were lax in their vigilance, their eyes firmly fixed on the main block of British fighters moving to intercept them from the front and not looking into the sun. The tactics were even more successful this time and the Prussians were sent into utter disarray when the brightly coloured machines suddenly appeared among them. One bomber pilot was so startled when Excalibur flashed past his cockpit that he completely lost control of his aircraft and swerved straight into the bomber next to him, destroying both.

The Prussians never recovered and never managed to regain their formations. As a result, most of them missed their targets and quite a few actually dropped their bombs early and turned for home in a panic.

It was a rout, but, following Sir Douglas Pewtall's strict instructions, the British didn't pursue the Prussians any further than the coastline, sending a clear message to the enemy - this is ours.

CHAPTER 6

'Stand down the bombers, please, Izzy. It's not worth the risk. Tell your boys and girls to get some rest before the night raid.'

'Yes, sir.'

Pewtall put down the telephone, then gazed down at the map table. The last of the four Prussian raids was on its way home and, while there was still time for them to send over one or two more before daylight ran out in a couple of hours, he doubted they would do so after the drubbing they'd been given; they'd want to come up with better tactics first. Or any tactics at all, actually, because so far all they'd been doing was trying to brute force their way into Britain.

That wasn't to say he and his people wouldn't remain vigilant and be ready to respond if the Prussians did try something.

Dee Fisher was hovering again and he smiled up at her.

'Yes, Dee.'

'Three of our radio stations are back up, sir, and two more say they should be able to resume operations in a limited capacity by tomorrow morning.'

Pewtall tapped a fist on the table in celebration, making his tea quiver. 'That's excellent news! Tell them well done from me and draw up another map of the coverage please.'

The woman smiled. 'Already being done, sir. And I've taken the liberty of standing down those elements of Sheepish Squadron that are no longer needed.'

'Good show! Give Sheepish my thanks as well, please.'

'Will do, sir.'

'And now give me the bad news.'

'Biggin, Manston, Kenley, Duxford, Tangmere and Hawkinge have all been effectively wiped out. There's very little left. Of our remaining principal fields, only two are still operational, the rest have closed, but most hope to be operational again in less than a week, assuming they're not bombed again. So far they haven't hit any of our secondary airfields, though, so we're still operating at full capacity.'

'That's something, then,' Pewtall said. 'We just have to hope they don't know where most of them are and keep hitting the ones we're not using anymore.' He smiled at her. 'Thank you. Let me know when the squadron readiness reports start coming in, please.'

'Yes, sir.' Fisher nodded, then hobbled away.

The smile faded from his face as he looked across at the light board on the opposite wall showing the status of the fighter squadrons under his command. As far as the overall picture was concerned it had been an excellent day's work. He just hoped that the boys and girls in the fighter squadrons had fared as well.

He stood to stretch his legs and gazed around the room, looking to see if there was anything that needed his attention. His team had everything well in hand, though, and, not for the first time, he wondered if any of them would even notice if he didn't show up tomorrow. However, there was one thing out of place and he chuckled at the sight of Scarlet skipping in a very unmilitary fashion across the room towards him.

'You don't have clearance to be in here.'

'When have you ever known me to need clearance to go anywhere?'

He tilted his head, conceding the point.

'I thought we were meeting for dinner at eight?' he asked.

'Yes, but I wasn't doing anything so I thought I'd see if you could get off earlier. You need to get some rest and relaxation while you can so that you don't burn out when it counts.'

'Rest?'

'Relaxation, at least.'

She smiled suggestively and he laughed.

'I should stay until nightfall, but I was just thinking that I might be able to get away earlier if nothing develops.'

'Alright then.' Scarlet dragged an empty seat over from nearby, then sat down and put her feet up on Pewtall's desk. A steward brought tea for the two of them, but she shook her head. 'Got any glasses down here?'

When the man came back with a water glass she winked at him, then produced a bottle from the thigh pocket of her flightsuit and poured a generous measure.

'Can I get you one, Dougie?'

He shook his head. 'I might have a sneaky little snifter in my office, but not in here.'

Scarlet looked at him, then looked around the room at the serious faces still working. 'Sorry,' she said somewhat shamefacedly. She pushed the glass away and put the bottle back into her pocket, then took her feet off the table.

Pewtall sat down beside her and pushed the glass back to her and picked up his tea. 'That's just me, though. You, on the other hand, have a reputation to keep up.'

He held his cup out and she clinked her glass against it.

'Confusion to the enemy!' he toasted.

'You've heard of my work, then?' she answered, grinning at him over her glass.

'Misfit Squadron stand down.' Derek announced to the ready room as he put the telephone down.

There was a collective sigh from the pilots, who'd been on the edges of their seats, clutching their helmets and prepared to run out the door. Everyone slumped back into their chairs for a moment, allowing themselves to finally acknowledge their tiredness, but then people began to stand and move from the room, loosening flightsuits and letting down hair as they went.

'Well done, everyone!' Abby called out after them. 'And Rob, Benedict, remember to let your fitters know how you'd like your aircraft repainted, please.'

The pilots quickly filed out, leaving behind only Abby and Penny.

Abby sighed. 'They all survived the day.'

Penny nodded.

'But how long is that going to last if things keep going like this?'

Penny shrugged.

'The new pilots have fit in well.'

Penny nodded and Abby frowned at her. 'Are you not going to say anything?'

Penny grinned and shook her head.

Abby rolled her eyes. 'I'm going to go change for dinner, then.'

She stood and started for the door.

'You need to stop worrying so much.'

Abby halted in the doorway and turned around.

'You've done all that you can. You've chosen the best pilots you could, you've given them the best aircraft you can and you've paired them up in the best way you can. There is nothing more you can do to prepare or protect them, unless you want to ground them all. And no,' she said, holding up a hand to forestall Abby as her mouth tightened anger flared in her eyes, 'I'm not saying you have to stop caring, but if you keep worrying about them then you're going to do something silly. You'll make a mistake, or have too many sleepless nights and you'll just make something worse. Do what you can to protect us, by all means, I would expect nothing else, but accept that we're at war and at some point someone is going to die - maybe you, maybe me, maybe one or more of the young 'uns.'

Penny stood up and strode over with that peculiar gait of hers. 'And make sure you enjoy life while you can.' She put her hand on Abby's shoulder and squeezed gently. 'Now, you said something about dinner?'

She wrapped her arm around Abby and manoeuvred her out of the door. 'Biffy found a couple of bottles of Chateau Podreaux '89 in the cellar last night and I stole them from him.'

'That'll make Derek very happy.'

'A few glasses will make everyone happy.'

Abby put her own arm around Penny as they walked towards the barracks. 'When did this become so hard, Penny?'

'Oh, about 1937, I think, when you let Georgie talk you into dealing with the likes of us.'

'Look out, Cotty, here comes trouble.'

Jack Brown, the man working beside Aviator Sergeant Felicity Cotter on the landing gear of the modified Spitsteam jerked his head over her shoulder and she turned to find Aerial Officer the Honourable Benedict Charles something or other bloody Wilberforce strutting towards them.

'Hell. What does he want this time?' Cotter muttered. She gave her companion a nod of thanks for the warning, then ducked out from under the aircraft just as Benedict arrived.

'Evening, sir, what can I do for you?'

'Cotter. I've been made a full member of the Misfits and I'd like you to repaint my aircraft please. In purple and white camouflage like Drake and Tanya's aircraft.'

'Like Squadron Leader Drake and Aviator Lieutenant Guseva's aircraft?'

'Yes.' Benedict nodded. 'That will be all.'

'Very well, sir, I'll...' Cotter started, but Benedict had already turned and was walking away.

Jack Brown came out from under the aircraft and joined her in watching the boy go. They turned to face the aircraft together.

'Well, at least she'll look good.' Jack said.

'Yes.' Cotter said. 'But that doesn't matter if what's inside is a steaming pile of...'

'Now, now, sarge,' Jack admonished with a grin. 'No need to go disrespecting an officer like that.'

'I know, Jack.'

'Not like *that*, anyway.' He winked.

Cotter smiled at him. Yes, there were other ways to show displeasure at an officer, especially if they relied on lower ranks to keep their aircraft serviceable. Not that she or any other RAC fitter would ever do anything to sabotage or otherwise make unairworthy one of their precious machines, but a snooty young officer might find an inexplicable smell in his cockpit one morning, coming from a rotten onion that had somehow managed to find its way under their seat, if he wasn't too careful.

Now, that was more like it, Gruber thought as he brought Hölle to a full stop on the airfield. *No Misfits, only inferior enemies and all the kills I could want.*

He climbed out of the cockpit and stood on his wing, watching the other Barons taxiing over. There were only twelve left - he had lost two in the first engagement of the day and another in this one - but that was of no matter; there were Blutsaugers to spare and plenty more pilots and the people in administration would have the squadron back to full strength by morning, even if it meant some other squadron was left wanting. The fact that Reitsch was one of the twelve survivors was rather annoying, though.

He jumped down from the wing and strode to the waiting autocar. Lang held the door for him, then climbed into the front seat next to the driver, but, before they could leave, the other back door opened and Reitsch slipped in.

He frowned at her, making his displeasure known without saying anything, but when she just smiled at him he turned away and looked out of the window.

'We should debrief,' the woman said as they pulled away.

'Very well.' Gruber said, looking at her expectantly.

'Not here,' she said, giving the driver and Lang a meaningful look.

Gruber rolled his eyes. 'All right then. Let's go to my quarters and get this over with.'

The autocar arrived at the chateau and Gruber stalked straight up the stairs to his suite without waiting for Reitsch. He tossed his helmet and gloves onto the sideboard and went to his favourite armchair.

Lang poured drinks for them, not the best schnapps, Gruber was pleased to note, then left after giving Gruber a nod and Reitsch a disdainful look.

Reitsch watched the steward go and when the door closed behind him she put her drink down and stalked over to Gruber. She stood in front of him, peering down her nose at him, and it was all he could do to stop from cringing back at the expected haranguing.

However, instead of berating him for the poor performance of the Barons, or the complete failure of the day's attacks, she brought up a hand and slowly started to pull down the zip on the front of her flightsuit. She opened it all the way, then shrugged her shoulders out of it and let it fall to the floor, leaving herself wearing nothing except a small pair of panties.

Gruber smiled and took a sip of schnapps to sweeten his breath, then stood and went to her.

Derek gasped in delight when a steward brought out the wine out that evening. The steward had been advised beforehand, though, and went straight to Derek, rather than Abby as the commander of the Misfits and highest ranked officer, or Penny, whose wine it actually was.

Derek could barely contain himself and, as soon as the steward had poured a splash into his glass for him to taste, he dived on it.

He swirled the liquid in the glass, holding it up to the light to inspect the colour, then stuck his nose in it and inhaled deeply. He made an appreciative noise, then lifted the glass to his lips and sipped. He sat, gazing into the distance as he slowly rolled the wine around his mouth, tasting it, savouring it thoroughly. Finally, he swallowed, but then he just sat there, gazing into the distance, a faint smile on his face.

Abby let out an exasperated sigh. 'Oh, for Darwin's sake, just pour for everyone,' she told the steward, 'I'm fairly sure he approves.'

The other Misfits laughed and Derek gave them a mock sour look.

'Philistines!' He mimed reaching out to stop the steward. 'Bring that bottle back here! They don't deserve it!'

The Misfits laughed again, but the food arrived at that moment and they quietened down as they dug in.

Half-way through the meal, Squadron Leader Algernon Billingsworth arrived, clutching a sheath of papers. He caught Abby's gaze and gave her a quizzical look, to which he received a nod.

Billingsworth had been in charge of the administrative side of Misfit Squadron at Badger Base and had moved to Bagshot with them before they'd gone to Muscovy. He had been assigned to another base while they'd been abroad and then disbanded, but Abby had insisted on him returning to the squadron when they'd been reformed. It was he who received the daily reports from RAC headquarters and his team had the job of interviewing the Misfits after each mission and compiling the after-combat reports.

'Good evening, everyone,' he said cheerfully, 'bon appétit and all that.'

The Misfits answered in various ways, from a simple wave, or Drake's "What oh!", all the way down to mumbles from Tanya, who didn't look up from her plate or stop pushing food into her mouth.

'Evening, Algie.' Abby said, after rolling her eyes at the manners of some of her pilots. 'What have you got for us?'

'Reports!' he said cheerfully, holding up the papers. 'First up, I've got the personal tallies. As per Misfit policy, any shared kills have been allocated to the regular RAC pilot who laid claim to them.' He looked down at the paper and began reading. 'Abby, two kills, three probables, two possibles. Penny, also two kills, two probables and four possibles. Tanya, *three* kills, oh, good show!' he said, looking up at her.

She acknowledged the cheers of the Misfits by regally waving a sausage on a fork at them and they laughed, then looked back at Billingsworth.

'Three kills, three probables and two possibles. Drake, one kill, four probables and one possible. Derek, two kills, one probable and three possibles. Gwen, also three kills,' he had to pause for more cheering, 'as well as five probables and four possibles. Kitty, one kill, one probable and one possible.'

He turned the page. 'As for our new and probationary members.'

'Full members now, Algie. All three.'

'Oh!' he exclaimed, then smiled at the three new pilots. 'Congratulations. And congratulations on your scores. Uh, Officer Wilberforce has two confirmed kills, two probables, one possible. Officer Sherborne, one kill and one probable. Officer Perkins...'

He paused, frowning. 'This can't be right, can it?'

'Yes it is,' Tanya said, waving a knife laden with butter at him. 'I saw them all.'

Billingsworth blinked at her. 'Well, then - Officer Perkins, *five* kills, one of which was a Baron, three probables and *six* possibles.'

For a moment there was a stunned silence, but then a roar went up from everyone, including the officers at the other tables and the stewards, all of whom had stopped whatever they were doing to listen the reports, and Ellie blushed as they applauded her.

It took a while for everyone to quieten down again, but then all attention returned to Billingsworth; he had the most important part of his report to give - that of the overall numbers for the day.

However, before he could, a voice, muffled by a mouthful of food, but still loud enough to carry to everyone spoke into the silence.

'I told you she was good.'

The results for the day were encouraging, but not outstanding. The RAC had managed to outscore the Prussians by just over two to one, which was barely good enough. The news of Ellie's score made everything seem better, more optimistic, though, as the word quickly spread through the base that one of the new pilots had become an "ace in a day", on her very first day in combat.

After dinner, even though they were off duty, every single one of the fitters returned to the hangar. There was some work left to do on a few of the aircraft, some repairs still to be made, some checks still to be done, but not all of them were needed for that. Instead, they were there to witness what was, to them at least, the affirmation that their hard work was worth it, that their pilots were worthy of the faith their fitters put in them and of the aircraft they entrusted them with. For most of the crews it was just a case of adding marks to the already impressive tallies already on the fuselage below the cockpits, but for three crews it was a very special occasion, a baptism almost, as they put the very first ones on their aircraft.

The paint on Benedict's aircraft was still wet, it wouldn't be fully dry until morning, but that didn't mean they couldn't put the two kill marks on it.

As the leader of the crew, it was Cotter's privilege and pleasure to paint the marks and she took the stencil and went to climb up, but stopped with one foot up, then smiled and turned.

'You know what? I have a better idea...'

Gwen painstakingly undid the buttons down the front of her dress uniform tunic and shrugged out of it. She put it on a hanger and buttoned it back up, then placed it in the wardrobe, making sure that it was hanging straight and wasn't at all rucked up. Only then did she stagger across the room and allow herself to collapse backwards onto the bed.

She groaned. 'What a day.' She ran her fingers through her hair, pulling out the pins holding it in place. 'I can't believe how out of shape I am. Although, I shouldn't really be surprised - Akio certainly fed us well and... and...'

Realising that she was performing a monologue she turned her head and stopped talking when she found Kitty standing by the door, still fully dressed, just looking at her.

'What are you doing over there? Aren't you tired?' She grinned, 'do you need help getting out of your uniform?'

When Kitty still didn't say anything or move, she propped herself up on her elbows. 'What's wrong?'

'We have to talk.'

A shock hit Gwen, like she'd bailed out into the North Sea in winter, and she swung her legs round to sit on the edge of the bed. 'What about?' she asked, feeling tears prickling at the corners of her eyes. 'Is it about us? Is something wrong with us? You don't want to end it, do you? Because... because...'

'What?' Kitty asked, frowning at her. 'No! No, darling, no!' she hurried over and sat down beside Gwen and grabbed her hand. 'Not that! Never that! Oh, darling...' she leaned in and kissed Gwen gently, but pulled back after only a moment, leaving Gwen wanting more. 'It's just... You have to stop checking up on me constantly while we're in battle. I can't fly with you if you keep doing that; you'll end up getting killed.'

Gwen shook her head and opened her mouth to deny it, but Kitty held up a hand to forestall her. 'No. You know I'm right. Every moment you're worrying about me is a moment less that you're worrying about the enemy. You missed several chances to get kills today because you were looking over your shoulder and you took damage because you were distracted.'

She looked down at their hands as she spoke quietly, hesitantly. 'If you can't trust me and treat me as you would a normal wingmate, then I'll ask Abby to swap me with Penny.'

'No, please don't do that.' Gwen said, quietly, but earnestly. 'You're right. I'm not treating you like a normal wingmate and that's not fair to you. But it's because the last time we fought together you almost died and there was nothing I could do about it because *I wasn't even there*!'

The tears started to fall in earnest now as Gwen thought back to the fight over Malta, remembering how the Misfits had split up and she had to watch impotently as Hans Gruber went after Kitty's group. Remembering not being able to find her afterwards. Remembering having to hear from a report that Kitty had been shot down and was riddled with bullets and fighting for her life. Having to abandon her on the island when the Misfits had fled.

When Kitty tried to pull her in to comfort her she didn't let her, she just wiped the tears away and met her eyes. 'So, yes, I suppose I have been treating you differently, but it's because I'm terrified of losing you and I'm terrified of not being there to help you again. So, please. Give me another chance.'

Kitty nodded. 'Of course, darling. Now come here.'

This time Gwen did allow Kitty to draw her into her embrace, but she quickly pulled back when the buttons of Kitty's uniform started digging into her face.

She smiled slyly. 'Are you sure I can't help you get undressed?'

CHAPTER 7

24th August 1941

Now, this is flying! Benedict thought as he wended his way through the crowded sky in the dawn light. He rolled over the top of a bomber, then under the next and out the other side of the formation where he found the pair of MU10s he'd had his eyes on. He gave the leader a three second burst and shouted in triumph as it come apart, but then had to pull hard to the side because he could feel that the MU9s that had been closing in on him were getting a bit *too* close.

He glanced to his nine o'clock, found Kite right where he'd known it would be and banked towards it, slipping in onto its wing, but then he saw an opportunity to hit an MU9 and was off again.

He was no longer so worried about straying from his leader's wing; Derek had pulled him aside after dinner the night before and told him that this was the best way he could use his superior awareness of what was going on and who was he to disagree? Besides, a few seconds here and there wouldn't do any harm and he knew where Derek was all the time anyway and made his way back whenever he could. Plus, this way he could keep above Sherborne in kills and maybe catch up with Perkins.

Ellie bit her lip as she led Tanya through the bomber formation, chasing a pair of MU9s. They had to swerve to make their way through a small gap and she found her guns already pointed right at it. She raked them as they went through, sending them spinning away before she went through herself. She was tempted to give the bombers a quick pass while she was at it, but Abby, following Sir Douglas Pewtall's instructions, had asked them to concentrate on the fighters and not use their limited ammunition on the bombers, even if the huge aircraft were tempting targets. She couldn't see that the strategy was paying off herself; the sky seemed just as full of small aircraft as it had been the day before, but that was what she had been told to do, so that was what she would do.

Besides, she had more to concern herself with than the choice of who to kill.

Like, when her luck would run out. Because she had been lucky the day before. Very lucky. And she'd only made as many kills as she had because of that luck.

She'd been congratulated by everyone she'd met after leaving the mess and had even found a few people waiting outside her barracks for her and some lovely gifts in front of her door. She couldn't help but think she didn't deserve their praise, though, didn't deserve the faith that they were placing in her and that Abby and Tanya were placing in her. She couldn't help but think that, as soon as her luck ran out, they would see her for what she was - a frightened little girl who was out of her depth and shouldn't be in the cockpit of a fighter, let alone flying with the best pilots in the world.

The HH190 that she was chasing rolled away, trying to outmanoeuvre her. Unfortunately for it, though, she'd quickly found that the capabilities of the clipped-wing Spitsteam were easily equal to the task and she didn't give up like most pilots would and quickly got the aircraft in her sights. It came apart as she gave it a quick burst, hitting the wing root, right where she'd been aiming, but, before she could even consider giving the wingman the same treatment, a call from Tanya warned her of some enemies trying to get behind them. She'd already been turning away, though, pulling hard in the other direction towards a group of MU9's harassing a pair of Harridans, almost unconsciously putting a bomber wing between her and the approaching enemies.

It was some consolation, at least, that she wouldn't likely be alive to see the disappointment on everyone's faces when they worked out how much of a fraud she was.

'Still with me, Ten?'
'Of course, Nine.'

Gwen grinned at the reproach in Kitty's voice. It was hard, but she resisted the temptation to look to make sure and instead put Excalibur on her back and pulled the stick into her lap, heading back into the storm the Prussians had sent to ravage the south coast that morning.

'They've changed their strategy again,' Pewtall observed, standing with his analysts and gazing down at the map table in the pit. 'Two raids at the same time and the other two already building.'

'The Misfits aren't going to be able to double up this morning.'

'No, they're not. Make sure they know that, please, and that they are to stay in the fight.'

'Yes, sir.'

One of the men hurried off to the radio operator, but the rest remained with Pewtall.

'Can we send our bombers over after the second set of raids?' he asked. He thought he knew the answer, but wanted someone else to confirm it.

'The second set of raids will likely hit half an hour after the first,' the head analyst said after glancing at his colleagues. 'We can't send out bombers on their coat tails, otherwise their escorts could just turn and engage, so we would have to wait at least half an hour. That gives the fighters escorting the first set of raids about an hour to rearm and rewind. They could have maybe half of them turned around and up again in time to hit our bombers. Maybe not before they hit their targets, but at least before they got back to safety.'

'What if we sent an escort?' Dee Fisher asked, pointing down at the markers of the squadrons in the air at that moment, engaged with the first raids. 'They could be back up in time.'

Pewtall scratched his chin and grimaced. 'It's risky. They won't be able to stop all the fighters getting through and hitting the bombers and we'd be losing people over water.' The one advantage the British had was that they were fighting on home turf - any pilot that bailed out could go straight back to their squadron, whereas the Prussians who survived were taken prisoner. Over France or the channel they would lose that advantage. He shook his head. 'No. It's not worth it. We're not that desperate yet,' he looked at the head analyst. 'Draw up a plan, though, I want this as an option for if we ever are.'

The Misfits landed within a few minutes of each other and parked up in front of the hangar in as close to a straight line as they ever got.

Each of them took their own time in getting out. Some, like Tanya and Kitty, leapt right out and exchanged words with their fitters, letting them know if any work needed doing. Others, like Penny and Derek, liked to sit a moment in their cockpit and chat with their chief fitter. However they did it, they all took at least a moment to show some appreciation for the men and women who kept them in the air. All except for Benedict, who usually climbed out in a leisurely fashion and exchanged as few words with his fitters as possible before leaving.

Abby liked to park up first so she could watch the others arrive and see any damage and that morning she scrambled out quickly. She told her fitters that she'd be back to have a word, but that Dragon was fine, and then hurried towards the end of the line where B flight had parked up, smiling at the pilots and fitters she passed on the way.

Rob was just finishing with his fitters and she nodded to him. 'Is your aircraft staying as she is?' she asked. They had taken off before light that morning and she hadn't been able to see Rob or Benedict's aircraft. Before a fight wasn't really the time to talk about paint anyway.

'Yes,' he said, smiling at his Spitsteam. 'I did want to add some rust patches so that she would look more like the aircraft that inspired the paint job, but Sergeant Pratt didn't like the idea very much, so I'm keeping her like this.'

Abby smiled. 'That sounds like interesting story, perhaps you can share it with the squadron some time?'

Rob nodded. 'When I'm ready.'

'Of course.'

Abby moved on down the line, past Derek's aircraft to Benedict's. Her steps slowed and she stopped when it was in full view, though.

Benedict had finished with his fitters and he came up to her. 'Did you want me, Abby?' he asked.

'I was just coming to see how you asked to have your aircraft painted. Is it exactly as you specified?'

Benedict smiled and turned to admire the new purple and white paint scheme he'd asked for. 'Why yes, I...' he trailed off and frowned.

Abby glanced to the side, where Benedict's fitters had gathered. They were the straightest-backed, most straight-faced, most interested in anything apart from their aircraft or the officers around them group of fitters she'd ever seen.

'So,' Abby asked loudly, as titters began to sound from the men and women who'd wandered over from the hangar and other aircraft. 'You specifically asked your fitters to paint *sausages* as your kill marks?'

Benedict flushed with anger, but then, to the surprise of everyone, including himself, he smiled. He searched out Tanya in the crowd and gave her a small nod of thanks for the talk she'd given him at DART about respect that he'd somehow forgotten all about when he'd been made a Misfit.

'Actually, ma'am,' he announced loudly, 'I think you'll find they're *bratwursts.*'

The Prussians came back almost as soon as they could, showing up on radar just as the British pilots were about to have their elevenses. Whether or not that was deliberate and the Prussians had wanted to deprive the British of their tea was a matter for debate in many messes that evening, but it certainly riled up quite a few of the pilots and gave them new purpose in the fight.

However, as so often is the way, just when it seemed that everything was going well and the Misfits were beginning to believe that the Prussians would never be able to touch them, everything fell apart and brought them crashing back to reality.

Sir Douglas didn't want the Prussians to be able to predict where the Misfits would show up or where they were based and had sent them to the raid coming over from the Netherlands towards Norfolk. It was a good idea, but it meant they had to fly about one hundred and fifty miles just to get there and didn't have a chance to get into position above the bombers. And without the possibility of diving on the Prussian aircraft to begin the engagement and sowing chaos among them, the resistance was much better organised.

Before the fight was even a minute old, Penny was raked from stem to stern by an MU9. Luckily, the damage to Kingfisher wasn't catastrophic, but several of the rounds hit her cockpit. Any other pilot would have been dead, but, ironically, she was saved by the fact that the Prussians had already taken her legs earlier in the war. Her artificial limbs were completely destroyed, though, meaning that she was no longer able to use her rudder pedals and was out of the fight.

Moments later, Drake went spinning towards the ground with half his wing missing after a few shots from one of the MU10's large calibre cannons tore into it. If he had been in one of the Spitsteams that would have been the end of his aircraft, but both Wolf and Lion were largely based on the Harridan and were extremely forgiving, so not only was he able to recover control, but he also managed to limp to the nearest airfield and put down safely.

Several other Misfits were hit, but the damage was largely superficial and they were able to stay in the fight until the Prussians had retreated back across the coastline. However, there was one last nasty surprise in store for them when they got back to Bagshot - when Rob went to put down his undercarriage, they found that one of his wheels had been completely shot to pieces. It was impossible for him to land normally and a pancake landing was far too dangerous, so he flew as close to the coast as he could with what little spring tension he still had, then pointed his fighter south, cut the throttle, put it into a shallow dive and jumped. His last view of his aircraft before she disappeared into the distance was of her descending peacefully towards the sea.

The fight could have gone a lot worse, pilots could have died, for example, but it was a rude awakening for the Misfits and a reminder that they weren't nearly as invulnerable as they'd thought.

Abby leaned against the frame of the ready room door and watched Hummingbird race towards the airfield. It passed over the manor house, buffeting the union flag flying on the roof, then passed over the trees - far too close. It was still going more than two hundred miles per hour by her reckoning when it crossed the perimeter fence and came directly towards the ready room. The nose dropped slightly and pointed directly towards her, but she forced herself not to turn away and instead kept her eyes fixed firmly on the windscreen. She couldn't see through it because of the glare reflecting from it, but she could well imagine the grin plastered on the Irishwoman's face. The aircraft kept coming and kept coming and kept coming until it seemed that the overhead rotors would chop the roof off the ready room, but at the last moment Scarlet pulled the nose up until it was pointing almost vertically, completely arresting her forward motion, then, as it stalled, she pointed the nose down and let the rotors hold her just inches off the grass for a moment before settling down, less than a dozen yards away.

The canopy swung up and Rob clambered out. He exchanged a few words with Scarlet, laughing a moment with her, then stepped down and came towards the ready room.

Abby chuckled when the smile immediately left the boy's face. 'Enjoy the ride, Rob?' she asked, the distinctively green young officer as he approached.

He grimaced. 'Next time I'm going down with my aircraft.'

She laughed and slapped him on the back as he went past, then waved to Scarlet. She watched, wincing, as Hummingbird lifted off and banked sharply over the top of the parked aircraft, making more than one fitter duck, then just set back down again in her place at the far end, all of fifty yards away. She rolled her eyes with a sigh, then turned to look into the ready room.

Algernon Billingsworth and his team had just finished taking everyone's operational reports and they nodded to her as they stepped through the door, but Algie himself had stayed behind to speak to Rob, who had collapsed onto a sofa. She was pleased to see he was being taken care of by Ellie and Tanya, a mug of tea already clutched in his decidedly shaky hands. He seemed to be recovering quickly, the colour in his cheeks returning to something more normal and, as she watched, he laughed at something Ellie said in reply to one of Algie's questions.

Satisfied that she didn't need to step in there, she looked around the room at the other pilots, assessing their mood. Drake was his usual self - the experience of being shot down wasn't a new one for him and he had already shaken it off. Penny was looking frustrated, but that was probably more down to the fact that she was having to use her spare legs - she had one of them off in her lap and was making adjustments to it with a tiny screwdriver and muttering to herself. As for the rest... She smiled; the Misfits were being the Misfits.

Scarlet came bouncing past her a couple of minutes later, but she waited a couple of minutes more for Algie to finish with Rob and leave before going to stand in the middle of the room. She didn't have to wait more than a few seconds before everyone had quietened down.

'I had the rest of the modified Spitsteams assembled and three are being prepared as we speak, but I have to ask - Drake, Rob, Penny, do any of you consider yourself unfit to fly?'

She looked to each in turn, receiving a simple no from Drake, a shake of the head from Rob and something rather more colourful, but still in the negative, from Penny.

'Good. Next: do we swap pairings around because of the change of aircraft or do we keep things as they are? My thoughts are we keep things as they are; you're building up an understanding with your partners now which I believe is worth more than pairing aircraft with similar performances. Anyone disagree? Anyone want to swap?'

When nobody chimed in she nodded. 'Good. But we're going to have to make some adjustments for tomorrow anyway,' she looked at Scarlet, 'as long as you don't mind making a run down to Plymouth this evening to pick Chastity up?'

There was a moment of silence as the pilots processed the information, but then excited chatter broke out. Abby let it go on for a moment, then held up her hand.

'I don't know about you, but I'm hungry and we might not have long before we're scrambled again. You can discuss the news over lunch and if someone can work out how to put eleven pilots into pairs that would be nice.'

Benedict ran with the other Misfits to the aircraft. His was one of the furthest away and he was somewhat out of breath by the time he arrived, but that didn't stop him from scowling in passing at the bare metal panels on the tail of his aircraft, spoiling the new colour scheme. It was some consolation that he had received the damage chasing and killing a pair of MU10s and would have another couple of kill marks to show for it, but still, as a Misfit he needed to look his best in front of the regular RAC pilots.

Cotter leaned in to help him strap in. 'There were a couple of badly frayed control cables in the tail, sir. We cobbled together a fix, but it might not be very strong. Are you sure you don't want to go up in one of the other Spits and let us take her apart and repair her properly?'

Benedict glanced across to where Drake and Rob were starting up their aircraft. The dull grey primer paint on them was enough to make even a beautiful aircraft like the Spitsteam look ugly. 'I'm sure whatever you've done will be fine. You'll have plenty of time to do whatever you want tonight.'

Cotter grimaced and jumped down as Benedict began to run through his final checks. She'd sent him a message advising of the state of his aircraft and suggesting he take one of the other Spitsteams, which were completely identical to his, but he had said no. She hadn't been able to understand why until she'd seen his face looking at the paintwork of the other Spits and realised that, incredibly, it was purely through vanity. She just hoped his decision didn't come back to bite him.

She shook her head as she ducked under the wing and went around the front of the aircraft. So much for the understanding she'd thought they'd come to only a few hours ago, but, then again, he had a life of privilege to overcome before he became a normal person.

'Sarge!' "Boy" Watkins called out as he came running in from the sunshine outside the hangar where he and a few of the others had been playing cricket. 'Tower just called - Sausage is on 'is way back. Declared an emergency!'

Cotter rolled her eyes. 'Of course he bloody did,' she muttered. 'Be right there,' she told the gangly boy who she suspected had lied about his age on his RAC application form.

The boy grinned and ran back out, but, knowing that it would still be at least a while before Wilberforce was in sight, she finished piling her plate with sandwiches before following.

The fitters had stopped playing and grouped up on the apron to look for the aircraft, shading their eyes and staring out to the east, towards which the Misfits had disappeared.

For a long minute there was nothing, but then one of the fitters called out. 'There she is!'

Cotter looked at where she was pointing, but she still didn't see anything for a good few seconds and even then it was only a dot. An aircraft travels very fast, though, and in another few seconds the dot had become a line and in ten more a recognisable silhouette.

"Ee's bobbing up and down like a bloody balloon.' Watkins said. 'What's 'ee doin'?'

'Shhh!' Cotter called out. 'Everyone quiet!'

She strained her ears, cupping her hands around them and opening her mouth slightly to try to listen. Her suspicions were soon confirmed - the pitch of the airscrew was constantly changing, becoming higher and lower in the same rhythm as the aircraft was going up and down.

'He's completely lost the elevator,' she said. 'He's having to use the throttle to control his height.'

Cotter slapped the side of her leg and gritted her teeth. She should have made more of an effort to talk him out of going up in a damaged aircraft. All for bloody show...

The rescue vehicles were already out and ready to race to the rescue, but the fitters were glued in place and they watched as Wilberforce took the aircraft around the airfield to the downwind side and began his approach. If it hadn't been obvious before that there was something wrong, then it was now as the aircraft approached the airfield far too low and far too fast.

They held their breath as the Spit passed over the trees, missing them by inches, then flashed over the fence and perimeter track.

Without elevators, Wilberforce couldn't carry out a normal landing, pulling the nose of the aircraft up as it decelerated until it settled gently to the ground. The only way for him to get his nose to come up was to increase the throttle, but that just increased his speed and height, which was the opposite of what he wanted. He floated across the airfield, rising and falling, trying to find a happy medium, but he couldn't quite get it right. He was swiftly running out of room, though, and in the end he apparently just decided to try his luck and applied just enough throttle to bring up the nose, then cut it completely.

There was a heart-stopping moment when the Spitsteam hit the ground and bounced and it looked like it was going to nose in when it came down, but a lightning-quick application of throttle controlled the crash and brought the nose up just enough. The airscrew still touched the earth, though, and it disintegrated, sending pieces of metal flying through the air for almost a hundred yards. In the end that was what saved the aircraft as that provided just enough resistance to slow it down and allow Wilberforce to apply the brakes, whereas otherwise he would have turned it over onto its back. As it was, the Spitsteam was still going at least twenty miles per hour when it ran out of room and was only prevented from going on a trip into the trees by the perimeter fence.

Cotter rolled her eyes, then looked around the fitters, finding her group among them. 'Who had the onion?' she asked.

Fitters and pilots alike stayed out of her way as Abby stomped past them and into the ready room, slamming the door behind her. She went over to where Benedict was relaxing in an armchair, reading a newspaper and drinking tea, and stood over him, uncomfortably close, not allowing him to stand.

'Cotter warned you about the damage, didn't she?'

'Yes, but...'

'She advised you to take one of the other Spits, didn't she?'

'Yes, but...'

'And you still decided to go up in yours.'

'Yes, but...'

'Because you know better than she does.'

'Yes! I mean, no, but...'

'There are very few pilots who know as much about their aircraft as their fitters and even they defer to them when it comes to matters of airworthiness.' Abby said, her voice rising as her anger mounted. 'That includes Gwen, who designed the bloody Harridan and half the bloody aircraft in the bloody squadron!'

She thrust a finger in his face. 'At one time or other I've had a mad Scotsman, a drunken Irishwoman, an insolent Muscovite, a smart-mouthed Australian, a circus pilot and even a bloody birdwatcher in my squadron, but I've never had an idiot and I'm not going to start now! So, buck up your ideas, stop being so bloody arrogant, vain and selfish and start behaving like a Misfit or you'll be out on your ear!'

Abby glared at Benedict for a moment, making sure he understood, then turned on her heel and stalked out. The rest of the Misfits had been waiting outside and they sensible waited until she had gotten completely out of the way before coming in. Billingsworth's team came with them and they all settled down into the chairs to make their reports.

None of them looked at Benedict.

'From the KBC studios in London, this is the news at eight.'
The radio wasn't usually on during dinner in the officers' mess - it just wasn't done - but Abby had asked for the news to be put on that evening for some reason and the head steward had obliged.

Today has seen more raids by the Prussian air force on RAC airfields around the south and east of the country. Twelve raids in total were launched by the Prussians, but, despite the large number of bombers sent over, the damage done was almost insignificant and sources in the RAC confirm that their ability to fight has not been at all compromised.'

The entire mess had gone quiet, everyone had stopped eating, and, even though it made no difference whatsoever, they were all looking towards the radio set behind the bar. All except for Abby, who was smiling faintly and looking across the table at her new pilots, the reason for which became quickly evident.

Joining the fight these last two days has been the newly reformed Misfit Squadron, who have been joined by three new members to replace those tragically lost or who have been moved on to tasks that are more important to the war effort. Aerial Officers Wilberforce, Sherborne and Perkins have already distinguished themselves, each of them shooting down several enemy fighters, but Officer Eleanor Perkins managed to accomplish a feat that had never before been registered - she shot down five enemy aircraft yesterday, not only becoming an "ace in a day", but

Whatever other news there might be was rendered inaudible by cheers as, for the second day in a row, the men and women in the officers' mess applauded Ellie.

Abby had stood while the others were cheering and she walked around the large round table, gesturing for Ellie to stand as she did. She held up her hand for silence, then pulled a piece of paper from her pocket. She didn't get a chance to read it, though, because the sound of cheering from the neighbouring building, where the enlisted men and women had their mess, sparked off a new round of cheers and then laughter when Ellie blushed and started to sit down, but was dragged back to her feet by her collar by Abby.

'Oh, no,' Abby said, 'you have to stand and suffer through the adoration of the people, like I've had to for three years.'

Drake blew a raspberry at that, to general amusement, and she gave him a scathing look. 'Taking over from Bruce as the squadron wag, Rudy?'

'Somebody has to do it, Abby.'

'No, they really don't.'

Drake blew another raspberry and Abby rolled her eyes when there was more laughter, but everyone went silent with expectation when she held up the piece of paper.

'A couple of telegrams came through half an hour ago. One was from a friend at the KBC who informed me of the contents of the top story of this evening's news broadcast. The second was addressed to Ellie.' She looked sideways at Ellie. 'Are you going to read it, or shall I?'

She chuckled when Ellie shook her head, a look of sheer terror on her face.

'It seems,' she announced to the room, 'that we scare her more than a thousand Prussian aircraft.'

She put her arm around Ellie's shoulders and pulled her in as laughter rang out again. 'We tease you because you're one of us,' she said softly. 'You'll get used to it. Try to enjoy it; it means we're alive.'

She released Ellie then frowned at the room. 'Are you going to let me read this or not?' she scowled, drawing chuckles, but when the room remained fairly quiet she nodded. 'That's more like it.'

She opened the telegram. 'Congratulations and thanks on behalf of all Britain. Stop. When duties permit come by for dinner. Stop. Elizabeth excited to meet you. Stop. As am I. Stop. Keep up the good work. Stop. GR.'

As the mess broke out in applause, Ellie smiled, but inside she was groaning; now, when she finally ran out of luck, she wouldn't just be letting down the Misfits and the RAC, but the king and the whole country as well.

'Ace in a day.' Gruber said, tossing the transcript of the KBC broadcast on the floor of his private dining room, leaving it for Lang or a steward to pick up. 'So? I've done that about twelve times.'

'But that was mostly against the Spanish, Muscovites and Norwegians.' Reitsch pointed out as she sipped at her wine. 'How many times have you done that against the British?'

Gruber fought back a snarl, not wanting to antagonise her before the evening had even gotten under way properly. 'Once.' He admitted, smiling his best smile. 'But the others still count.'

Reitsch shrugged, but didn't say anything else and Gruber applied himself to his dinner. She wasn't the best dinner guest he'd ever had, or the worst, by a long shot, but she was one of the better looking, especially in the tight black dress she'd put on for the occasion.

They finished their dinner mostly in silence and after a steward had cleared the plates Gruber reclined back in his chair and smiled charmingly.

'Shall we retire to my suite for a nightcap?'

Reitsch stood and gazed down her nose at him. 'I think we should keep our relationship strictly professional from now on.'

'What?' Gruber asked, leaping to his feet. He strode around the table to her and grabbed her arm as she started to walk away. 'Why?'

She stared down at his hand and he hurriedly pulled it away.

'I thought we had a good time?' he said, wincing inside at the whining tone in his voice.

She looked at him and he thought she was going to change her mind for a moment, but then she seemed to come to a decision and her eyes turned ice cold.

'No,' she said. '*We* didn't. And now that I've ticked you off my list I have better things to do with my time. I only deigned to dine with you because your food is better than the muck in the mess. Goodnight.'

Lang opened the door for her and she sashayed out.

Gruber collapsed back in his chair and stared at the closed door.

Eventually, he shrugged and picked up his wine glass - it wasn't as if that hadn't happened before either.

Schmidt balanced his plate on his hand and picked at the sausage and vegetables on it with a fork while he stood and studied the huge map on the wall that he'd had marked for the operation. The RAC bases, aircraft factories and radio direction finding station each had their own colour pins, but at that moment he was only concerned with the green ones that denoted the RDF stations. The British were reacting to his raids too well for them to be as blind as he had been expecting them to be, but was that because some of the stations were still operational? Or were there stations he didn't know about?

An aide knocked and came straight in. 'I have the numbers for the day, Herr Generalfeldmarschall.'

'Mmm!' Schmidt beckoned the man over with his fork while he finished chewing. He swallowed, then wiped his mouth on the back of his hand. 'Give me a summary.'

'The new tactics seem to be working. We've had far fewer casualties and the ratio of our kills to theirs is now in our favour, except in those raids where the Misfits show up.'

Schmidt grunted and the aide paused and looked up from his notes, but when no other comment came from the old general he continued.

'More of our bombers are getting through to their targets and our pilots report that there are noticeably fewer British fighters in the air each time.'

The aide finished and looked up.

'Good.' Schmidt nodded, but didn't look away from the map. 'Tell the army and navy commanders to continue making their final preparations for the invasion - we are still on schedule for two days from now.'

'Yes, sir.'

'And the Misfits?' Schmidt asked, walking over to a second, much smaller map with pink pins showing the locations the enemy squadron had been sighted. There was no pattern he could discern. 'Have we got any idea where they're based yet?'

'No, sir. Beyond what we already knew - that they have to be somewhere in the south or around London because of their behaviour in the raids on the east of Britain.'

'Hmmm.' Schmidt nodded again, then tapped the map. 'What about their old base in Kent?'

'The one that was destroyed?'

'Yes. Has anyone checked to see if it was repaired?'

'Uh, I'll have to make sure, but I don't think so.'

'Have someone do so, please. Just in case.'

Schmidt ran his finger across the map from one of the pink pins to another, as if he might feel where the Misfits were. They were the only unknown, the one variable that could possibly spoil things.

'In the meantime, prepare orders for Gruber. Tell him that his priority is the Misfits - I want him to knock them from the sky.'

CHAPTER 8

25th August 1941

'Alright, we're going to try something different this morning.' Abby said when everyone had grabbed a tea and found a place on the sofas and armchairs. 'I had a lovely little chat with Sir Douglas last night and, once he'd finished adding his congratulations to Ellie and the rest of us on top of those of the king, the KBC, every single newspaper in the country, all the squadron commanders who made a point of ringing me and so on and so on and so forth, we eventually managed to find a moment to speak about how the war is going and what he'd like the Misfits to do today.' She gave a blushing Ellie a smile before continuing. 'He shared a few figures with me.' Abby walked over to the chalkboard and picked up the chalk but didn't write. 'It seems that we're not doing very well. In fact we did worse yesterday than the day before.' She started writing. 'On the first day, we shot down one point nine enemy fighters for each one of ours on average, but that dropped to one point four yesterday and he expects it to drop even further today, possibly even to one for one.' She underlined the last number and turned back to her pilots. 'That is unsustainable and we will not prevail if it continues. However,' she turned back to the board, 'when the Misfits are part of the intercepting force the average kill ratio goes up to *three point five*.' She emphasised the number and underlined it several times on the board, then drew a circle around it for good measure before putting down the chalk and facing them.

'We are losing, ladies and gentlemen, there's no other way to put it than that, and even our efforts are not going to be enough. So, Sir Douglas and I very quickly came to the conclusion that the Misfits need to intercept more raids.'

'How?' Drake asked. 'We can't get down and rewind fast enough and even if we took up spare springs I doubt we'd have enough tension to get from one raid to another and still fight.'

'Quite right,' Abby nodded. 'So today we're going to split up. A flight will go to one raid while B and C flights, under Gwen's command, will go to another and we're going to see if we can have the same effect on the Prussians as we do when we stick together.'

Benedict went out into the early morning and walked with the other Misfits towards the line of aircraft. He didn't join in with their banter, though, or even really hear their jokes, because he was too focussed on squinting ahead to where his aircraft was parked the end of the line. It was still fairly dark and at first he couldn't see which aircraft his fitters had gotten ready for him, but he was fairly sure he knew which one it would be. However, when he got near enough to make it out, it was the distinctive patterning of his own one and not the dull silvery grey of the spare Spits that he found, the lovely royal purple that was his favourite colour looking black in the faint light from the hangar.

Cotter stumbled towards him as he approached, wiping her hands on a cloth. The black under her eyes was clear to see, even in the low light, and he tell from her posture how exhausted she was.

'You got her ready.' Benedict stated, rather redundantly, the words catching in his throat for some reason.

'Just about, sir.'

'So... she's airworthy, then?' he asked carefully.

Cotter shrugged. 'As far as we can tell, sir. She is fully repaired, but we haven't had time to test her.'

Benedict looked longingly at the paintwork and the markings underneath the cockpit - they were still sausages, but there were five of them now after yesterday's fights, making him an ace, and he would dearly love to display that to both friend and enemy alike.

'Well done. Thank you for your hard work, but it's probably best if I take one of the spares. I'll test her when I come back. If that's alright with you, of course?'

Cotter sighed in obvious relief and smiled. 'Yes, sir. That would be fine.'

'Which one shall I use, then?' Benedict asked, turning to look at the spare Spitsteams that were parked up just in front of the hangar, ready in case they were needed.

'This way, sir.' Cotter said, lifting a hand to signal the group of fitters responsible for the preparation of the spares.

Abby grunted in satisfaction as Cotter led Benedict towards the spare Spits and turned to walk back along the line of aircraft. It would take more to get back into her good books than a sensible decision and a bit of respect, but it was a good start.

The Misfits were never going to have the same kind of physical effect when it was only four or six of them diving onto the Prussian formation than they did when it was all ten of them, but the psychological impact was just as great and they sowed just as much chaos among the Fleas as they had before. The Prussians had finally gotten wise to the Misfits' tactic of hitting them just before the main force of British fighters arrived, but it seemed they were still under orders to stay with the bombers and not counteract them directly. The only answer they'd been able to come up with, therefore, was to ignore the Misfits' attack, mostly by hiding underneath their own bombers, absorb whatever losses they took, and try to concentrate on the incoming Spits and Harrys. It worked, up to a certain extent, and the Misfits weren't able to get as many kills in that first pass as they had before, but it still left the Fleas distracted, more vulnerable than they would have been otherwise and easier prey for the RAC.

Schmidt entered the theatre through the ornate front doors, receiving the salutes of the four guards with a nod. However, instead of going through the double doors where the next set of guards were posted and into the stalls he headed for the stairs leading up to the dress circle. There were no lights on up here and the thick carpeted muffled his steps as he went down the stairs between the seats to the brass railing at the front of the balcony-like area and leaned on it so that he could look down into his command centre unseen and unnoticed.

Rather than find some damp basement, or purpose build a bunker to hold his command centre, Schmidt had come up with the idea of commandeering something suitable and had immediately thought of the theatre he'd driven past on his way to the main army base where his offices were located. Situated in the middle of a small French town, it was flanked by houses that were still occupied by French families and, rather than presenting a security risk, he believed that meant there was less chance that it would be bombed. The building itself had been easy to convert to his needs and there were now no sign of the previous occupants or the show that they'd been putting on - something French and frivolous, no doubt. The seats in the stalls below had been ripped out to make room for an enormous map table, the backdrop and wing curtains had been torn down to open up the stage and desks had been set up, his own in the middle, looking down at the map table, and radios had been installed in the left side wings, where the electrical circuits controlling the lighting system had been. It was warm and rather more comfortable than any other command centre he'd ever had and the supply of coffee and pastries from the bakery two doors down was unlimited and already putting inches onto his waistline.

He watched his men going about their jobs, doing what they did when they weren't under his watchful gaze, rather than what they wanted him to see them doing.

To his satisfaction, everyone and everything seemed to be in place and doing their job well and he nodded and retraced his steps down to the stalls entrance.

'Achtung!'

Generalfeldmarschall Weissman, the commander of the Fliegertruppe, called the command centre to attention as Schmidt came in, officially this time.

Schmidt acknowledged the salutes quickly, then went straight to his seat. 'What is the situation?' he asked, as he accepted a cup of coffee from a steward.

'Raids one and two have just engaged the enemy.' Weissman said. 'Raids three and four are formed up and beginning to move.'

'Good.' Schmidt sipped his strong black coffee as he gazed down at the map table.

'Any sign of the Misfits yet?'

'Yes, sir.'

Schmidt leaned forward, searching for the pink token among the sea of red and black ones. 'At which raid?'

'Both, sir.'

'What?' Schmidt spluttered, nearly spilling his drink over himself. He put it down and wiped his hands on a napkin.

'The Misfits have split up to attend both raids in lesser numbers.'

'And?'

Weissman grimaced. 'Early indications are that they are having the same effect on each raid as if they were at squadron strength.'

'What?' Schmidt slammed his fist down on the desk and this time the coffee went flying, the cup rolling off and smashing on the floor, unnoticed by either officer. 'Both? How is that possible? Dividing their strength should just make it easier for Gruber and his circus to deal with one group of them! What the hell is that fool doing?' He peered at the table again, trying to find the Barons' token among the aircraft over Britain. He couldn't, though. 'Where the hell are they?'

Weissman pointed to the single blue token on the board, hidden in amongst the dozens of black tokens grouped over Belgium. 'With raid three, sir, which is assigned targets in the county of Essex.'

'Ha!' Schmidt barked. 'Of course they are! Exactly where that coward Gruber knows the Misfits are not going to be.' He slammed the table again, then thrust a finger at Weissman. 'As soon as they come down I want you to get that Reitsch woman on the telephone. Let her know in no uncertain terms that the Barons are under orders to accompany the raids over the south of England from now on. Tell her that if Gruber tries to do anything other than that then she is to deal with him appropriately. Is that understood?'

Weissman frowned, slightly puzzled, but still nodded. 'Yes, sir.'

When the Misfits landed back at Bagshot they found Chastity Arrowsmith waiting for them at the side of the airfield. She wasn't alone, though, she had brought an old friend of the Misfits - Freddy Featherstonehaugh, a reporter for The Times - with her.

Scarlet had gone to get her the evening before, but, instead of bringing her to Bagshot, she'd let herself be persuaded to take a detour to London and had dropped her off at Hyde Airfield before going on to Bentley Priory. Chastity had met up with Freddy there and he had driven her down that morning.

The Misfits swamped Chastity, welcoming her back. They'd heard about her adventures in Egypt and across North Africa - the news of her survival and the subsequent retreat across the desert had been widely reported - but they still bombarded her with questions.

'Give her some space, people!' Abby eventually had to call out. 'You can interrogate her over tea after we've debriefed.' She looked at Chastity seriously. 'For now there is only one thing we need to know - are you alright and are you going to need to rest before you come back to us?'

Chastity smiled, her teeth looking very white in her sunburned face. She looked thin and rather under-nourished, but happy, standing hand in hand with Freddy. 'I had plenty of time to rest on the boat. I just want to get back into the air.'

'I'm afraid all we've got for you to fly is a modified Spit.'

Chastity glanced over at the aircraft and gave a contented sigh. 'Just like old times, then.'

While Chastity went to find herself an aircraft, Freddy Featherstonehaugh accompanied the Misfits to the ready room, however, he pulled Abby to one side before she went in.

'I think you know what I'm going to ask,' he said.

'After last night's KBC broadcast I figured it was only a matter of time before someone came knocking.'

Freddy nodded. 'I made some calls this morning and got the other newspapers to agree to go back to our previous arrangement of it being only me here, as long as I share my material with them, but if I don't come up with something on your new pilots quickly, then they're going to send their own people. Sir Douglas was busy and I couldn't get hold of him to make sure it was alright, but the king has signed off on it.'

Abby grinned. 'So I'm stuck with you.'

'I'm afraid so.'

They peered in at the new pilots.

'Talk to Wilberforce first,' Abby said. 'Of the three he'll be the most willing to blow his own trumpet and it'll give the other two more incentive to talk and make sure they tell their side of things.'

Freddy frowned. 'Is he likely to lie to me?'

'No!' Abby chuckled. 'But he is the kind of person who will twist things slightly to make himself look better.'

'Understood.'

'And leave Perkins for last.' She held up a hand when he frowned. 'Yes, yes, I am fully aware it's her that everyone wants to know about.' She glanced at where Ellie was speaking quietly to one of Billingsworth's assistants. 'However, unlike Wilberforce, she will play down her role in the fight and will barely give you anything more than the bare bones of her story. If you talk to the others first you can ask them about her and it'll give you something to fill the gaping holes in with.'

Freddy nodded. 'Will do. And thank you.'

'When do you want to get started?'

'As soon as possible, really. I'd like to have something for this evening's edition.'

'Alright, then.' Abby turned and went into the ready room. 'Benedict!' she called out. 'Once you've finished giving your report, Freddy Featherstonehaugh from *The Times* would like a word with you.'

'Me?' Benedict asked, surprised. He smiled slowly. 'Of course.' He smirked at Rob and Ellie, then gave Freddy nod. 'I'd be delighted.'

'Good,' Abby said. She jerked her thumb over her shoulder. 'He can wait for you outside. Take him some tea and biscuits when you go and remember you have a test flight to take.'

'Yes, ma'am.'

'And don't forget to tell him about sausages.' Tanya called out from behind a plate of sandwiches.

'They have no reply to us!' Benedict gloated as he dismantled another Prussian fighter. That was the second already and, added to the two he'd scored that morning, he only needed one more to become an ace in a day like Ellie. He'd make sure that the journalist knew about that before he published his story about him. And he'd get Cotter to repaint the kill markings properly that night too, so that when the photographer came tomorrow the world would be able to see how good he was.

'Seven,' he said over the radio, 'you have a pair of MU10s angling towards you, four o'clock high.'

'I see them, Eight. Thank you.'

He banked back towards Derek, in case he was needed, but a flash of red beyond the formation of bombers just below him caught his eye. There were two of them, dogfighting with a pair of Harridans, turning hard and rolling around each other. Only one of them was a red *Blutsauger*, though, the other aircraft was black with red only on the tail. It looked like a modified MU9 or something - it was probably a provisional member who had been put in an inferior aircraft, like Abby had stuffed him into a Spit.

He smiled; Ellie had killed a Baron, so it couldn't be that hard and it would look very good in the papers if his fifth kill of the day was a Baron. He was never going to catch up with Ellie, especially seeing as the Muscovite woman was letting her lead the pair for some reason, but at least like this he'd get some renown of his own.

A quick check on Derek showed that the man had the MU10s well in hand, so he reversed his turn and headed towards the bombers and the pair of Barons. He put the bombers between him and them, hiding his approach - just because the outcome of the fight was a foregone conclusion, didn't mean he wasn't going to make use of any advantage he could get.

One of the Harridans went into an uncontrolled dive, the pilot either unconscious or dead, but there was still one left fighting, keeping them busy and from seeing him coming.

He lost sight of his prey for a couple of seconds when he pulled up over a last, tightly-packed group of big bombers, but he knew exactly where they would be and rolled his aircraft onto its back, ready to pull down directly onto them. The only trouble was, when he got past the bombers the Barons were no longer where they were supposed to be. He scanned the sky below him frantically and immediately found the second Harridan and the Blutsauger falling towards the ground, shedding bits of themselves, but of the black aircraft there was no sign.

He continued his search, but then started when he realised just how long he had been flying straight and level, albeit inverted. In a panic, he pulled the stick back and sideways, kicking the rudder hard, swerving aside just as tracer fire leapt out at him from behind a bomber. He was too late to avoid it completely, though, and a line of holes appeared as if by magic in his wing. The black aircraft flashed past him as he corkscrewed and he craned his neck and pulled hard on the stick in an attempt to follow it. The enemy fighter was extremely agile, though, and, try as he might, he couldn't get it in front of him. In fact it was out-turning him by quite a considerable margin.

However, there were other ways to conduct a dogfight than just trying to turn tighter than your opponent and he watched for his opportunity, waiting until the turn took him back towards the Prussian formation. A group of bombers loomed large in his windscreen and he straightened out and raced for it, all thoughts of making his fifth kill of the day now gone, replaced by the simple desire to survive.

There were RAC aircraft in amongst the bombers and Derek would be there somewhere - they would be safe together.

The bombers were further away than he'd thought, though, their sheer size making him misjudge the distance, and, well before he could get amongst them, the enemy fighter appeared in the mirror over his head.

Derek saw off the second of the pair of MU10s, sending it limping away out of the fight with a big chunk gone from its wing, only one airscrew working and the rear gunner dead, then searched the sky for Benedict. The boy hadn't come back for a while now and he was concerned that he might have done something foolish; it was no secret that, after the dressing down that Abby had given him, he was trying hard to prove himself. Was he trying too hard?

He eventually found his wingman on the far edge of the bomber group, much further away than he usually got, and was about to turn towards him when the purple and white aircraft came apart, its wings folding up and coming off as it just stopped in the sky. It fell, disappearing from view, and a black aircraft rolled through the space it had previously occupied.

Derek's heart sank, even as his eyes narrowed and his hands and feet worked on the controls, turning him towards it.

Reitsch saw the brown and white aircraft coming from off her two o'clock and recognised the ridiculous bird shape of Derek Niven's *Kite*. She wondered if he would prove more of a challenge than whoever that had been in the garish purple aircraft, but, by the way he was coming directly at her, she doubted it.

She banked slightly as he drew closer, feigning an attack on a pair of Spitsteams, then just as she knew he was about to open fire she pulled up sharply and rolled towards him. As expected, points of light winked on his wings, but the shots passed harmlessly below her and moments later so did he. She continued her roll and pulled sharply, right up onto his six o'clock. Now it was her turn. She depressed the button on her stick, saw the impact of her fire on his wing, and nudged the rudder to direct it at the cockpit. Her aim was true and she saw the man's canopy shatter, but then her guns stopped, her ammunition gone.

She swore, but she didn't wait to see if she could claim another kill, she just pushed her nose forwards and dived through the vertical, only pulling up for home when the needle of the speedometer was nearing the nine hundred kilometres per hour mark.

Abby handed Dragon over to her fitters with a smile, then walked to the edge of the airfield and looked up at the aircraft of B and C flights circling to land. She frowned as her count came up short.

'Abby.'

'Algie.' She nodded a greeting to Billingsworth as he came over to stand with her, but didn't stop scanning the sky.

'Derek and Benedict missed their check-in and we can't reach them.'

Abby's eyes shot to him. 'When did you last hear from them?'

'I looked at the transcripts and the last thing they said was about halfway through the fight. Benedict warned Derek about a pair of MU10s and Derek thanked him.'

'MU10s?' Abby frowned. 'Well, *they're* not likely to have taken them both down.' She looked towards the aircraft now landing. 'Let's see if anyone saw anything before jumping to conclusions.'

'Righto.' Billingsworth stood in silence with her for a second, but then he turned to her. 'Actually, I think I'm going to check with control one more time, just in case.'

He hurried away without waiting for an answer and she was too caught up in her fears and dreads to give him one, or even really hear him.

The Misfits had all landed and gone into the ready room by the time Billingsworth came back, but Abby was still standing on the apron. She just couldn't leave; it felt like she would be abandoning her pilots if she just turned her back and gave up hope.

'No word.' Billingsworth said, shaking his head. 'Nobody has called to say they diverted to their airfield or reported either of them crash landing. It's not looking good I'm afraid.'

'None of the pilots saw anything, either,' Abby said.

'They could have put down in a field somewhere with no phone, I suppose.'

'Both of them?'

Billingsworth shrugged. 'Anything's possible.'

Gwen came back out of the ready room and they turned to her as she walked towards them.

'Something I didn't mention before,' she said quietly, for their ears only. 'The Barons were covering our raid and they were rather more keen than usual. They were up high, at the same altitude as we were and they were posturing for a head-on pass. I didn't take them up on it, obviously, but still, they haven't tried that with us for a while.'

'Hmm,' Abby said thoughtfully. 'Do we think Gruber has finally found a backbone?'

Gwen shook her head. 'I think it might have more to do with someone new. I'm not sure, I'll have to check with the others, but I'm fairly sure I spotted a strange aircraft with them. It's black and red and looks more like an MU9 or an HH190 than a *Blutsauger*. Maybe he has something to do with it.'

'Maybe some of the regular RAC boys and girls have seen it,' Abby said, looking at Billingsworth.

He nodded. 'I'll ring around and find out as soon as we've finished here.'

'Thank you.'

The three of them went into the ready room, but, while Gwen sat down next to Kitty and Billingsworth went to interview Drake, Abby just leaned against the door frame and watched.

The room was far quieter than usual, the laughter gone. Serious pilots made their reports while clutching to the comfort of a hot cup of tea or each other. They knew just as well as she did that sooner or later a phone call was going to come and the news wasn't going to be good. It couldn't be. They would have heard *something* by now if it was.

'Can I have your attention, please?' she announced, pushing herself away from the wall and walking into the middle of the room. 'Whether Derek and Benedict have fallen prey to the Barons or not we don't know, but I don't care. It looks like they've finally worked up the courage to give us a fight, so we're going to oblige them. Next time we see them we're going to disrupt the fighter escort as we've been doing, but after that we're going to concentrate on them. I want to kill enough of them to make them think twice about trying it on with us again. And if we can take out Gruber or whoever that is in that black aircraft while we're at it, so much the...'

She was cut off by the sudden sound of the telephone. Billingsworth, who happened to be closest, picked it up.

'Misfits.' He listened for a long moment, but then he exhaled slowly, his chin dropping almost to his chest. 'Understood. Thank you. Keep me informed of his condition, please.'

He put the phone down, then turned around.

'Derek bailed out near Maidstone. He's badly hurt and has been taken to the hospital there. And...' He swallowed. 'And...' he took a deep breath, then tried again. 'And the remains of a purple aircraft have been found. It looks like the pilot went down with it.'

Abby nodded. 'Thank you, Algie.' She looked around the room, taking in the sad or shocked faces. 'This changes *nothing*,' she said forcefully, causing more than one of her pilots to flinch. 'But what I

said before applies even more now - I don't care whether the Barons
had anything to do with this or not, we are going to *destroy* them.'

CHAPTER 9

'Barons. Twelve o'clock. Directly over the first group of bombers.'

Tanya's cold, almost emotionless, voice had them lifting their eyes from the vast bomber force below to scan the skies ahead of them.

'Got them,' Abby said.

'I count sixteen.' Ellie said. 'They've been bringing in replacements.'

'It doesn't matter.' Penny chimed in. 'We only need to kill two of them.'

'Exactly.' Abby said. 'Stick to the plan.'

Ellie settled herself in her seat, feeling the flightsuit gripping her thighs and midriff tightly, the straps over her shoulders and around her waist holding her in with just enough give that it didn't restrict her ability to look around. She shifted her hand slightly on the spade grip, wringing the leather wrapping, feeling her gloves squeak over it more than she heard it, before settling it back in exactly the same position as it had been before.

She slotted lenses over her goggles and studied the approaching Barons. They were in four groups of four, with only a slight gap between them. They were too far away to make out colours, but she thought that the leaders of the two middle groups might have had slightly different silhouettes. It might have been only her imagination, though, making her see what she wanted to see.

These were the Fliegertruppe's elite pilots, their equivalent to the Misfits and she should probably feel frightened, or at least a little apprehensive going into combat against them. However, despite her doubts about her own abilities and her fear that she would let everyone down, to her surprise, all she felt was determined to do her best and to at least take some of them down with her if she should fall.

'On my mark.'

Abby's voice brought her back to thoughts of the job at hand and she peered forwards, over the side of the nose, and found that they were almost up level with the bomber formation. The Barons had accelerated ahead of them, racing to meet the Misfits, but that didn't matter, in fact it would make their plan all the more effective.

'Now!'

All four Misfit aircraft instantly rolled onto their backs and pulled hard down.

Most of the Barons started shooting in that moment, but it was too late and their fire went harmlessly high. One of them had somehow anticipated the move, though, and had adjusted their aim accordingly.

Ellie's aircraft juddered as it was hit and she saw two holes appear in her wing, but she ignored them; she wasn't dead and she'd find out soon enough if her aircraft could still fly and she could still kill Prussians.

She pursed her lips and concentrated on remaining in formation with Tanya. Abby had told the Muscovite to take the lead for this flight and neither she nor Ellie had argued; while Ellie was good, she still lacked the Muscovite's killer instinct and it would be needed against the Barons.

As they cut through the bombers, Ellie gave whatever fighters she found in her way a quick squirt, but she didn't allow any of them to distract her for more than a moment - her main focus was on the red aircraft following them down.

'They're closing.'

'I know.'

Tanya pulled up under one of the groups of big Hoffmans, surprising the group of MU10s escorting it. The two of them shot straight through the middle of them, sending one falling from the sky, then cut sharply across the front of the bombers, close enough for Ellie to see the terrified look on the faces of the pilot and copilot of one of them. The manoeuvre hadn't just taken the bombers by surprise, but the Barons as well, because they found the two Misfits suddenly pointed back towards them, guns already blazing. One of the crimson aircraft flew apart as it was riddled with cannon fire and another went into a spin with half a wing missing before the pair of Misfits were through.

Ellie growled her elation, but didn't allow herself to celebrate any more than that, instead she was already scanning the sky.

'The targets weren't in that group.'

'No.' Tanya replied calmly. 'The black one is behind us.'

'Happy hunting.' Abby muttered as they blasted through the bomber wing and she lost sight of Tanya and Ellie as the two elements separated and flew in opposite directions.

The forces acting on her body were fierce as she pulled up hard, but it was nothing she hadn't experienced hundreds of times before and she roared out her rage at the loss of one of her pilots to help keep the blood in her head. An MU9 appeared in front of her and disappeared just as quickly as she ripped it apart with Dragon's cannons, but that did nothing to satisfy her.

'Six o'clock high and coming fast.' Penny reported from her wing.

'Got it.'

There was a likely looking group of Funkel 88s ahead in a tight formation, like sheep huddled against a wolf, and she pointed her nose directly at them.

'Gruber's with them,' Penny said. 'No sign of the black aircraft.'

'Shame. We'll just have to kill them one at a time.'

Fire came from the gunners in the noses of the 88s and she dipped below it, applying some rudder to slew Dragon to the side, then returning to point at them again.

She wasn't actually going to carry out a head on attack, but any confusion she could sow among them would only help to confuse the pursuers.

At the last moment she dipped beneath the bombers, going between then and a group of MU9s that either hadn't seen them coming or hadn't wanted to risk opening fire and hitting the crimson aircraft beyond them, but as soon as the formation was past she slammed Dragon on its side and pulled around behind them.

Dragon creaked and groaned as Abby subjected her to more punishment than she ever had before and Abby screamed this time as blackness encroached her vision. The world started to fade, but she barely needed her eyes or other senses anymore; after so long in combat her instincts were perfectly capable of keeping her alive.

And killing others.

She rolled out of the turn with her nose pointing back the way she'd come and found a red aircraft directly in her sights.

One down, fifteen to go.

'Leader, we're coming right at you.'

Ellie pulled up next to Tanya and adjusted her heading slightly to aim past Abby at one of the Barons chasing her. She grinned, wondering if the Prussians had realised yet that there was a rather nasty surprise in store for them.

'I see you, Three. We've got Gruber plus six.'

'We've got black plus five. Looks like Ellie and I are winning.'

'Don't count your chickens *yet*!'

Penny's last word came out almost as a shout as the four Misfits passed each other and opened fire almost simultaneously, immediately destroying four of the red aircraft.

Ellie saw her chance to take a potshot at Gruber after killing her chosen target and she kicked her rudder, slewing the Spitsteam sideways to point her nose at him, but her shots only grazed the bottom of his tail. She had the great satisfaction of seeing his tail wheel fly apart, though.

That was as far ahead as the Misfits had planned and Ellie followed Tanya as she banked sharply in an attempt to follow Gruber while simultaneously trying not to give the following Barons a clear shot.

'Black is still behind us.' Ellie called out.

'I know,' Tanya answered tensely. 'That pilot is good, and his aircraft...'

'He's firing at me!' Ellie called out as shots flashed past her canopy.

'Split up,' Tanya ordered, 'evade and survive and I'll come around behind him.'

'Roger.'

Ellie rolled and dived, using the incredible rolling rate and acceleration of the clipped-wing Spitsteam to the best advantage. She passed below the solid layer of bombers and into the loose cloud of British and Prussian fighters, seeking to lose the black aircraft in among them. A quick glance in her mirror showed the enemy aircraft still right behind her, though.

She led the enemy fighter on a merry dance, rolling and banking, climbing and diving, seeking to stay just that one step ahead of it - that one step that was the only thing between her and death. Tracer rounds flashed past her canopy more than once as the man tried his luck, but only once was she hit and she gained another hole in her wing to go with the two already there.

'Almost on you, Four, hold on.'

About bloody time, Ellie thought, but, even as she did, she knew she was being harsh on Tanya; the whole sequence of desperate manoeuvres had only taken about twenty seconds, thirty at the most - barely enough time for Tanya to have banked around behind the enemy.

'Bring him back to the right now and I'll have a shot.'

'Roger that.'

Ellie was in a maximum rate turn to the left, trying desperately to stay out of the more manoeuvrable enemy's sights, so doing what Tanya wanted her to do wasn't as simple as it might seem - if she simple reversed the turn she would just pass right in front of the enemy and give them a clear shot. She couldn't see any other way of doing it, though, not quickly enough for Tanya to get her chance anyway. At least the time she would be vulnerable would be minimal and the enemy would have to be very good to capitalise. She might even take him completely by surprise; they wouldn't be expecting her to do something so incredibly stupid.

She took a deep breath, entrusted herself to Tanya, and rolled her aircraft as sharply as she could onto its other wing.

Unfortunately, it seemed that the enemy *was* a *very* good pilot and he didn't miss the opportunity Ellie had afforded him. The Spitsteam was buffeted by multiple impacts and Ellie screamed as a jagged hole appeared in the canopy next to her and several dials on the instrument panel exploded.

The world began to swirl around her and she was thrown against the side bulkhead as her aircraft spun sickeningly. She shoved the stick sideways and pushed with her foot to stop the spin, but nothing happened. Neither control had any effect, they were just limp and loose. She found out why a moment later when she saw that there was very little aircraft actually attached to her cockpit anymore. Her mind, confused by the sickening spin and sudden change in her circumstances, still tried to work out how to save the Spit for a few seconds, but eventually she came to the realisation that there was only one thing she could do.

She struggled to lift her arm against the forces trying to pull it down and grabbed hold of the canopy release. There was a worrying moment when the canopy stuck only slightly open and she thought that there might be broken glass or something obstructing the slide, but gravity was working in her favour now and, once she got a good grip, she applied her full, amplified weight to the problem and the glass cover slid open with a crash. She hit the quick release for her straps, then struggled to her feet. It took a lot of effort, but then something broke off the wreckage of her aircraft and suddenly she was thrown free.

The ground was less than a thousand feet away and rushing up towards her incredibly quickly, but she knew she couldn't just deploy her full glidewings; she was rolling too fast and falling too rapidly and something would give. She deployed a single panel and used it to orientate herself, then another panel, which allowed her to control her descent, a third shortly after permitted her to pull up and stop her fall. Only then did she fully extend the wings, but, even as she sighed in relief and before she could fully take stock of her situation, there was a loud crash and she jerked and looked around, thinking that she might be in danger. It had only been the sound of her aircraft hitting the ground almost directly below her, though.

'Thank you,' she told it, 'I'm sorry.'

Her eyes prickled as she took in the mangled mess that had been the first aircraft that had really been her own, but then she tore her eyes away; she needed somewhere to land. Preferable close to a town so she wouldn't have to walk very far in her flightsuit.

Tanya gnashed her teeth as Ellie's aircraft flew apart.

Damn this pilot's good, she thought. *Not good enough, though.*

The black aircraft started to roll away, but it was too late; Ellie had given Tanya the opportunity she needed and she wasn't going to waste it. She squeezed the trigger and saw tracers reach out and connect with the enemy, ripping big chunks from the aircraft's wing. However, before Tanya could adjust her aim, tracers were flashing by her own cockpit and she was forced to evade. She quickly lost the new enemies, but by that time the black aircraft had gone.

Never mind, she thought, *there are plenty of other Barons to kill.*

Please be alright, Ellie.

Dragon and Kingfisher were better aircraft than the *Blutsaugers* they were up against, but that wasn't the only thing that counted in a dogfight, or even what counted the most, instead it was the quality of the pilot that mostly determined who won and who lost. Unfortunately for the Barons, they were completely outclassed in that respect as well. Penny and Abby were confident enough in their abilities to split up and, while Penny kept the Barons busy and proceeded to shoot them out of the sky one by one, Abby set her sights on their leader.

When the four Misfits had led the Barons into their trap, Gruber had been directly behind Abby, with all the advantage he could possibly want over her. Something must have happened to him in the crossover, though, because he'd been slow to react when she'd started angling towards him and when he finally did they were on almost an even footing, looking at each other through the tops of their canopies across a large invisible circle in the sky.

Gruber had built his aircraft, *Hölle*, more than six months before when he'd realised that his previous aircraft, *Flamme*, a triplane, wasn't anywhere near good enough for a modern air war. He had stolen design elements from *Wasp* and *Dragonfly*, the aircraft of Gwen and Abby at the time, in an attempt to build a superior machine to theirs. Unfortunately for him, the Misfits had already been working on improving their aircraft and, while Hölle might well have been better than Dragonfly, it wasn't nearly as good as Dragon.

If Gruber hadn't known that before, it became perfectly obvious now as Abby began clawing her way around the circle to him and she saw him craning his neck every which way, searching for help, saw the panic bloom in his face when he realised that it wasn't coming, and she grinned at him and gave him a cheerful wave when he looked up at her again.

His next move - run for home - was perfectly predictable, she just wasn't expecting him to do it quite so soon, and it took her by surprise when he rolled and dived for the ground. She was on him in a flash, though, diving behind him.

It seemed that the one thing Hölle did better than the Misfit aircraft was run away and Gruber was getting further and further ahead with each passing second. She wasn't going to catch him and she doubted he was going to come back, so Abby fired, holding down her trigger for a full three seconds, longer than she would normally do for a single target that wasn't a bomber. She saw at least a couple of the rounds impact, but couldn't tell if they'd had any real effect. She was pretty sure he would have gotten the message, though, so she pulled up, not wanting to dive too far away from the fight and have to spend too long getting back.

Gruber getting away wasn't the outcome she'd wanted from that day's fight, but she'd take giving him a fright and shooting down more of his squadron as they ever had, as long as she didn't lose any more pilots in the process.

Ellie banked her glidewings towards the town.

Of the two or three she could have reached it was the largest, with maybe a hundred houses, some outlying farms and what looked like a parade of shops. She hoped it was big enough that someone would have a telephone, or that there would be a post office that would be able to send a telegram. Failing that she'd take an autocar, a springcycle or even a bicycle if it got her to somewhere she could contact the base and let them know where she was.

Not wanting to risk someone coming out of one of the houses unexpectedly and crashing into them, Ellie alighted just outside the town, on the road leading into it. Despite being one of the best landings she'd ever made under glidewings - soft and with barely any forward motion - her legs gave way beneath her and she stumbled and fell to all fours. She fumbled with the handle as a gust of wind threatened to topple her sideways and retracted the wings, then pushed herself back onto her knees. Only then did she see the group of children watching her warily from the edge of the field next to the road.

'Hello there,' she said, giving them her friendliest smile.

'You a Prussian?' asked one of the girls. She was the biggest among them and stepped forward, lifting the cricket bat she held threateningly.

Ellie laughed, even as she eyed the bat nervously. 'There aren't any women in the Prussian air force. So, no,' she tugged the strap of her glidewings to one side to show them the RAC badge ever her heart. 'I'm British.' She looked along the road to the town. 'Is there a telephone anywhere?'

'The pub's got one.' The girl said, lowering the bat and pointing to the town. 'We can show you.'

'Thank you,' Ellie said. She struggled to her feet and resettled her glidewings on her back.

'Come on!' the smallest of the children, a boy no older than four or five, said, running forward and grabbing her hand.

The pub was in the middle of the town and not far, but the strange procession drew quite a few people from their homes and when the children took her inside they crowded in after her or peered in through the window.

'Oi! Dad!' the biggest girl called out. 'Got a pilot here wants to use the telephone!'

The man in his late twenties standing behind the bar beckoned Ellie over. 'Over here,' he said as a greeting, pointing her towards the large black box on the wall at the end of the bar next to him.

'Thank you.' Ellie went over, but before she picked up the receiver she shrugged out of her glidewings and lowered them to the floor. She rubbed her shoulders, wincing at the pain and rolled some life back into them before reaching out.

'Operator.'

'Hello, Bagshot one-one-two, please.'

'Hold please, caller.'

Ellie smiled at the barman while she was waiting, but he didn't see; he, like just about everyone else at the bar, including the children who had followed her, was staring at the patch on the right side of her chest that had been revealed when she'd taken off the glidewings.

'Hello?'

Billingsworth's voice on the other end of the line brought her back to the telephone. 'Hello, Algie? It's Ellie.'

'What?'

'It's Ellie!' she said, raising her voice slightly. 'I've been shot down. I'm fine, I just need a way to get back.'

'Understood, where are you?'

Ellie looked at the barman. 'Can you tell me where I am, please?'

'You're in the Fox and Badger, Frinsted, Miss.'

Ellie relayed the information to Algie, who noted it down, then told her to stay put near the telephone. She thanked him and put down the receiver, then smiled at the barman. 'Could I have a glass of water, please?'

The barman stared at her for a second, the glass in his hands forgotten, but then he nodded. 'Of course.' He stomped away from her down to the end of the bar furthest from her and she saw for the first time that he had a wooden leg.

He came back seconds later and put a glass of water in front of her.

'Sorry,' he said as she drank thirstily, 'I couldn't help overhearing, or miss that patch you've got there...'

Ellie finished drinking and smiled weakly. She knew where he was going and found that she was dreading it. She'd already heard the excited whispers spreading around the room and knew exactly how the Misfits were treated when they appeared in public.

'Would you happen to be Eleanor Perkins?' he asked.

The pub went deathly quiet as everyone waited for her answer and for a moment she wished she could lie and say no; she really didn't want the attention, or feel that she deserved it like the older Misfits did. She couldn't, though. When they'd joined, Abby had given them a talk about their role as Misfits and responsibilities that went beyond just shooting down Prussians, telling them that they were going to be role models and public figures as well and that there would be articles written about them, photos published of them and perhaps even radio interviews to do. She had told them that what made the Misfits so effective wasn't their success in the air, but the positive effect they had on the morale of the British people and the other RAC pilots. As well as the negative one they had on the morale of the Fleas they went up against. She had finished by telling them in no uncertain terms that, when the time came that they were thrust into the spotlight, they were not to hide from it or waste the opportunity.

She took a deep breath, then tried a bigger smile. 'Yes. Ellie to my friends.'

The pub descended into chaos as Ellie was surrounded and bombarded with questions. At some point a plate of food and glass of shandy was put in front of her and, after her protests of not having any money were waved away, she ate hungrily, stuffing in mouthfuls while she described her battles.

In a way, it was far more exhausting than dogfighting and she was very glad when, just over half an hour later, she heard the familiar sounds of a rotor blade, a shadow passed over the pub and people called out first in alarm, but then in wonder as Hummingbird put down in the village square right outside.

It was only much later, after several more missions, that she realised that that half an hour had done more for her than all the praise from her instructors, her friends and the other Misfits, done more for her than being chosen as a Misfit even. That half an hour of conversation, of connection with the very British people who she was flying and fighting to defend, accomplished what nothing else had been capable of doing, dispelling every single doubt she'd ever had about herself and giving her the strength and determination to face what lay ahead.

Reitsch had landed aircraft in much worse condition and with much worse handling characteristics when she was a test pilot so she had no trouble bringing Vixen home and setting her down, even with gaping holes in one of her wings and no flaps. She taxied to the hangar and began to climb out, but stopped before jumping down from her wing when she spotted another aircraft banking onto the downwind leg. She hadn't heard any calls over the radio to say anyone else was on their way and she put her goggles back on and increased the magnification of the lenses to see who it was.

It was Gruber and the reason for his silence became obvious when he got closer and she saw the holes in his aircraft. He landed and she chuckled as he slewed across the airfield, digging a furrow into the grass as he went because his tail wheel was missing. He parked in front of the hangar, but left the aircraft pointing the wrong way because he couldn't swing it around. She jumped down and sauntered over, planning to meet him once he'd gotten out, but he didn't get out and there was no movement from the cockpit. His fitters looked concerned, but they were just waiting around; they had been told not to approach until he signalled them, in case he was "taking a moment" and were obviously afraid to do so, even though something was quite obviously wrong. She had no such qualms and she climbed up onto the wing and peered into the cockpit, wondering if she would find him dead. Hoping she would, really.

Gruber looked back up at her, alive, unfortunately, but definitely not well. There was an expression of horror on his face and his gloves were slick with blood as he desperately tried to put the large flap of skin hanging from his cheek back into place.

It was the funniest thing she'd seen in a long time and as she jumped down and started calling for the medics, she couldn't help but laugh.

'Ellie got two. Penny four. Tanya three. Me two. That makes eleven Barons down.' Abby said as she noted down the numbers on a piece of scrap paper, 'but Gruber and the black aircraft got away.'

'And Barons seem to be a fairly disposable commodity anyway.' Penny pointed out.

'While Misfits definitely are not.' Drake said.

'Indeed.' Abby turned to Freddy Featherstonehaugh. 'Which reminds me - will you keep Benedict's death out of your report tonight, please? I don't want his family or girlfriend reading it before we've had a chance to tell them.'

Freddy shook his head. 'There's no need to ask; we're used to this kind of thing and always give a day's grace. However, it'll already be out there because of the crash report and the rumours will be spreading quickly. So if you want to keep ahead of them you'll have to hurry.'

Abby nodded. 'Algie is already trying to get hold of Benedict's father,' she looked at Rob and Ellie, who had been dropped off by Scarlet not long before, 'but I thought you two might like to tell his girlfriend. It'll have to be by telephone, I'm afraid - I can't spare either of you for however long it would take you to go to Wales and back.'

Ellie looked at Rob, who just nodded. 'We'd like that,' she said.

'You have some time if you'd like to try to get hold of her now.' Abby said, looking at her chronograph. 'Algie should be in the radio room, but if he's not just tell them I authorised it.'

Ellie nodded. 'Come on then,' she said to Rob.

Rob still had half his jam roly-poly left, but he pushed it away without a second thought. 'Coming.'

Ellie started to leave, but as she was passing Tanya, the Muscovite reached out to take her arm. 'I'm sorry, it was my fault you got shot down.'

Ellie smiled at her. 'It's alright. It was worth taking the chance and I'm still alive.'

Tanya smiled back and nodded. She released her arm, letting her go, but then grabbed Rob as he tried to follow Ellie. 'You going to eat that?' she asked, jerking her thumb over her shoulder at his abandoned dessert.

They managed to get a telephone line directly to Group Captain Wyvern's office at RAC Gwynedd. He wasn't there, but the call was answered by the adjutant, Aviator Lieutenant Pierce. They told him why they were calling and asked him to get Sandra and Lottie as well, if possible, so that she would have someone there with her. He informed them that Lottie was no longer there, but told them he would get Sandra and would find someone to be with her.

Sandra was in the mess hall, at lunch, and it took her more than ten minutes to come to the telephone. They didn't even have a chance to greet her before she said "it's Benedict, isn't it?" Apparently she'd known that it was only a matter of time before she got a phone call or message, especially with the Prussians throwing aircraft at Britain the way they were. She finished by telling them she would miss him, but was glad that Benedict had died doing what he loved.

It was a strange conversation and one that they unfortunately had to cut short to return to duty and they left Sandra sounding a lot more cheerful than they themselves felt.

'Sandra's right,' Ellie said quietly, as they hurried to the ready room, 'Benedict *would* have been content to die doing what he loved doing, after all, we all know we could die every time we go up and we accept that. It's just a shame he didn't get to enjoy being a Misfit for longer.'

There was no sign of the Barons during the third set of raids of the day, which proved to be the last, and that evening's papers made a big deal of how the Misfits had "seen them off", as one paper put it and at least three qualifying the engagement as an "unprecedented victory". Mention was made of one fallen Misfit and one more who had been badly injured, but, as Freddy had said it would be, Benedict's name was left out of the reports.

A tired and haggard-looking Billingsworth showed up just as the Misfits were finishing dinner and flopped into a seat at their table. He knocked back a glass of wine, then stared at it for a moment before looking up at the men and women watching him.

'Derek is out of danger,' he said bitterly, 'but he's never going to fly again.'

CHAPTER 10

26th August 1941

One of those summer storms that spring up, seemingly from nowhere, sprung up the next day, seemingly from nowhere, and as soon as it was clear that there weren't going to be any raids, or much in the way of flying, Abby gathered her pilots in the ready room.

'Benedict's remains have been taken to his parents,' she said once everyone was settled on the sofas and the door shut against the downpour. 'They are planning to have a small remembrance ceremony tomorrow morning before burying him in the family plot. The rain is supposed to let up by then, so I had to tell them that we couldn't attend, I'm afraid. We'll raise a glass to him later in the mess, but we can't do any more than that. Sorry, Ellie, Rob.'

She looked at them and they nodded their understanding.

'As for Derek,' Abby continued, 'he still hasn't regained consciousness and they're not allowing him any visitors yet, but I'm planning to go later tonight anyway and anyone that wants to join me is welcome to do so. First, though, we need to take stock.'

She perched on the edge of the table and looked around the decidedly less crowded room. 'Yesterday was a good day for the RAC. Losses went down and kills went up and Sir Douglas is confident that if things continue this way then we have a chance to prevail.'

'But?' Gwen asked quietly.

'But *we* are reaching the limit of our effectiveness.' She lifted a hand to indicate the chalkboard where the names of the pilots and their flight assignments were written.

'The loss of two pilots is a blow, but on its own is something we can deal with; we can still field two full flights, with one pilot in reserve, which means we can still attend the two closest raids. However, our aircraft are another matter. The fitters will do what they can today and are undoubtedly praying that the weather remains inclement to give them more time to carry out badly needed repairs, but none of us are flying a completely intact aircraft anymore and it can only be a matter of time before we have to ground them for a complete overhaul. To make matters worse, we're down to the last of the modified Spitsteams that Supranaval supplied us with. I've asked them for half a dozen more, but they will take a week or more to arrive and by then it might be too late. They were only supposed to be a stopgap anyway, until we built ourselves some new aircraft.'

She looked around the room. 'The bottom line, ladies and gentlemen, is that if things go on like this we are going to have to start using standard issue RAC aircraft and adjust our tactics to suit the reduction in performance of our machines.' She pulled a face that was half grin half grimace. 'We might even have to start behaving like a proper squadron.'

Drake huffed. 'It's not as if most of us haven't flown Spits or Harrys before. I'm sure we can make do perfectly well.'

Many of the others, including Rob and Ellie, who had trained on the latest production model of Spitsteams, made their agreement known, but they all fell silent and looked at Penny when she raised her hand.

'Before we all resign ourselves to becoming ordinary RAC pilots, not that there's anything wrong with that, of course, I think there's something you should see.'

Penny refused to elaborate any further, but instead insisted they all got in the squadron's bus and took a trip down the road into Bracknell, a few miles away. She refused to say anything about where they were going or why until they reached a large warehouse on the outskirts of the town and even then "here we are" was all she said.

The driver got them as close to the door as she possibly could, but there was still a good yard and a half gap and they were sopping wet when they got into the warehouse, but they instantly forgot about any discomfort and stumbled to a halt to gape at the four silvery machines within, aircraft in various stages of construction, glowing almost magically in pools of light coming from overhead.

'I bought this place while you were in Malta, after I heard you lost half of your aircraft on arrival.' Penny said, 'They made tea urns here before the war, so there were full metalworking facilities and electrical wiring in place and all we needed to do was bring in some hoists and whatnot before we could begin. I originally planned to build eight aircraft, but then Cummerbund disbanded us and I couldn't put them on the RAC books or go to Georgie for money, so I had to reduce that to four - that was as far as my budget extended, I'm afraid.'

They had been seen arriving and Alasdair Patterson, the man who had looked after the airfield and Penny's aircraft before she'd rejoined the squadron, hopped down from one of the aircraft and hurried over.

'Alasdair!' Penny called out. 'How is it going?'

'Well...' the Scotsman said, drawing out the word, then sucking air between his teeth as he turned to look at the aircraft. 'Ye c'n have mebbe the first two in a couple of days - one of each - but the others... a week?'

Penny nodded. 'Well done, thank you.'

She turned to the group. 'Alasdair is building two Lion-pattern and two Excalibur-pattern aircraft for us. Unfortunately, because of the way I had to bring the pieces in bit by bit when I could buy, beg, or steal them, none of them are fully built. A couple are close to being ready, though.'

'But we still have no guns or springs.' Alasdair interjected, looking pointedly at Penny.

'Yes,' Penny said, 'we are still short a few bits and bobs, but I'm sure we'll be able to find them now, won't we, Abby?'

'Indeed.' Abby said, her eyes shining as she gazed at the beautiful machines. She smiled at Alasdair. 'We lost a couple of aircraft so I have some fitters hanging around without very much to do now, unfortunately. If I got them here could you finish those two aircraft by tomorrow?'

'Depends how soon ye c'n get them here.'

'Have you got a telephone?'

'Aye.'

'Then half an hour.'

Alasdair nodded grudgingly. 'Aye, that'll do it.'

Penny took Abby to the design room at the back of the warehouse, where the telephone was, and after Abby had called for reinforcements and supplies, they stood at the window looking out over the workshop.

'Why didn't you tell me about this before?' Abby asked. 'We could have helped.'

'I probably should have, I realise that now, but when you brought in the modified Spitsteams I thought we wouldn't need them. After yesterday, though... Besides, I knew *this* would happen.' She waved her hand at the workshop. Kitty and Gwen had already stripped off their uniform jackets and were working on one of the Excaliburs, Rob and Drake had done the same and Drake was showing the boy what to do on one of the Lions. Even Ellie, Chastity and Tanya had found something to help with. 'You would have had a lot of tired pilots and fitters who would rather have been here than resting or doing badly-needed maintenance.

'I see what you mean.' Abby said. She started unbuttoning her jacket. 'Shall we?'

'If you insist.' Penny went to a metal cupboard next to the door and opened it to reveal a set of coveralls with her name embroidered on them.

Abby rolled her eyes. 'This is where you've been disappearing to every night? And here I was, thinking you were fraternising with his lordship.'

Penny laughed. 'Well, there's only so much fraternisation a woman can stand. Sometimes she just wants the embrace of a good aircraft.'

The doctors and nurses couldn't get out of her way fast enough as she stomped through the hospital. Whether it was the look on her face, the imposing figure she presented in her flightsuit and leather greatcoat, or simply that her reputation had preceded her, she didn't know or care; she didn't need anything from them so their fear of her was just amusing. And not a little gratifying.

Gruber's room was at the very end of the hall on the top floor. He had been isolated from the other patients in case the sight of him destroyed what little morale they had left. The door was closed and there was a sign forbidding entry, but she just went straight in. She found him in the room's only bed, covered in crisp white sheets. Peacefully asleep. The doctors had given him blood, pumped him full of chemicals for shock and used electrics to knit the skin of his face. The machines were gone now, though, and the room was completely empty except for a single vase by the bed. The red of the flowers reminded her of the sight of him in his cockpit and almost started her laughing again, but she managed to control herself and stalked over to the bed. The sight of his face nearly made her lose that control, though, and she leaned down to peer at the white scar running down the side of his face. It went from the corner of his eye all the way to his jaw, pulling the eye slightly out of shape and his mouth into a bit of a grimace. He hadn't quite been made monstrous, but he certainly wasn't going to be a Hollywoodland heart-throb anymore.

She reached out a finger and prodded the scar.

Gruber started awake with a gasp and recoiled from her, but then frowned when he recognised her. 'What are you doing here? Why aren't you still in France?'

He lifted his head and looked around the room, taking in the sparse, military-style furniture. 'Where am I? This is...' His eyes narrowed. 'Why aren't I in Berlin? I ordered them to take me there for surgery.'

Reitsch took a piece of paper from the pocket of her long black leather overcoat and brandished it at him. 'Message from the Kaiser,' she said. 'A reply to the request you made before you fainted and my report that accompanied it. It reads,' she cleared her throat, even though it was unnecessary. '"Permission to return to Berlin denied. Gruber is to remain where he is and continue to fly with the Barons. He will be their commander in name only, though - Melitta Reitsch is to take over all decisions regarding the squadron's activities and deployment." Then there's some instructions about the running of the squadron,' she said, waving the paper at him vaguely, 'but that's all for me - you needn't concern yourself with that anymore. There is something for you here at the bottom, though, it says: "he can keep the scar as a reminder of his failure."' She looked up and smiled. 'I think you'll agree that this is far more than you deserve. My recommendation to the Kaiser was actually that you be shot and your body disposed of quietly.'

'Give me that,' Gruber growled, sitting up and leaning forward to snatch the paper. He scanned it quickly, going so pale that the scar stood out starkly red.

'How can he do this to me? Why?'

Reitsch moved closer to the bed, looming over him. 'Why? Because all I've seen you do since I got here is drink and eat and run from any fight that involves the Misfits. Because even after you were directly ordered to engage them you still disobeyed, going behind my back to assign us to a raid you knew they wouldn't be at. Because, when you finally do deign to do as you're told, you manage to lose three quarters of your squadron and half your face in a single fight.'

She leaned over, putting her hands on the railing at the side of the hospital bed until her face was inches from his.

'You are an embarrassment and a fool, but worse than that you are a *coward* and the Kaiser doesn't want you to have any more opportunities to expose yourself as such and destroy the morale of his army. So, you are going to stay in the squadron and you will keep shooting down a few Harridans and Spitfires, but *I* will be making all the decisions and *I* will deal with the Misfits.'

She snatched the piece of paper back from him as she straightened and put it back in her pocket. 'The weather is bad, so you can wallow in your self pity today, but tomorrow I want you back on the flight line. The invasion is coming and the people will expect their hero to be at the forefront.' She started to walk away, but then stopped when something occurred to her. 'If you are not there then I will assume you have deserted and I *will* have you shot.'

Schmidt stood at the window of his office looking out at the rain.

'Where did this come from? Why didn't we see it coming?'

His aide shrugged. 'Sometimes winds just change, sometimes...'

'Shut up!' Schmidt shouted at him. 'Or I will have you shot, alongside the meteorology experts who promised me two weeks of good weather!'

'Yes, sir.' The aide swallowed. 'They have said that it will clear overnight, though, sir.'

'One day lost.' Schmidt growled. 'One whole day. No matter. Send word that the invasion is to be pushed back a day.'

He waved his hand, dismissing the aide, who hurried gratefully from the room.

He went to his desk and pushed the latest reports around until he found the one from Reitsch. He smiled as he read it; at least there was something to be happy about, he thought, as he read again the contents of the Kaiser's cable and her graphic description of Gruber's injury.

'I don't think I've ever been glad to see rain before,' Ellie said, staring out at the thick rain pouring vertically down onto the road outside the warehouse.

She and Rob were sitting on the doorstep, under the cover of the overhang, their feet pulled back to avoid being splashed. They cupped their hands around tin mugs of tea and sipped occasionally, but they had them more as an excuse to be there than because they were actually thirsty.

'Certainly not since I started flying, anyway,' she added after a moment.

Rob nodded. 'Hmm.'

For a while they just sat, watching and listening, letting the rain wash away their thoughts and feelings.

'I wonder where Lottie is.' Ellie said eventually. 'Do you think she dropped out and went home?'

'I don't know. I don't think so. I think if she'd done that then Pierce would have told us.' He shrugged. 'Actually it sounded to me like she's doing something he couldn't talk about. Like she's gotten roped into something hush-hush.'

Ellie chuckled. 'I hope she's not becoming a spy; I can't see Lottie doing much sneaking around.'

'I can see her blowing things up, though.' Rob said with a smile. 'She always did say she wanted to drive a big bomber.'

'I hope she's alright, whatever she's doing.' Ellie said.

'Hmm.'

They fell silent again, one of those comfortable silences where two people who had been through a lot together could just be with each other, without the need to keep saying something to stop it from being awkward.

Ellie looked at one of the puddles for a while, watching the rain falling into it and sending perfectly circular splashes up. It was hypnotic and extremely relaxing and she began to feel like she was sinking into the concrete of the steps.

She turned her head to comment to Rob and found him looking at her.

Their eyes met and caught and Ellie found her heart racing as something inexplicable and wonderful passed between them and for some reason they began to lean towards each other. Unfortunately, before whatever it was that was happening could fully happen, something actually physically passed between them and they recoiled in surprise.

'Do you know what I want to know?' Tanya asked angrily, going to stand in front of them. She looked from one of them to the other, completely unconcerned about the fact that she was getting soaked.

'What?' Ellie asked, concerned that she or Rob or both might have done something to upset her friend.

'Why are they calling them *Lion* pattern aircraft? Why not *Wolf* pattern? Eh?' she snarled. 'They were built at the same time! The exact same time!'

The Muscovite threw her hands in the air, then stomped between them again and disappeared back into the building.

Ellie and Rob looked at each other, but the mood had completely changed and the moment had gone forever, perhaps to be found again, perhaps not.

'We should, uh...' Ellie said, tilting her head towards the door.

'Yes.' Rob said with a smile. 'We should.'

With the help of the Misfits and the twenty fitters and mechanics Abby had called in to help, all four aircraft were finally assembled, with the guns and springs they'd brought from Bagshot installed, about an hour before the sun went down.

Abby went to the door and looked up into the sky.

'What do you think?' she asked Penny.

'Rain's letting up a bit and there's pretty good visibility up to about two or three thousand feet, I reckon.'

'Me too,' Abby said. She turned to look at the table against the side where everyone was gathered, having a quick cup of tea before getting on the bus back to Bagshot. 'Rob! Ellie! Chastity! Front and centre!' she shouted.

Ellie and Rob were fresh out of the discipline of basic training and immediately dropped what they were doing and ran over, to the general amusement of the fitters and other pilots, but Chastity just sauntered slowly over, still sipping her tea.

'What's up, Abby?' she asked, but then grinned. 'Really?'

Abby nodded. 'Really.' She took in Rob and Ellie's puzzled faces and rolled her eyes. 'Do I have to spell it out for you?' she asked. 'Alright then - Chastity gets an Excalibur, but the Lions now belong to you two; that way you'll have the same type of aircraft as your wingmates.'

Ellie looked at the aircraft and her eyes widened. 'Really?'

Abby laughed. 'Really!' she pointed to the design room. 'There are glidewings and helmets in there, but there's no need for flightsuits; you can fly in what you've got on.' She pointed a finger at them. The ceiling is only a couple of thousand feet, so no playing silly buggers, alright?' she grinned. 'At least not until we're sure everything works, anyway?'

Penny gave her a sour look. 'I suppose you're taking the fourth bird?'

'Of course,' Abby said smugly. 'Commander's prerogative. Besides,' she said, looking at the Excaliburs greedily. 'I've always wanted to fly one of those.'

There was a nice straight road outside the warehouse and, after extensive and exhaustive checks, the four aircraft taxied out and lined up next to it. The road was bordered mostly by empty lots and abandoned warehouses, so the chances of someone wandering onto the road right when they were taking off weren't high, but it was better to be safe than sorry and the fitters and the rest of the pilots spread out along the length of the improvised runway to make sure.

Ellie was extremely glad to be last in line to take off. While she'd been getting ready, Tanya had given her a long talk about how Wolf handled, about her little mannerisms and foibles, going on and on until it felt like Ellie knew the aircraft back to front and could fly it in her sleep. The reality of it, though, was that it was an unfamiliar aircraft with an unfamiliar cockpit layout and she now had to not only fly it back to Bagshot, but get it into the air on a bumpy, badly maintained, rather narrow road that went between buildings, rather than a nice flat open airfield. She used the time, therefore, to dance her hands and feet over the controls and scan the instrument panels to memorise the slightly different layout. She was so engrossed in the task that she actually missed Abby, Rob and Chastity take off and didn't see if they had had any difficulty.

There was no control to ask whether it was clear to take off, instead Penny was acting as a ground controller and Ellie obeyed her waved instructions and taxied into the middle of the road. She couldn't see the road in front of her because the aircraft's nose was just a little bit too long so she had to trust that Penny had her lined up properly.

The woman gave her a thumbs up, then dramatically pointed down the road and Ellie laughed, feeling her anxiety lesson a little, but it returned in full force when she pushed the throttle forwards and the aircraft lunged forwards. All aircraft tended to yaw to the side during takeoff because of the slipstream from the airscrew hitting the rudder and it was something she had learned to compensate for automatically, but this aircraft was quite a lot more powerful than the

Spitsteam she'd been flying, with a bigger airscrew, and the amount of rudder she applied was insufficient. The aircraft began to drift to one side and she pushed her foot further down in a panic, only to have the aircraft swerve back in the other direction. Luckily, by now she was going fast enough to push the nose of the aircraft forwards and as soon as it was out of the way she had a clear view down the road. She straightened up, aimed for the horizon, and after only a few more seconds she pulled the stick back into her lap and leapt for the sky.

Unable to contain her elation she whooped and slammed the aircraft into a roll before pulling sharply towards Bagshot.

'I thought I said no silly buggers, Four.'

Ellie winced at the mildly reproachful tone in Abby's voice, but couldn't help but keep grinning as she raced after the other machines. 'Just making sure everything works, Leader.'

It was already late when the Misfits took off, but they squeezed as much juice as they could out of their flight and only landed when they could barely see their airscrews in front of their noses.

Everyone was waiting for them, standing in the shelter of the hangar against the drizzle and they taxied up to the apron and were pushed right in by an army of grinning mechanics and fitters. The remaining Spitsteams had already been pushed right to the back to make room and their teams of fitters welcomed their new charges lovingly.

Ellie's chief fitter, Aviator Sergeant Tonbridge, saluted her as she climbed down. 'Evening, ma'am. We'll only have time to put a coat of primer on her tonight, but how would you like her painted and have you got a name for her yet?'

Ellie blinked at him, then shook her head and smiled wryly 'You know, it hadn't actually sunk in yet that she's mine.' She reached up to run a hand along the wing as she thought back to the flight she'd just had. Short as it had been it had still been memorable because of the remarkable performance of the machine. 'I really like her like this actually,' she said, half to herself, then looked at Tonbridge. 'Do you have any silver paint?'

'Yes, ma'am!' the man said with a smile.

'And as for a name...' she mused, considering. She smiled slowly as a memory from a long time ago, a much happier time, came to her - a vision of a beautiful silver sculpture her mother had had on her dressing table. '*Heron*.'

Tonbridge nodded. 'Thank you, ma'am.'

'Thank you, Sergeant.'

She gave him a last smile and a nod, then patted Heron and went to Rob, who had landed before her and wandered over while she'd been talking to Tonbridge. Together they walked towards where the other Misfits were standing at the side of the hangar, out of the way.

'How was it?' he asked.

'Absolutely fantastic!'

He grinned. 'It was, wasn't it? Your aircraft is going to look fantastic as well.'

'I think so.' She looked at him thoughtfully.' Let me guess - you asked for yours to be painted green and called her Finch?'

Rob chuckled. 'You know me too well!'

They smiled at each other, but then saw that the other pilots were waiting for them and hurried their pace slightly.

Billingsworth was with them and he started speaking as soon as they arrived.

'Derek regained consciousness a few hours ago...'

'Let's go then!' Abby said.

'Wait a moment!' Billingsworth called out, stopping her as she turned to leave. 'He has asked not to have visitors.'

'What?' Abby asked incredulously. 'Not even us?'

Billingsworth shook his head. 'Not even you.'

'Did you see him?'

'No,' Billingsworth said. 'He sent a message through the hospital with the request, along with a brief report of his final flight.' He wet his lips. 'Wilberforce was indeed killed by the pilot in the black aircraft and Derek was shot down by it in turn, but only after an extended fight, during which he was able to ascertain that the pilot is, in fact, a woman.'

'I knew there was something familiar about the way they flew!' Gwen said.

Everyone turned to stare at her.

'It's Melitta,' she said. 'Melitta Reitsch. She was at Oxford with me, in the same class. We were in the Oxford University Flying Club together and were friendly for a while, but she tried to steal...' her voice cracked and she coughed to clear it, 'she tried to steal Richard from me. He wasn't my husband yet, but...' she trailed off, her eyes welling up with tears and Kitty put her arm around her and pulled her into a hug.

'Melitta Reitsch.' Billingsworth said, making a note. 'If she studied at Oxford there must be some record of her. I'll see what I can find out.'

CHAPTER 11

27th August 1941

Schmidt turned up early to his command centre that morning, while it was still fully dark and none of his aircraft were even in the air. He was so early that the lights in the theatre were still warming up and the enlisted men who controlled the map and operated the radios were still gathered around in groups, chatting and drinking coffee. When they saw him they stood to attention, but he waved for them to go back to what they were doing and went to his desk on the stage to prepare signals and orders.

He was still writing fifteen minutes later when the first officers arrived and he beckoned a couple of aides over.

'Send these,' he said, 'and get me an open channel to our aircraft as soon as they are all up.'

With that done, he sat back in his chair, accepted a cup of coffee and watched the map filling with Prussian symbols.

'Sir. Your channel is ready.'

Schmidt nodded at the aide. He scanned the piece of paper laid out in front of him one last time, then stood and went to the radios in the wing of the theatre. The aide showed him the radio that was ready for him, the operator out of his seat, but standing by to flick the switches for him.

Schmidt settled in the chair, then picked up the microphone and nodded at the operator, who turned the radio to transmit, then nodded back at him.

Schmidt took a moment to compose himself, then began. 'Attention pilots and crews of the Fliegertruppe. This is Generalfeldmarschall Schmidt, addressing you from my command bunker.' The fact that he was in a theatre among the comforts of a French town, rather than a concrete hole on an army base somewhere, was a secret, even to his own men, and one that he didn't particularly want the British, who would undoubtedly be listening, to find out. 'Soon now you will fly across the water once more. The British are expecting us to continue our attacks on their airfields and we will not disappoint them. They do not know that we have been watching them, though. They do not know that we have been learning. And they will not expect the surprise you have in store for them today!'

He took a breath and wet his lips, readying himself for the big finale. 'When future generations study this war they will trace the ultimate victory of the Prussian Empire back to here. They will say that it was now, on this day, over the skies of the Kingdom of Great Britain that the Fliegertruppe defeated the Royal Aviator Corps. They will say that it was on this day that your courage and bravery ultimately won the war! Long live the Kaiser! Long live the Empire!'

He was almost shouting by the time he finished and he gestured curtly to the operator to cut the feed, then sagged back in the chair and took deep breaths to recover. He smiled, satisfied; it hadn't been the longest speech he'd ever given, by any means, and he had taken a leaf out of the Kaiser's book and used more simple rhetoric than he usually did, but it had served its purpose - the pilots had been sent off on this most vital of missions with a fire lit under their seats and, more importantly, it would look good in the history books.

He stood and stalked across the stage towards his desk, already thinking about the orders he needed to write, but he only made it half way before he became aware of a commotion and he frowned and came to a halt. Peering around for the source of the noise he found that his men weren't applying themselves to their work, but were applauding instead.

Their behaviour went against his sense of military propriety and his first instinct was to reprimand them all and order them back to work, but then he reconsidered. Why should the Kaiser and Gruber be the only ones adored by the public? Why should it be their names that were always in the media? Why should they get all the recognition for how the war was going? He had done far more than them over the last two years and it would be his plan that finished

Britain off once and for all, removing the last obstacle to the Prussian conquest of Europe and the world.

He rewarded the men with a rare smile and raised his hand in salute, but he only allowed himself a couple of seconds to bask in the adoration before turning and striding to his desk. After all, if he permitted himself to relax and assume that the job was done before it actually was, then his name might be on the lips of the Prussian people for an entirely different reason.

Air raid sirens weren't unusual at Bagshot and they didn't interrupt the cricket game the fitters and mechanics were playing on the airfield while their aircraft were up in the air. The drone of aircraft directly overhead and the whistling as the first bombs fell certainly wasn't usual, though, and sent the men and women scrambling in a panic for the shelters. They barely made it before the first explosions and the last of them in, Aviator Sergeant Potter, Abby's chief fitter, who had made sure everyone was safe before seeking safety himself, was the only witness to the direct hits which brought the roof of the hangar down and collapsed its walls.

'They've hit almost all of our secondary airfields.' Dee Fisher said. 'Including Bagshot.'

Sir Douglas Pewtall stared down at the map as the last of the markers denoting the Prussian aircraft was moved off of British soil.

They'd been hoodwinked, fooled, lulled into a false sense of security by the way the Prussians had carried out their attacks in exactly the same way as they had last summer.

It was brilliant.

They'd been hitting the primary airfields over and over, making sure they were completely destroyed and preventing any rebuilding attempts, forcing the RAC to move to secondary fields. And then, when they'd settled in and gotten comfortable, they'd hit those. Every last damn one of them. They must have had dozens, perhaps hundreds, of spies, let in by Cummerbund and his cronies, no doubt, mapping out the airfields locations, making sure they got all of them.

Brilliant.

'How many are still operational?' he asked, hoping for the best, but expecting the worst.

'Five are still open, but of those only three were completely ignored. The other two took extensive damage and have extremely limited repair and rearming facilities.'

Pewtall sighed. 'Just as well we have your tertiary airfields.'

'Yes, sir, but they were never supposed to take so much traffic at once - they're only there for overflow. I thought only one, or at the most two squadrons would be moved in at a time while repairs were carried out to primary and secondary fields. They have little to no repair facilities and their rearming and rewinding facilities are extremely limited. They'll be lucky to turn around one squadron and make them ready for the next raid. They certainly won't handle two or three.'

'And what if they bomb those? Do you have any more airfields up your sleeve?'

'No, sir. Not within range anyway. Many smaller flying clubs just don't have airfields big enough for us, or haven't been in use for years and are too badly maintained to open. We'd have to move our fighters back to bomber airfields, or to Wales, and they would struggle to get into position before the Prussians arrived.'

Pewtall pursed his lips and twisted his mouth to the side as he weighed the possibility. 'That's not good, but at least they would be able to intercept the Prussians on the way home. For now, get as many ground crews as you can to each of those tertiary fields - they can wind springs the old-fashioned way by hand if they have to. A few more aircraft in the air to meet the next wave might make all the difference.'

'Although...' He leaned forward to peer down at the map as something occurred to him. 'We do have *one* airfield available.' He pointed to London. 'Find out how many squadrons can we cram into Hyde if we commandeer all of the civilian facilities. And divert the Misfits there right away. It won't be ideal, but it's the best we've got right now and they'll be better protected there by London's ack-ack than they will anywhere else.'

'Yes, sir.' Dee Fisher turned to hurry away.

'Oh, and Dee!' Pewtall called after her.

'Sir?'

'Ask His Majesty if we can borrow his Royal Guard flight, please. I have a feeling we're going to need as many aircraft as we can get.'

'Yes, sir.'

As Fisher left, Pewtall looked around the balcony at his fellow officers, all scrambling to get their aircraft down safely, then at the men and women down below, who were using the excuse of the empty map to relax for a moment. He wondered how many of them had realised yet what this change of Prussian targets meant. He wondered how many of them realised that the invasion was only days, or perhaps hours, away.

The four aircraft of A flight were running extremely low on tension when they entered London's airspace. They'd been about to descend into their backup airfield when they'd received the order to divert to Hyde and Abby had almost countermanded it and landed anyway, knowing that it would take them to the limit of their range. She'd seen the sense in it, though, and thought that the risk would be worth it. She just hadn't counted on there being other aircraft landing ahead of them.

They entered the pattern orbiting Hyde, waiting to land and found that almost an entire squadron was ahead of them in the pecking order, undoubtedly all just as low on tension as they were.

London control set them to circling to the north of the airfield, near Regent's Park, within visual range, and they watched the Spitsteams and Harridans of the other squadrons landing one by one in quick succession. While they were there B flight joined them and Gwen reported in.

'Five here, Leader. I'm on reserve and so are Seven and Eight.'

'We're not much better here ourselves, Five.' Abby answered.

'Leader, Two here. Switching to reserve.'

'See what I mean?' Abby said as laughs greeted Penny's deadpan announcement.

A tense silence descended after that, though, interrupted only by most of the remaining pilots switching to reserve one by one.

After a minute or so with no word from Hyde there was a click as Abby switched to the control frequency. 'London control, this is Badger Leader, we're down to our last ticks here. Is there a hold up?'

'Badger Leader, this is London control. Yes, sorry, one of the Harrys of 145 squadron crashed on landing and we are clearing the wreckage... wait one, please.' There was a moment of silence, then the woman's voice returned. 'Badger Leader, you are clear for landing. Wind is ten knots from one seven five degrees.'

'Thank you, control, Badger Leader on approach.' There was a click as Abby switched back to the squadron channel and a sigh. 'Alright, I don't think anyone has enough tension to hang around waiting for the others to land, so form up in flights; we're going to land in formation. B flight first.'

Landing in formation on a field as large and as wide as Hyde wasn't as dangerous as it might have been, but it still wasn't advisable, as any wrong step or miscalculation would be disastrous for more than just the pilot who made the mistake. The Misfits didn't have much choice, though, as any one of them could completely run out of tension at any moment and there weren't many other places to safely put down in central London, not in an emergency anyway. They were such good pilots that it was just an interesting exercise to them, though, although it did get a bit scary for Ellie for a moment when Tanya tucked herself in rather a lot closer beside her than was necessary.

Everyone got down fine, but Gwen completely ran out of tension as soon as she turned off the field, proving just how low she had been, and she waved at A flight as they went past her.

The Royal Guard hangar was positioned at the very end of the airstrip, so that their aircraft had a straight run along the length of the strip and could be at full unwind before they were even out onto the field, without any need to waste time taxiing. Abby had naturally assumed that was where they would be stationed, so that the Misfits could get into the air as quickly as possible. They were guided towards the east side of the field instead, though, towards one of the large hangars up against the Airfield Lane wall.

Things started to make sense when they got a glimpse inside the hangar.

Unfamiliar fitters and mechanics ran to meet them. There were only two or three for each aircraft, rather that the five or six that was more usual in an active squadron, but they had no problem keeping the aircraft moving and pushing them into the hangar. There was an airship inside, one of the sleek models that the rich had used to travel the world in style and comfort before the war, but it was suspended from the high roof and there was more than enough room below the envelope for their fighters. It was a spring-powered model and the owner had apparently spared no expense in its upkeep because there was not one, but four spring-winding machines waiting for them and what looked like a complete repair shop in the corner.

This wasn't a shack in a village airfield with a few spanners and a hand-winder, it was a fully equipped base all in itself, just on a much smaller scale than they were used to.

'This'll do,' Abby said, climbing down from Dragon and looking around.

'Wait until you see the rest of it,' a woman said, coming through a door at the back.

'Dot!' Abby shouted, breaking into a run.

The other woman spread her arms as she approached and they embraced joyfully.

'Dot?' Ellie asked Tanya quietly as she joined her in front of their aircraft.

'Sky Commodore Dorothy Campbell.' Drake said, wandering over and putting his arm around Tanya. 'She was with Abby right from the beginning, doing the administration side of things while Abby was finding pilots and aircraft. She was in Malta with us, but we had to leave her behind in Gibraltar when the war minister had her attached to a navy taskforce as RAC liaison. I suppose she came back with Chastity.'

The two women released each other and wandered over towards the Misfits.

'Sorry I didn't come to see you,' Campbell was saying, 'they've had me locked up in a debriefing room at Bentley Priory since I got back. They wanted my side of the Gibraltar and Malta stories.'

She looked around the Misfits and smiled. 'Some new faces I see. And some old ones.' She nodded at them. 'It's good to see you all again. Let's get you some food and we can have a chat while your aircraft are seen to.'

She led them towards the door she'd come through and they found themselves in what was, to all appearances, a lounge in a stately home - there was a fireplace to one side with an antique mirror over it, a grandfather clock in the corner, a dozen or so paintings and portraits on the walls showing hunting scenes and aristocratic ancestors, a dining table seating at least twenty people and several sofas and armchairs. A large buffet table was against the wall opposite the fireplace and a couple of stewards were working frantically at it, laying sandwiches and biscuits on plates and preparing pots of tea.

'This will be your ready room,' Campbell said.

Abby frowned. 'It's very nice, but we don't need all this. We'd be happy with the Royal Guard and a quick takeoff.'

Campbell nodded. 'Sir Douglas appreciates that, but the trouble is that if we stuff you in there then there won't be enough room to turn you around quickly and they don't actually have the repair facilities that this hangar does. There's also this.'

She beckoned to them and they followed her to a door on the far side of the room. Through it was a short corridor with a few door on either side, but she ignored them and walked to the door at the far end and went through.

The Misfits found themselves on the side of Airfield Lane. Directly opposite them was a place that they were all very familiar with - The Dorchester.

Campbell turned and grinned at them. 'It's the closest hangar to your billet.'

'This is Lord Henry's hangar, isn't it?' Drake asked, gazing up at one of the portraits on the wall once they were back in the lounge.

'It is.' Campbell said. 'How did you know?'

'I've been here before. A long time ago. When I was seven. He had half a dozen or so aircraft back then, though, not just one airship.'

'He has more now, we moved them into the hangar next door to make room.'

Drake chuckled and shook his head. 'Daft old man was crazy about aviation.' He turned away from the portrait and walked over to the sofas in the middle of the room where everyone had settled in with food and tea. 'He took me up in a two-seater biplane when I was seven. It was fully aerobatic and he didn't hold back. It was the first time I'd ever been up in an aircraft and it scared the life out of me some of the things he did with that thing, but that was the day that I fell in love with flying. He was seventy-three at the time, if I remember correctly, and was always up in the air. Spent more time in an aircraft than on the ground. It must have broken his heart when they closed Hyde down to civilian traffic.'

Campbell grinned. 'Last I heard, he had moved to Wales and the king had given him special dispensation to keep flying.'

'But he must be ninety by now!' Drake said, astonished, then laughed. 'Good on him! I hope I'm still flying when I'm ninety.'

Most people nodded their agreement at the sentiment, not speaking because they had their mouths full.

'So,' Campbell said, looking around the group. 'As you may or may not know, the Prussians hit all our secondary airfields this morning.'

'All of them?' Abby asked.

'All but three. Which means they had better intelligence than they did last year and better planning.'

'They're coming.' Ellie said quietly.

Campbell pointed at her. 'Got it in one. Sir Douglas has been in conference with the king and the commanders of the navy and the army and they are in agreement that the Prussian invasion fleet will sail within the day. Most likely before dawn tomorrow.'

Silence greeted Campbell's revelation, the only noise for a few seconds coming from Tanya as she continued to munch on biscuits.

'What do we do?' Abby asked eventually. 'What *can* we do?'

'The same as you've been doing.' Campbell answered. 'Stay in the air and answer today's raids, then be ready for whatever you are asked to do tomorrow, whether it is providing cover for the navy, attacking enemy ships, or strafing Prussian troops as they try to land.' She looked at her chronograph then stood. 'I have to get back, but I'll be liaising with you until this is over, one way or the other. Your mechanics and fitters will join you here soon and you have parts and spares coming, but if there's anything else you need just ring the Priory and I'll sort it out.'

She looked around the group before her gaze settled on Abby. 'I don't have to tell you how critical the next few hours and days will be, so keep your squadron at full readiness, please.'

'Of course.'

Campbell gave them all a last smile, then started to go, but immediately came to a halt and turned back. 'Oh! I almost forgot.' She carefully brought a thick cream envelope out from her RAC issue handbag and gave it to Abby. 'You've all been invited to the palace this evening.'

Ellie's mouth opened and she gaped at Campbell. 'I'm going to meet the king?'

Abby looked at the envelope, then chuckled. She showed it to the other Misfits, letting them see the symbol on it - not the kings, but the feathers of the Princess of Wales.

'Better,' she said, 'you're going to meet Liz.'

CHAPTER 12

'Where's everyone else?' Rob asked, completely forgetting radio discipline in the moment.

None of the other Misfits could blame him; they were in range of the raid approaching Kent and the Prussians were a sea of hundreds of dark dots in the distance, while the British fighters that had been sent to face it numbered in their dozens.

'Don't worry, Eight.' Drake said. 'It just means there are more Prussians for us.'

'Thank you, Seven, Eight,' Gwen said. 'But let's try to keep the chatter down, please.'

'Roger that, Leader. Seven, keeping the chatter down.'

Rob glanced over at Drake and laughed when he found him grinning back at him - ever since Gwen had been put in charge of B flight she'd become less and less like herself and more like Abby, even down to using the same exasperated voice when the rest of them joked around.

'It seems there are no Barons to worry about; they must have gone to the other raid...'

'A flight get all the luck!' Drake quipped.

'So, we're going to do things a bit differently,' Gwen continued, ignoring him. 'We're not going to make much of a dent in this formation if we spread ourselves thinly like we did before, so we're going to stick together and punch a few big holes instead. I want both elements within sight of each other at all times and Nine will act as a wildcard between them. Chastity, I want you to concentrate on warning us of any threats that come our way and intercept them if possible.'

'Roger, Five.'

The Prussian formation was closing fast now, the dots fast becoming aircraft.

'Prepare to dive on my mark.' Gwen said. 'Happy hunting, Misfits... Mark!'

Rob waited a split second for Drake to begin his manoeuvre before carrying out his own, settling comfortably a wingspan from him as the five Misfit aircraft began their dive in line abreast. He liked to imagine this moment as being akin to a cavalry charge, their guns the lances flashing in the sunlight, and he wondered if they inspired the same kind of panic in the Prussians as that would have done in hapless infantry forced to stand up to tons of horseflesh and metal.

He hoped so.

With the flaps out and the throttle back, the Misfits' dive was a sedate three hundred miles per hour and Rob had plenty of time to see that the Prussians were trying something new, their fighters trailing behind the bombers instead of among them. Unfortunately for them, Sir Douglas Pewtall had also sent new instructions to his pilots for this second raid of the morning.

The Prussians had thrown the British into chaos that morning, but now it was time for them to sow a little bit of chaos of their own in return.

Reitsch watched the four Misfit aircraft diving away and frowned; they had dived too early to hit the fighters that Schmidt had ordered to form up behind the bombers until the British engaged, instead of flying with them.

'What are they...?'

Her eyes widened. 'Dive now!' she ordered, even as she pushed her stick forwards. The Misfits were attacking the bombers!

'They're coming down, Leader.'

'Thank you, Four. Ignore them for now; they're too far away to hurt us. Concentrate on your target.'

Ellie looked down at the massive bomber formation. Strangely, the fighters weren't mixed among them, but were in a gaggle trailing behind. She wasn't going to complain; it made getting through the formation a much less dangerous prospect. They also might be able to get in a couple of runs before the Fleas could catch them.

'I'm going for the leader, Four. You take the one behind him.'

'Roger, Three.' Ellie adjusted her course minutely, drifting slightly away from Tanya and settling her sights in front of her target, leading it slightly. The bomber loomed closer and closer, getting bigger and bigger and her finger twitched as it reached the size the fighters were when she opened fire on them. That was far too early, though, and she waited until the wings had spread almost across her windscreen and it seemed like she was going to collide before finally pressing the button on the yoke.

Her bullets impacted on the bulbous cockpit of the 111 and she saw the glass shatter. That wasn't going to bring down the aircraft unless she got lucky and completely destroyed the controls or hurt the pilots, though. However, they were diving on the bombers from in front and slightly to the side, at their ten o'clock, more or less, and it was a simple matter for her to walk her fire to the wings and spray the engines on the side closest to her. The bomber almost filled her entire windscreen now and she was forced to stop firing and pull up, but all that did was bring the next bomber in line into her sights and she repeated the process with it. There was another behind it, but Tanya was banking away and Abby had warned them to stay together, so she abandoned her run and accelerated to catch up with the Muscovite. She couldn't resist looking into the mirror over her head, though, to check on the results of her work, and was gratified to see both of the bombers starting to drop from the formation, the cannons of Heron having dealt untold damage to their systems.

'Barons, five o'clock! Break, break!'

Ellie swivelled her head rapidly to find an entire flight of red fighters almost upon her and she slammed Heron into a reverse turn and pulled hard towards them, berating herself for forgetting about them in her jubilation.

Tracer rounds reached out at her from the enemy aircraft, appearing to be coming directly for her, but her manoeuvre had taken the Prussians by surprise and the bullets seemed to swerve, passing harmlessly behind her, only yards away. The Prussian fighters flashed by and she instantly reversed her turn again to give chase, but then remembered her orders and instead lined up on another bomber and pumped two seconds' worth of cannon and machine gun fire into it before turning to head after Tanya.

'That's Reitsch leading the first flight, Leader.' Penny said calmly as the four aircraft dived towards her and Abby. 'Looks like Gruber's leading the second flight.'

Abby laughed. 'Seems like Gruber's been pushed off his pedestal.'

When they'd counted only two flights of Barons, eight fighters in total, she'd wondered if they'd split their forces, just as the Misfits had done, but when she'd seen that both Reitsch and Gruber were there she'd realised that they hadn't. It looked like their resources weren't as unlimited as it had seemed they were and they hadn't stocked back up on pilots. Or Blutsaugers, either, because she thought she spotted a few MU9s among them. It was extremely encouraging and something that Freddy would certainly be interested in as a follow up to his story about how many Barons the Misfits had shot down the day before.

That was all something to worry about when they got home, though; first they had to survive the fight.

'I know we've been told to concentrate on the bombers, Penny,' she said, breaking radio protocol for once in her uncertainty, 'but how do you say we do a little hunting first?'

'Sounds good to me, Abby darling.'

Abby smiled. 'Alright, then, break on my mark and I'll meet you on the other side.'

'Roger that!'

When the order came, Penny rolled Kingfisher sharply onto her side and pulled hard. Abby had judged it extremely finely and Penny clenched just about everything she had left of her body as tracer rounds came towards her and only missed by what looked like inches. She really didn't like playing the mouse in these cat and mouse games with the Barons, but she'd rather it was Abby and her doing it than the younger pilots, or one of the poor boys and girls in Harrys and Spits.

She continued the roll she'd started, pulling Kingfisher's nose down and around, gathering speed as the aircraft described a corkscrew in the air. She completed the manoeuvre in quick succession and found herself back on Abby's wing, only now they were behind the Barons, who were struggling to pull their noses around. Reitsch, confirming everything Gwen had said about her, was turning the hardest and swiftly leaving her companions behind.

'We kill her, then we go back to the bombers.' Abby said. 'You take the high road.'

'Roger,' Penny said, even as she pulled up and away from Abby, who continued to hone directly in on the Prussian woman.

What are they doing? Reitsch thought as she frantically tried to pull Vixen round to face the two Misfit aircraft bearing inexorably down on her. *Why are they wasting their time with me instead of doing their job?*

She looked back and forth from one of the two enemy aircraft to the other, looking for a way to get the advantage back, to maybe destroy one and even the odds. There wasn't one, though, and she knew there wouldn't be; she recognised the aircraft and knew that neither of the pilots would make a mistake.

There was only one conclusion she could come to, therefore - if she stayed, she died.

She put Vixen on her back and dived for the deck and home.

Abby blinked in surprise as the black aircraft plummeted from the sky. 'Well... That was...' she said. 'I guess we're going back to the bombers, Two. But if you get the chance, see if you can knock a Baron or two from the sky while you're at it.'

In the second engagement of the day it was the RAC's turn to take the Fleas by surprise. They ravaged the unprepared Prussian bombers, destroying dozens of them for the loss of only a few aircraft, preventing many from reaching their targets and harassing others so much that they were unable to hit them properly.

It was a victory, but ultimately a rather meaningless one, because the damage had already been done in the earlier raid.

'Welcome back, Officer Perkins! Officer Sherborne!' the man behind the desk of The Dorchester said with a wide, welcoming smile when he saw them. 'Congratulations on your posting and your success!' The smile went away immediately, though. 'I was sorry to hear about Officer Wilberforce. All of us here at The Dorchester were.'

'Thank you,' Rob said, taking his key and passing Ellie hers.

They smiled at the man, then hurried to join the other Misfits at the lifts.

'Ten minutes to freshen up a bit, then straight down to lunch, please.' Abby was saying. 'Sorry, but we're going to have to eat in flightsuits, in case we get called.'

Most of the Misfits had been assigned rooms on the first floor, as close to the ground as possible so that they could run down the stairs if need be, but there hadn't been enough rooms for everyone and Ellie, Rob and Chastity were on the second floor. Chastity just to the right of the lift and Rob and Ellie in the two rooms immediately to the left.

Rob and Ellie went to their doors, but stopped before going in and looked at each other. Last time they had stayed at The Dorchester had been immediately after their friend Tayler had died. They'd seen the sights of the city and taken advantage of the luxury of the hotel - Drake had been paying, so they hadn't held back at dinner or in the bar - but they hadn't been able to fully enjoy themselves and didn't have the best memories of the hotel, or London.

They smiled sadly at each other, then went into their rooms without a word.

The Prussians were pushing hard to get as many raids in as possible and the Misfits barely had time to finish eating before they got a call to tell them that one was building and they were needed.

There were more British aircraft in the air for the third Prussian raid, but once again the enemy had switched tactics. This time they hit coastal defences and shipping and then immediately returned home, giving the RAC little chance to engage them because of Pewtall's standing order not to pursue over the water. They continued to employ the tactic during a fourth raid and even managed to fit in a fifth before it got too late. It was a rather puzzling tactic by the Prussians, especially because the damage they caused was minimal - the defensive positions were heavily fortified and ships were tricky targets to hit at the best of times - but they didn't necessarily know that what they were doing wasn't very effective.

Even though they hadn't been fighting as much as usual, flying five sorties was tiring in itself and the Misfits were near exhaustion by the time they were released from readiness. None of them were going to say they were too tired to go to the palace, though; they were all looking forward to it too much. Princess Elizabeth, who insisted on being called "Liz" by the Misfits, was one of the nicest, kindest people they had met, she was also an engineer and an aviation enthusiast and the conversations they'd had with her in the past were always interesting.

Two huge autocars flying the Princess of Wales' colours were sent to The Dorchester for them, even though they could have walked to the palace in little more than five minutes, and they had attracted quite a crowd by the time the Misfits came out. They spent a few minutes shaking hands and all of them signed autographs, although Ellie seemed to be most in demand among them, to the delight of Gwen and Abby, who were the ones usually swamped whenever they went out in public. The Royal Guard drivers were getting nervous, though, so they extracted themselves as best they could and piled into the vehicles.

The autocars took them through the main gates of the palace at the end of The Mall, but, instead of driving through the east facade and into the interior courtyard where guests were usually received, they were taken around the side, to the entrance of the West Tower, more popularly known as the Brunel Tower. They were taken through the military checkpoint outside the door and then went up to the tenth floor in the lift.

Their Royal Guard escort showed them into a laboratory and there they found Princess Elizabeth. She wasn't dressed for dinner, though, she was wearing coveralls and was being helped into a set of glidewings by a boy.

'Hello, everyone!' she called out with a grin. 'Won't be a mo!'

With that, she nodded at the boy, then took off at a run towards a large window that had been opened to the night and leapt, instantly disappearing from view.

The Misfits looked at each other, then at the boy.

The boy said nothing, though, he just grinned at them and, after a few seconds of awkward silence where nothing happened, Abby cleared her throat. 'Are we supposed to wait for her to come up in the lift? Or do we go down to meet...?'

She trailed off and laughed, leading the rush to the windows as Liz buzzed softly past outside, waving and grinning widely.

'Be right there!'

They watched as she banked away from them, then curved back and they scattered as she headed directly towards them.

Ellie had been in the middle of the group and was slow to get out of the way, but that just meant she was in position to catch the princess when she stumbled on landing and almost fell.

She struggled with her for a moment, the weight of the wings threatening to topple both of them over, but then the Liz pulled the lever to retract them and they straightened up together.

'Thank you!' Liz said. She stepped back and smiled, then blinked. 'Oh! You must be Eleanor Perkins. I've heard so much about you!'

She thrust out a hand and Ellie took it automatically before remembering herself and sketching a quick curtsy.

'Oh, don't bother with all that,' the girl said, pulling her up. 'Misfits don't do that.'

She released Ellie's hand, then looked around at the astonished Misfits. 'Well?' she asked, raising her eyebrows.

Predictably, Gwen and Kitty were the first ones to come forward.

'They're powered, but there's no room for the motor, or the spring,' Gwen said. It wasn't really a question, more an observation, but Liz nodded.

'They're electric?' Kitty asked, noting the lightning bolt warning symbols on the backplate.

'Yes,' Liz said, grinning at her. 'I expanded on some of the discussions we had about Nicole Tesla's work.

'*You* made them?' Abby asked.

'Not these, these are the first production model, but they're based on my prototype. The people at the Scott Brothers Company tweaked my design a bit and refined the engineering far more than I could in my lab, but they're still essentially the same as when I first put them together.'

As the Misfits continued to bombard Liz with questions about the glidewings, Ellie found herself retreating steadily, and as they continued the attack she found herself standing with the boy and she smiled at him.

'Ellie,' she said, by way of introduction.

'Isaac.'

'You're not a prince or anything are you?' she asked nervously, wondering if she was committing some kind of social faux pas by not calling him "my lord" or curtseying.

He laughed. 'No, I'm just a boy from the East End.'

She sighed in relief and he laughed again.

'And you work with Princess Elizabeth?' she asked, looking at the white coat he was wearing.

'Not really,' he said, shrugging. 'I just help her out every so often when she needs another pair of hands.'

'Oh.'

'My laboratory is on the sixth floor.'

'Oh! So you're a scientist too!' she exclaimed delightedly.

'Yes, but...'

He couldn't say any more than that because at that moment the crowd of pilots parted and Liz came towards them, shrugging out of the wings. They were immediately pounced upon by Gwen, who carried them to a bench, taking Kitty and Drake with her.

'I see you've met Isaac,' the princess said to Ellie. 'Everyone!' she called out, 'this is Isaac Richardson. We saved each other's lives last month and he has a lab a few floors down.'

Penny frowned at Isaac. 'Richardson. Any relation?'

The boy nodded. 'My father.'

'Oh, I'm terribly sorry. He was a great man. A good man. He is sorely missed.'

'Thank you.'

Liz reached out and touched Isaac's sleeve comfortingly, but he just shrugged and smiled at her.

She turned to Abby then gave a meaningful look at Gwen, who had found a screwdriver. 'We should really go down to dinner before they dismantle my wings.'

Abby chuckled. 'Children!' she called out, 'time to put your toys away.'

'Aw, mum!' Drake whined, stomping his foot and making a face.

'Don't worry!' Liz said. 'That's a production model. The first batch is being delivered as we speak, so they'll be waiting for you tomorrow morning. A leaflet will be with them, explaining their use and capabilities, but I can tell you all about them *over dinner.*'

She gave them a meaningful look and Gwen sheepishly put the screwdriver down.

They had an informal dinner in one of the smaller dining rooms, which was still big enough to seat a few dozen people. Liz sat in the middle of the table, instead of the head, and the Misfits gathered around her in no particular order. The first course was taken up entirely by Liz describing the capabilities of her glidewings, which were being manufactured under the name "Windsor Wings". The second course was then dominated by Liz answering Gwen's questions about how she'd put them together and Kitty's questions about the electrics. When it looked like the conversation was going to continue in the same vein during the third course Abby stepped in and banned all talk of the wings. Unless, of course, she added hastily, Liz wanted to say anything else, which the princess quickly and laughingly asserted she didn't.

After that, the dinner became more of a usual Misfit affair, with the same kind of joking around and storytelling that there usually was, with Liz joining in almost as if she were one of them, rather than being the focus of things, which was probably what she had intended all along with the informal setting.

Dessert had just been served when the king came in. They started to stand, but he waved them back to their seats.

'I'm not here,' he said with a smile, 'not officially, anyway.'

He flopped down into one of the spare chairs, startling Ellie, who not only found herself meeting him for the first time, but sitting next to him. He accepted a glass of wine from a servant, then looked around the table.

'Sorry to disturb you, but I couldn't have you coming to my home and not pop in to say hello.'

His eyes settled on Ellie and he smiled. 'You must be Officer Perkins.'

'Yes, sir.'

He peered around. 'And Officer Sherborne, is he... Ah!' he said, spotting Rob. 'There you are. Welcome to the palace, both of you. It's nice to finally meet you.'

'Thank you, sir.' Rob said, nodding.

'I spoke to Sir Douglas about promoting you both, but he said it was already in the pipeline, so that should come through in a few days and he told me that there will be some kind of commendation for you, Officer Perkins, for your remarkable achievements.'

Ellie blushed. 'That's not necessary, sir, but thank you.'

'Tosh!' the king said, 'of course it's necessary!' he smiled at her, then looked across the table. 'And Chastity, the field promotion to aviator lieutenant you were granted by Brigadier Cholmondeley-Warner is to be confirmed, but I'm afraid you'll only hold onto it very briefly... because your promotion to squadron leader has already gone through in recognition for the bally good work you did holding things together in Africa. There's also a gong coming for that, as well as commendations for the bravery of the other pilots that were with you.' He gave her a sad smile. 'I know it'll be little consolation for their families, but there's not much else we can do except keep the memory of them alive as we fight.'

'Thank you, sir.' Chastity said softly.

The king nodded to her, then sipped at his wine. He looked tired - there were bags under his eyes and he was hunched over slightly in his chair, his posture not as straight as it usually was.

'Have you eaten, father?' Liz asked, obviously concerned.

'I had a sandwich, oh I don't know when, but...'

'Bring some food for my father, please,' she said to the head servant

'I don't really...'

'This is my dinner party, father.' Liz said imperiously. 'You walked into it so you can play by my rules.'

'Yes, Elizabeth.' The king looked around the table and grinned. 'This is one war I refuse to fight.'

'Because *this* one you won't win.' Liz said, smiling sweetly.

The king laughed. 'So, has she bored you all to tears with her wings, yet?'

'Not at all,' Abby said dryly. 'Gwen and Kitty have.'

'Yes, well,' he said, after the laughter had died down. 'I'm authorising pursuit of the Fleas over the water for whoever is issued them. As far as necessary. Even to within sight of France.'

'What kind of range do they have, then?' Gwen asked, leaning forward eagerly.

'I flew my prototype clear across London and back.' Liz said. 'About six miles. And that was straight and level, not gliding from a height. I haven't fully tested the production model, but I can only assume it has a greater range.'

'Yes,' the king said. 'I didn't say anything to my daughter before, because I didn't want to give her any ideas, but I asked the engineers at Scott the same question when I was debating my order. They told me that the wings were perfectly capable of taking off from a standing start from the beach at Calais and then fly home clear across the channel.'

More than one of the pilots looked very intrigued at that revelation and the king laughed. 'Sorry, Abby! Seems like my daughter isn't the only one I should have kept that from.' He finished his glass of wine, then stood. 'I'll leave you to it. Happy hunting tomorrow.'

The Misfits chorused thank yous and good nights as the king left. There was silence for a moment before Gwen leaned towards Liz again. 'Are the glidewings...?' she began, but was quickly silenced by a hail of napkins.

None of the Misfits was a heavy drinker, apart from Scarlet, of course, and she wasn't there because she'd been off doing something secret for the last couple of days. However, even though none of them had had more than a couple of glasses of wine, they were still rather unsteady on their feet as they staggered up the steps of The Dorchester a bit before eleven, their tiredness, more than anything, catching up with them.

Nobody even mentioned the possibility of a nightcap in the bar or a desire to prolong the evening, so they piled into the lift, too weary even to climb just one or two flights of stairs.

After saying goodnight to Chastity, Rob and Ellie went down the wide corridor to their doors. They said goodnight to each other and Rob turned to go, but his hand was caught and he found himself being pulled back around. Their eyes met and suddenly they were in each other's arms, their lips locked together.

This was what Rob had wanted for so long, for as long as he'd known Ellie, in fact, and his heart leapt with joy. It felt good, it felt right, but...

He pulled back, gasping for breath. 'I'm so sorry,' he said, kicking himself inside, 'but I can't. I want to, believe me I do. But not now. Not yet.'

There was hurt in Ellie's eyes and he almost gave in and pulled her back, but then her face softened in understanding and she nodded.

'Not yet,' she whispered softly. She smiled and reached up to stroke his cheek, then turned and went into her room.

Rob stood in the corridor for a long moment after the door had closed behind her, cursing himself as a fool, but at the same time basking in the promise for the future that her smile had held.

CHAPTER 13

28th August 1941

'Control, this is Tapir Leader, preparing to engage the enemy.'
'Roger, Tapir Leader. Happy hunting.'
The Misfits had been instructed to take off late and then orbit over the Kent Downs at two thousand feet, ten miles back from the coast, and they were forced to listen as their fellow pilots engaged the enemy. They could picture the scene - the hundreds of British fighters that had made it into the sky that morning, racing towards more than double the number of Prussian fighters and bombers, which had been sent to clear a path for the Prussian invasion ships that were even now steaming from ports in France, Belgium, the Netherlands and the Channel Islands. It had to be terrifying and it was increasingly hard to hear as the calls became steadily more frantic and losses were reported, but there was a reason they were listening rather than participating and that reason was the rockets that had been delivered overnight and installed under their wings - rockets filled with acid, which their friend Wendy Llewellyn had first cobbled together on Malta and called "meltrockets" and which the Misfits had used to great effect. They had been little more than thick metal tubes back then, heavy, unwieldy and rather inaccurate, but these new versions were sleek and looked very dangerous and were light enough that they could each carry eight of them. They were the fruit of Wendy's work in a secret weapons research facility and had come with a note from her that had simply said "Enjoy!"

'Control, this is Badger Leader. We're wasting tension here. When are you thinking of sending us in?'

'Badger Leader, this is control. Your escort should be arriving momentarily.'

'Our what, control?'

'Your escort, Abby!' a new, but familiar voice announced.

The Misfits had all been gazing intently towards the sea and the unfolding battle with their lenses at maximum magnification in an attempt to see how it was going, so they didn't notice what was approaching from behind them until a huge shadow fell on them and a massive aircraft buzzed past, buffeting them in its wake.

'Come on, little duckies! Follow mother!'

'What the hell is that?' Ellie couldn't help but ask, staring at the six-engined monstrosity painted in eye-watering colours.

'That,' Tanya said, her glee clear in her voice, 'is Dreadnought!'

'Wendy!' Abby said. 'Shouldn't you be in a workshop somewhere?'

'What? And miss all the fun?'

The Misfits spread out on either side of the huge aircraft and Ellie found herself next to Dreadnought as they descended to one thousand feet and sped towards the coast. She split her focus between peering forward to assess the battle and scanning the sky, looking for stray Fleas, but her eyes kept wandering back to the aircraft next to her and eventually she realised that someone in the cockpit was waving at her, trying to catch her attention.

'Uh, hello, Dreadnought, this is Badger Four, uh, is something wrong?'

'Ellie!' The figure in the window waved even more enthusiastically, 'it's me! Lottie!'

'Lottie!' Ellie blinked in surprise, then laughed and waved back, just as enthusiastically. 'Why am I surprised? You always wanted to fly a bomber.'

'And now I get to fly this! It's...'

'Children, children!' Wendy's deep voice cut them off with a laugh. 'Clear the airwaves, please! You can catch up when we get home! One minute to target.'

Ellie gave Lottie a last wave, then peered out over Heron's nose. Her mouth went dry when she saw that the land had come to an end while she'd been chatting and there was now only water beneath her. This was the first time she'd ever been over water, without the safety of home soil beneath her, and she found it strangely unnerving.

However, that feeling was nothing compared to the dread that the sight of what awaited the Misfits sparked in her.

Her imagination hadn't even come close to picturing the vast Prussian fleet. There seemed to be more ships than there had been aircraft in the sky at the beginning of the offensive, their wakes, shining white in the dawn, almost obscured by the smoke of their labouring engines as they steamed across the channel as fast as they could.

The Royal Navy had formed a picket line a few miles out from the shore, but it looked pitifully weak to Ellie, spread out along the coast as it was, and she doubted if it would be able to prevent a landing on its own. Fortunately, though, the navy wasn't on its own.

'Spread out. Aim for the biggest ships,' Wendy ordered, taking command, 'the biscuit bangers can deal with the small stuff.'

'How many of these things of yours do we you think we'll need to sink a ship?' Abby asked.

'Oh,' Wendy said casually, 'one ought to do it, if you get a direct hit. Best fire two at each, though, just in case.'

The Misfits extended their line until there was almost a quarter of a mile between them and Ellie scanned ahead for a target. There were so many to choose from, but one of them caught her eye, one of the very biggest, flying a huge red Prussian flag. She sincerely hoped someone important was on it and flicked the first two switches on the shiny new panel that had been bolted under her instruments.

'Incoming aircraft!'

'Where away, damn you?' Admiral Haas, second in command of the Reichsflotte and commander of the western fleet, shouted back at the lookout.

The man pointed, panicked. 'Dead ahead!'

Haas rushed to the forward windshield and stared out at the aircraft. He laughed. 'It's only a single fighter! What does he think he can...?'

He stopped abruptly as twin lances of flame sprouted from the wings of the tiny aircraft and something impacted on his ship just behind the forward guns. He ducked down behind the bulkhead in case the explosion shattered the windows, but, aside from a slight tremble running through the ship and a soft rumbling noise, there didn't seem to have been any effect. He smiled and stood.

'Get me a damage report!' he bellowed, 'and call the Fliegertruppe - ask them where in hell's name they are!'

Before anyone could act on his orders the shipboard communication set rang and the officer of the deck picked it up. Haas snatched it from him before he could say anything.

'Report!' he barked

'It's some kind of acid! It's eating through the decks!'

'Acid?'

The officer of the deck heard him. 'Sir! I heard of this in the Mediterranean, when we attacked Malta. The Misfits attacked with rockets containing some kind of acid.'

'And how did you counter it? What do we do?'

'The Italians had a counter-agent which they distributed throughout the ships. Dousing the acid with it stops it.'

'Do we have any counter-agent?'

'Uh, no, sir.'

'No?!?' Haas swore under his breath. 'So, what else do we do, man?' he yelled.

The officer shrugged. 'We abandon ship, sir.'

Tay would have loved this, Rob thought as he banked around, his wingtip only feet from the waves, and searched for another ship to target. *And he would have been so much better at it than me.*

He flipped two more switches, arming the next two rockets, and centred his sights on his last choice.

Tracer fire was all around, flung out by the ships in a desperate attempt to bring down him and the other Misfits, but the fighters were moving too fast for them and the Prussian gunners were hampered by the fact that their targets were in their midst and low, and, more often than not, they hit each other when they missed. Dreadnought was the only one taking any damage, but it seemed she could absorb it and she was giving back as good as she got, silencing every gun that dared to target her.

Rob waited until the last moment, then pressed the button under the switches. His aircraft rocked, slowed down perceptibly by the release, and he watched as the trail of fire and smoke sprang out. The impact wasn't as impressive as he would have liked and the explosion was definitely underwhelming, but he grinned as he pictured the panic spreading as they realised that they were doomed nonetheless.

Enemy ships were sinking all around now, but none of them was showing much in the way of damage. There were no billowing clouds of smoke, no huge explosions and the only enemy fire was coming from a handful of fighters, but still ship after ship was just slipping beneath the waves calmly and gracefully while their crews dived into the sea all around them.

It had to be extremely unnerving for the Prussians, but he couldn't say he had any pity for them whatsoever.

The Misfits sank more than twenty ships and Dreadnought accounted for another ten before Prussian fighters descended on them and they were forced to abandon the attack and defend themselves. It was a drop in the bucket, though, and the fleet steamed on without pause, almost as if nothing untoward had happened.

As they approached the coast, the ships began to form lines, following the unseen paths plotted by their leaders from the maps and documents acquired by spies working with the erstwhile war minister - paths that would allow them to pass safely through the dense minefields set up all along the British coast.

'There they go, just as you said they would.' Admiral Sir Dudley Witherow, the commander of the Royal Navy, said. He growled. 'That damned Cummerbund has a lot to answer for, giving them maps of our defences like that. Just as well you chaps found out they had them, eh?'

He moved aside, giving the man and woman standing with him access to the telescope pointing out across the channel from the small opening cut into the white cliffs of Dover, directly beneath the castle.

Squadron Leader Yaxley put his eye to the optical device and swung it back and forth slightly to take in the ships moving towards the British coast. He had no idea what he was looking at, though; he barely knew one end of a ship from another, so working out whether they were doing what he'd predicted they would do from a glance was beyond him.

'Yes,' he said, standing up again and giving the woman beside him a look. 'Yes, indeed. What do you think, Scarlet?'

The woman hid a grin, then bent to the telescope, however, instead of looking at the ships, she tilted it back slightly and looked at the sky over them.

'I think... that it's time for a drink,' she said, after she'd drunk her fill of the sight of the Misfits racing back to land, the anti-aircraft guns of Dreadnought covering them and accounting for not a few Prussian fighters in the process.

Admiral Witherow laughed and turned to lead the way back down the access tunnel. 'I suppose the sun is over the yardarm somewhere in the world! Is rum alright?'

'Of course not!' Scarlet scoffed, smiling widely, 'I would think, for the favour we've done you and your biscuit bangers today, you could at least break out the good stuff!'

Witherow laughed again. 'I'll see what I can do.'

The tunnel opened out into a wide circular chamber, cut into the bare rock. There were a couple of dozen men and women bustling around busily and the admiral called over a petty officer waiting attentively nearby and whispered in her ear. When she rushed off, he turned back to his visitors. 'Take a seat and let's watch the situation unfold while we wait, shall we?'

Scarlet took in the row of chairs on a small platform at the side of the room and grinned at the sight of the symbols on the backs of the two in the middle. She jumped up onto the platform and plumped herself down in the one with the royal crest on it, swinging her legs up to dangle over one of the arms.

Witherow raised an eyebrow at her, but said nothing and just sat in the one with the Royal Navy crest on it - his own chair.

Yaxley hesitated, saw that if he sat in the chair next to Scarlet he would have her feet in his face, then sat in the one next to Witherow.

The petty officer returned with a silver tray, on which were three glasses and a bottle of Scotch. She looked at Witherow questioningly and he shook his head, then tilted it at Scarlet.

'Ice, ma'am?' she asked.

'No, thanks.' Scarlet said, grinning up at her. 'Just fill it up.'

The woman poured a couple of fingers and went to put the bottle back down, but caught Scarlet's expression and tipped it up again. Only when the glass was more than half full did Scarlet nod in satisfaction and accept it.

The petty officer gave her a sly smile, then moved to Yaxley, but he shook his head. 'Just tea, please.'

With the pleasantries out of the way, Scarlet joined the other two officers in gazing down at the floor of the chamber.

The floor was taken up almost in its entirety by a map, painted on wooden panels. It was unlike any map the two RAC officers had seen before, with only the outlines of the south and east coasts of Britain and the coasts of France and the Netherlands marked on it thickly in black. The coast of Britain, with Dover in the centre, was directly in front of the platform, so it was if they were sitting in the map and looking out, just as they had done with the telescope. The sea was coloured white, instead of the usual blue, which, presumably, was so that the thousands of inscriptions and symbols drawn on it would show up better. Men and women with felt-soled shoes walked over it, pushing markers around as the positions of ships were reported and from this point of view it was easy to make out what Witherow had seen with the telescope - both Prussian fleets, the one approaching from the south and the one from the east, were bunching up and funnelling into several clearly defined paths.

'Your Misfits have done a marvellous job of thinning the herd a bit,' Witherow said approvingly, pointing at a few dozen wooden markers lying on their sides to the south. 'It's a shame they can't do the same with the other fleet.' He looked to his left, where only a couple of wooden markers were lying down, ambushed by the few undersea boats that had been able to sneak into the area.

'Never mind,' he said. 'Thanks to your warning we've had time to prepare a few little surprises for them.'

Scarlet raised her glass to him. 'Don't thank us, thank the boys and girls in France getting this info for us. All I did was hop over the channel to pick it up.'

Witherow stared at her. '*All* you did...'

Scarlet knocked back the rest of the whisky, then grinned at him as she held her glass out towards the petty officer.

The captain of the *Mühlberg*, one of the Reichsflottes biggest, most sophisticated and most powerful battleships, stood at the front windshields of the bridge. The coast of the Kingdom of Great Britain was barely in sight - just a slither of darkness on the horizon, with the smoke of the aerial bombardment from the Fliegertruppe of only minutes ago still hanging over it - but it was in sight and it was something he'd begun to think he would never get to see. At least not while the war was still raging, anyway.

In his orders, that piece of land was called "*Landing Point Buschgroßmutter*", but on the chart it was labelled as Dunwich Beach and, undoubtedly, once the conquest was over, it would bear another name, something Prussian and patriotic. Whatever its name, it was a lovely long flat piece of land that the armour and men in the ships following up behind his shock group would easily roll up onto before continuing on to roll over the British army.

There were some British ships anchored in a line a couple of miles off shore, presenting their broadsides to him, and a few more in the distance to either side, racing to join them, but they were far too few and far too small and would do nothing to stop his ship.

He tore his gaze away from the view and went to join his navigation officer at the chart.

'How long until we get to the minefield?'

The lieutenant had a large chronograph on the chart and he glanced at it, then adjusted a pair of compasses and used them to measure a distance on the map before answering. 'Fifty three seconds until we reach the edge, sir.'

The captain nodded, then turned to his second in command. 'Are all ships in position?'

'Yes, sir. In two lines, as ordered.'

'Good, then take us to flank speed.'

The Mühlberg surged forward powerfully, throwing foaming white water from its bow. The captain and crew held their breath, knowing that they were now entering the minefield, but when long seconds passed and nothing happened they began to relax.

An explosion off the port side threw spray into the air and they all ducked, but the captain just laughed as he straightened up. 'It is just the British pop guns!' he called out to his men, turning in place to give them a reassuring smile. 'Don't worry, they don't have anything big enough to hurt us!'

'Sir!' The lieutenant at the chart called out. 'We will be out of the minefield in fifteen seconds!'

'Excellent! Prepare to turn ninety degrees to port. Order the starboard side guns...'

He never got the chance to finish his order, as a massive explosion tore the Mühlberg apart, sending fire and shrapnel surging through it, killing most of its crew, including everyone on the bridge.

At each of the five beaches chosen for landings on the east coast of Britain and the four on the south coast, the ships in the vanguards of the attack met the same fate. Massive mines, the biggest that the British possessed, supplemented by as much explosive as could be packed into the shell and studded by armour piercing steel lances, had secretly been placed across the safe paths through the minefields.

Those ships were the biggest, most powerful ships in the Prussian Navy and were supposed to smash the way through the Royal Navy so that the smaller, weaker troop ships could land their precious cargoes. Instead, they came to a sudden halt, creating a deadly blockage in the narrow channel, which forced the ships coming up close behind them to frantically turn to avoid ripping themselves apart on the wreckage, which in turn forced the ships behind them to manoeuvre and so on down the lines. Many of those that hadn't yet entered the channel were able to turn aside and come to a stop, but those that had weren't so lucky. Several collided with each other at speed, causing catastrophic damage, while others wandered too far off the safe path and into the minefields before they could stop and paid the price. A few managed to make it past the wrecks, only to run into more mines in the supposedly safe channel. All the while, the Royal Navy continued to bombard them, adding their own damage and confusion to the mix.

The invasion stalled as the ships of the Reichsflotte found their way blocked and their captains filled the airwaves with requests for orders from admirals who were either dead, abandoning stricken ships, or simply unable to see a way forward.

Sir Douglas Pewtall watched the markers on the map table closely, judging the moment. The Fleas had sent their entire force out together that morning to bombard the landing zones that they had chosen, hoping to soften up the resistance and detonate any mines sown on the beaches. It was a fine tactic and would have paid off *if* the ships had been able to reach the beaches because the Prussian troops would have been too close to the British defenders to risk a full scale retaliation by the RAC. They hadn't, though, so the boys and girls in their bombers would get to have a little low-level bombing practice.

The closest of the retreating Prussian markers reached a point about fifteen miles from the British coast and Sir Douglas looked over at Di Fisher. 'Tell Izzy to go, please.'

'Yes, sir!' Fisher said before pointing at the radio operator who had been watching her for the last few minutes.

The woman immediately bent over her radio set and sent the order to put the Royal Aviator Corps' entire bomber force into the air.

Give them hell, Pewtall thought, watching the lights on the wall starting to shine as the bomber squadrons took off, *send them packing back to where they came from.*

'Generaladmiral Weber and Admiral Haas are both requesting permission to fall back, sir.'

'No!' Schmidt shouted, slamming his hand down on the desk. 'Tell them to push forwards!'

'But, sir, they report heavy losses.'

'I don't care! We have plenty of ships. We have plenty of men. The losses are insignificant! Tell them I don't care how they do it, but they are to get our troops on the beach now! And tell them that these orders have the full authority of the Kaiser behind them and any captain, or admiral, that refuses them will be shot!'

'Yes, sir!'

Schmidt snarled as the man fled. It was almost as if his men had been expecting the British to roll over and capitulate without a fight - all the waiting and the rumours about the British war minister surrendering and the war being as good as over had made them soft.

Of course the British would defend their homeland like lions! *Of course* there were going to be heavy losses! But pressing forward bravely, no matter the cost, would ensure that the war ended in weeks, perhaps days, not drag on for months or years and would ultimately result in far fewer lives lost.

'I don't believe it...' Admiral Witherow whispered, lifting his eye from the telescope and staring out over the water open-mouthed. 'They're still coming.'

A massive fountain of water flew up into the air a few miles offshore among the dark grey Prussians ships. The rumble, like nearby thunder, followed about a dozen seconds later, and by that time it was obvious even to the naked eye that the ships were turning and once again pointing their bows towards shore. More explosions followed and a few of those ships stalled, swerving or capsizing, or in one spectacular case ripping completely in half. The others seemed unbothered by the sight and white water appeared at their bows as they picked up speed.

Witherow ducked as the tunnel echoed to a roar far louder than any explosion so far and he and the two RAC officers lifted their eyes to watch as dozens of bombers, Nelsons and Splendids mostly, flew overhead seemingly within touching distance.

Anti-aircraft fire reached out from the ships towards them, filling the air with bright filaments. A handful of the bombers were hit, their engines bursting into flames or pieces flying off them, and a couple fell from the sky, hitting the water and disintegrating before the occupants could possibly have had time to get out. The rest flew through the storm, though, and released their payloads over the ships.

Fresh huge explosions covered dozens of the ships with smoke, but, curiously, a couple of dozen more were peppered with small explosions, as if firecrackers had gone off on them.

'What the dickens...?' Witherow muttered, puzzled.

He looked at the two RAC officers and Yaxley just shrugged, but Scarlet grinned.

'It seems that Wendy Llewellyn has been busy,' she said. 'If I'm not mistaken those are what she calls "meltbombs". Nasty little things that contain metal devouring acid. Completely harmless to people, although I wouldn't advise bathing in the stuff, especially if you have fillings, but it'll eat straight through a ship if you don't have the counter agent...'

They watched as an apparently undamaged ship sank beneath the water, far too rapidly for something of its size.

'Which it appears the Prussians do not have!' she finished gleefully.

Their job done, the bombers swung wide around the fleet and headed back to land. The undamaged Prussians chased them with gunfire, bringing down one more Nelson, but the rest disappeared back over the white cliffs, heading home to, presumably, pick up more ordnance.

Witherow bent to the telescope again and soon grunted in satisfaction. 'They've stalled. Most likely picking up survivors. We'll have to wait and see what they do, but I can't imagine that the poor souls out there have much will to fight left in them, even if they do make it to the beach.'

He turned to walk back down the tunnel. 'This is only one invasion fleet, though: there are eight others. Let's hope they're going just as well.'

CHAPTER 14

'These are the last of the rockets, there are no more after these,' Dot Campbell said, as she stood with Abby, watching the fitters finish rearming the Misfits' aircraft. 'Some of the chemicals used to create the acid aren't exactly easy to come by and Sir Douglas asked Wendy and her people to concentrate on creating bombs because they're a lot cheaper. And, besides, we thought the Italians would have given the Prussians counter-agent, or at least warned them to stock it.'

Abby chuckled and shook her head. 'Heads are going to roll for that oversight.'

'Oh, I do hope so.' Dot said, grinning at her. 'But let's hope they don't correct their error too soon.'

'Tea?' Abby asked, motioning towards the lounge.

Dot checked her chronograph. 'Oh, alright, then, I've got a few minutes.'

They went back inside and wandered over to the buffet table.

'What are we supposed to do when we've run out of rockets?'

'It depends on the Prussians, really.' Dot said, spooning sugar into a cup. 'If the Prussians manage to get a foothold on the beaches there will be a fair amount of ground attacks to be done. If they don't then it'll be back up top to take on the Fleas again.'

'Is it likely that they will land?'

Abby had asked the question quietly, but silence fall over the room nonetheless and they turned to find the other Misfits looking at them.

'We honestly don't know.' Dot said, turning to address the room. 'The last I heard before I left the Priory was that the Prussians had hit the minefields and had taken heavy casualties, but that they were still pressing forwards.'

Drake nodded. 'Sounds like the Kaiser's gotten a bit impatient and has put a rocket up them.'

Rolling eyes and a few groans greeted his pronouncement and he frowned, puzzled, but then realised what he'd said and chuckled. 'No pun intended, sorry.'

'Even though Rudy could have chosen his words better, he's correct. Usually, the kind of losses we're seeing would at least provoke a revision of strategy, if not an all-out retreat, but the Prussians are just blindly continuing to sail through our minefields.'

'Do we have more mines than they have ships?' Gwen asked softly.

'Probably not.' Dot said. 'But we don't just have mines to stop them, fortunately.'

The telephone rang and Drake, who had claimed Lord Henry's wingbacked armchair as his own, picked the receiver up from the small table beside him.

'Misfits... Understood, thank you.' He replaced the receiver and looked up at Abby. 'Dreadnought is ready. We're to take off in ten minutes.'

Abby nodded. 'Alright, everyone, you know what to do.'

As the pilots began to stand and stretch and move away to the bathrooms or finish their food, Abby turned to Campbell. 'Sorry, I have to get ready.'

'I should be going anyway,' Dot said, checking her chronograph again.

'Have you got a romantic rendezvous?'

Dot huffed. 'Chance would be a fine thing... No, I have an inter-service meeting at Whitehall.'

'Going up in the world I see!' Abby said, following Campbell as she started towards the street door.

'Not really. I'm fairly sure nobody wanted to go and I got the short straw because I'm the most junior.'

'I'm sure that's not true,' Abby said, grabbing her hand and pulling her to a halt in the doorway. 'You are one of the best and most experienced commanders we have and you need to go into that meeting *knowing* that. You mustn't just sit back and let others talk because you think you're the most junior, you have to use that experience and find a way for us to win this fight.'

Dot stared at Abby for a long moment and then smiled. 'You know, I'm rather glad we met. Life would have been so dull otherwise.'

She squeezed Abby's hand, then walked out to her waiting autocar.

'One minute to target.' Wendy said, her voice strained with tension that hadn't been there during the previous flight. 'Happy hunting.'

It was understandable that she was nervous. Dreadnought had taken heavy fire during the first assault and, while it hadn't been nearly enough to bring her down, one of her crew had been killed and half a dozen more had suffered injuries, including both Wendy and Lottie, who had been cut by flying glass when the cockpit had been hit, although thankfully not too seriously. Not only that, but the Misfits had also been directed towards Bournemouth, where the largest invasion fleet had broken through the minefield and was getting dangerously close to shore, so the stakes could not have been higher.

Smoke had been visible in the distance for quite some time, the black haze rising into the sky on a wide front that covered almost the entire horizon, so they had expected to find a certain amount of destruction, but they were in no way prepared for the scene of utter devastation awaiting them in the water.

Everywhere they looked, ships were burning.

Close to the shore at least half a dozen light grey ships flying British colours were stricken, a few sinking where they lay, with men and women jumping from them, swimming for shore or being picked up by small boats, and a few more limping away, trailing smoke and firing defiantly as they did so. The Prussians were having a far worse time of it, though. Dozens of the dark grey ships were burning, sinking, or capsizing, while all around them thousands of men struggled in the water, thrashing it white, many of them laden down with full equipment that their life preservers, if they even had them, were unable to deal with. There were lifeboats everywhere, packed with more men than they could handle and with more hanging off of them for dear life, but none of the ships had stopped to help and there very obviously weren't nearly enough to go around.

It was carnage, but the losses were almost insignificant compared to the size of the force that remained and the remaining Prussian ships were now clear of the minefield and racing for the beach through the gap they had blown in the Royal Navy.

The Misfits descended on them, through a storm of anti-aircraft fire, and loosed their rockets, this time not at the biggest, best armed ships, but at the ones they'd been shown photographs of, the ones that intelligence had flagged as carrying armoured vehicles and supplies.

Ellie spotted one of the priority targets in amongst the main pack of ships and shifted slightly towards it. She glanced across her wing to make sure that Tanya wasn't going for the same one just in time to see half of the Muscovite's wing get ripped off in a puff of anti-aircraft fire. She recoiled, throwing an arm up to cover her face as shrapnel flew towards her. It didn't reach, but by the time she looked back, Wolf was rolling into an uncontrolled dive.

'Get out, Tanya! Get out!' she screamed, but the aircraft disappeared behind her and out of sight before she saw if she was able to bail out or not and she was forced to put the Muscovite out of her mind as her target approached.

She released her first pair of rockets and banked hard, but instead of looking for the next supply ship she searched the sea for Wolf. She found the aircraft immediately, the wreckage bobbing up and down in the wake of a large ship, and looked for signs of Tanya, but she wasn't there - the canopy was back and the cockpit was empty.

Something caught her eye, something completely out of place amongst the ships and she selected magnifying lenses to take a better look while she continued to roll and bank in an attempt to confound the enemy gunners. She lost it for a moment and had to remove the lenses, but then found it again and brought it into full clarity.

'Yes!' she shouted, as she found Tanya calmly flitting across the waves in front of the leading ships, slowly outpacing them.

'Leader, this is Four. Three is down, but she's on those new wings and heading home.'

'Understood, Four.' Abby replied. 'Keep up the pressure, Badgers, let's keep their eyes on us instead of her.'

'Good luck,' Ellie whispered, then threw Heron on her wing and searched for a ship to destroy.

Between them, Wendy and the Misfits accounted for another two dozen or so Prussian ships, but they weren't the only ones trying to keep them from shore and, even as they turned for home, hundreds of small spring-powered boats were launching from hidden bunkers tucked away under piers or carved into sea walls and into the paths of each of the enemy flotillas. The boats were carrying a heavy load, but they had been designed for speed over a very short range and they raced over the sea towards the enemy.

The Prussian gunners rapidly shifted their aim to this new threat, giving the retreating Royal Navy ships and the shore batteries a temporary reprieve, but by the time they had brought their guns to bear it was already too late; the boats were already turning for home and the torpedoes they had carried out were already in the water.

Schmidt watched as the markers edged closer and closer to their objectives. Fleets one, three and eight were through the minefield and only a few miles from shore now, with nothing in their way, and fleets five and nine were not far behind, but it looked like fleets two, four, six and seven were stalled and wouldn't make it through the mines in sufficient numbers or force to complete their attack.

'Sir...' an aide approached nervously and placed a message slip in his hand.

Schmidt glanced at it just enough to note the names and codewords of the fleets, then shook his head and screwed it up. 'Request denied. Keep them going forward.'

'Yes, sir.'

'And send out the fighters now to cover the landings.'

'Yes, sir.'

Schmidt turned back to the map as the man hurried away. He had never expected all of the attacks to reach the land, had planned for it, in fact, and had placed his best men and materials on the convoys with the best chance of doing so. The other fleets had only ever really been distractions, something to absorb some of the punishment the British would mete out. They had done their job and would continue to do it, whether they liked it or not, while the real invasion army made landfall.

All that was needed was a few holes in the wall the British had put up and then the flood would pour through and wash them away.

'So, it seems like we're going to have to accept that enemy troops are going to land, whether we like it or not,' the king said, gazing at the map laid out on the round table, around which representatives of the Royal Navy, the British Army, and the Royal Aviator Corps sat with him.

'Yes, sir.' Admiral Uxbridge said, hanging his head, 'the Royal Navy has failed.'

'Pish and tosh, Eustace!' the king said, banging his hand softly on the table. 'You've done your utmost. You all have. This is all Cummerbund's doing; we wouldn't be in this situation if it weren't for him. The question now isn't who is to blame for the situation, but what to do about it. Basil?'

Basil Foxbrush, second in command of the British army, reached out to draw on the map with a finger. 'Thanks to the intelligence brought back by the Tactical Air Squadron a few days ago, we were able to throw cordons around the Prussian landing areas in time and place land mines on the beaches.' He drew semicircles around each of the beaches under attack. 'We will pull troops from those beaches where the landings have failed to reinforce the others and we have reserves standing by to plug any gaps that form.'

'Good,' the king smiled, then turned to the woman sitting next to him. 'Dot?'

'We are actually in a much better position now than we were yesterday. With the Fleas concentrating on bombarding their landing sites rather than us, we've had time to repair and reopen one of our primary airfields and two of our secondaries, which has allowed us to finally get on top of repairs. Bomber losses are mounting, though; the decision to carry out low-altitude attacks means greater accuracy and effectiveness, but it also means our aircraft are much easier targets.'

'Right,' the king said, stroking his short beard as he stared at the map. 'The way I see it, if we can't stop them landing we need to at least cut them off, which means disrupting their supply chain.' He looked at Admiral Uxbridge. 'Can the Royal Navy get in position to at least slow down their resupply and reinforcement efforts?'

Uxbridge stroked his own full beard as he looked at the map, unconsciously mirroring the king's gesture from before. 'I believe so, sir. Stop it, no, but at least make it costly for them to keep making the crossing.'

'Good; we'll have to force their battle ships to choose between protecting their convoys or the ground troops.' He looked at Dot. 'Your boys and girls will be best suited to hitting the landings now. They'll be at their most vulnerable then, before they've had a chance to dig in. Concentrate on their armour and machines. Troops can always be mopped up later.'

Dot nodded. 'Yes, sir.'

The king smiled and returned the nod, then turned to General Foxbrush. 'There's not much to say about your deployments, Basil, but there is still this.' He tapped one of the many papers in front of him - the TAS report on the thousands of paratroopers marshalling near airfields in France and Belgium. 'I haven't yet seen any plan on how you're going to deal with these.'

'I'm afraid our response to them is going to have to be fairly reactionary,' Foxbrush said with a grimace. 'We're pretty sure they'll come tonight, but the TAS were unable to get any information on where they will land.' He waved at the map. 'There are just so many places they could go - bridges, roads, airfields, the list is endless and we don't have enough resources to cover everything. We've placed our reserves in certain key positions and put the local observer troops and police forces on alert and asked them to watch the skies tonight, but beyond that there isn't much else we can do.'

'Very well.' The king nodded, but then fell silent and leaned forwards on his elbows to gaze down at the map. He remained that way for quite a while until, eventually, he lifted his head and looked around the small group. 'Is there anything we've missed? Anything at all that we could be doing that we're not already?'

There was silence again, but then Dot Campbell cleared her throat. 'Well, Sir Douglas assures me that he has another one of his surprises in store for the Prussians, but I don't know what that is or how it will help us...' She looked a question at the king and he gave her a sly smile.

'I do,' he said, 'and the Prussians really aren't going to like it. But I'm not going to let the cat out of the bag. That's for Sir Douglas and the Hawkings to do.'

'Depth is decreasing rapidly, captain. Twenty-five metres. Twenty-four. Twenty-two.'

The man at the depth gauge continued to call out ever-decreasing numbers as Kapitänleutnant Lister of supply vessel B235 picked up the speaking horn attached to his chart desk.

'Attention! Seal and prepare for release!'

He felt a series of vibrations pass through the deck below him, like someone had beaten on a bulkhead with a tool, and nodded in satisfaction, but then ducked as another explosion sent water fountaining into the air from only metres off the port quarter. He grimaced as the boat wallowed as it took on more water. It had never been the most seaworthy of vessels, but it had been pushed to its limits on this, thankfully short, voyage. Overloaded and almost swamped, with damage from a near hit to the bows, it was perilously close to sinking and the cargo couldn't be jettisoned soon enough for him.

'Thirteen metres. Twelve. Ten!'

'Release!' Lister shouted, pointing at the man standing at the panel of red-painted levers that had been roughly welded to the bulkhead.

The man pulled the levers down and the boat was rocked by small detonations below the waterline. It creaked and groaned, its already tortured superstructure complaining at this fresh insult, but even as it did so, its movements became more controlled as the weight it had been carrying dropped away.

'Four away, captain!'

'Hard to port!' Lister called. 'Set course for home!'

He'd done his job, delivered the cargo he'd been ordered to deliver, and he was damned if he was going to hang around any longer; he'd seen enough of his friends and comrades have their ships sunk underneath them for one day. He would leave this foolishness, this damn stupid invasion, to everyone else, pick up as many survivors as he could on the way back to France, then go and get drunk in the mess.

'What in Victoria's name are those, major?'

'I haven't the foggiest, sergeant, but I don't think we should let them finish whatever they're doing, do you?'

'No, sir!' the sergeant said with a grin before turning to bellow at the men and women at what she considered *her* guns. 'Adjust your fire! I want those things turned into scrap *yesterday*!'

As the gunners spun wheels to lower the guns and point them at the new threat, Major Peregrine bent to the triangulation lenses set solidly into the earth of the hill where his guns had been set up. The enemy was so close now that his people didn't need the exact measurements from the instrument and its pair twenty yards away to hit their targets, so he used the magnifying lenses just to inspect the strange Prussian vessels.

The boats, or whatever they were, had come to a halt about an eighth of a mile from the beach and swung around to prevent their sterns to the land. They were odd-looking things, like metal coffins, almost, with an enclosed, slightly pointed, featureless roof, and they reminded him of one of the models of siege weapons they had on display in York castle - a battering ram in a cart with a roof over the top to cover the assailants. It would make no sense for the boats to hold battering rams, though, but they could well be hiding some kind of weapon.

It took him a moment to realise that the boats had stopped rocking and a further moment to notice that they were now slightly higher in the water, but it wasn't until their shapes started to change, becoming longer, that he realised what they were.

'They're building bloody piers!' he exclaimed. 'Sergeant! Get those guns firing! I want...'

His mouth went dry and the words died in his throat as the first of the huge Prussian tanks breached the waves, blew the seals that had kept it watertight, and started firing as it advanced onto British soil.

CHAPTER 15

'Sir Douglas...' Di Fisher hobbled across the room to Pewtall, frowning. 'That callsign you gave me...'

'Volcano?' he asked.

'Yes, that's the one. Uh, I have someone reporting in with it. They say that they will be in position in ten minutes.'

Pewtall grinned. 'Acknowledge, please. Give them the frequency and callsign of the commander on the ground at Dunwich and tell them they have permission to attack when ready.'

'Yes, sir.' Fisher hesitated, but she knew better than to push for more information rather than carrying out orders and hurried away after only a moment.

This should be good! Pewtall thought to himself, rubbing his hands together in anticipation. He hadn't wanted to call on the Hawkings so soon, had been asked not to, in fact, by the Hawkings themselves, but the Prussians had left him little choice. However, if everything he'd been told about the Hawkings' airship, the *Hephaestus*, was even half true and if they had only had time to get it working at half its capacity, then the Prussians wouldn't know what hit them.

'Harriet, darling, we're listing again...' Sheridan Hawking said, grabbing hold of the leg of the control panel he was under so as not to slide across the smooth metal deck they hadn't had time to bolt the fire-retardant rubber matting to.

'I know! I know! I'm trying! But the number three fan is playing up again and it's not as if I've ever flown something like this before!'

'It's an airship, not a fighter. How hard can it be? And hasn't Hamish locked that down yet?'

'I'd like to see you come and give it a go! And no; he says every time he fixes one connection another one comes loose.'

Sheridan swore under his breath. Something was causing a worrying vibration in the number three fan. At the moment it wasn't too serious, but if it became too much worse it was going to shake itself apart.

That, thankfully, touch wood and all that, was the worst of the multitude of problems that had cropped up since taking off the day before - so far at least - but, by all rights, they shouldn't be in the air at all, let alone flying straight into a full-scale battle.

'Got it!' he cried out in triumph. He screwed the inspection hatch back on and slid out from under the console. He stood, staggering slightly as the deck righted itself suddenly.

'Well done!' Harriet gave him a warm smile, then frowned at the control panel. 'What exactly did you just fix?'

'Not sure...' Sheridan scanned the switches quickly, then grinned sheepishly. 'The landing lights.'

Harriet rolled her eyes. 'Very helpful.'

'We're almost in range!' the RAC officer at the charts called out.

'Thank you, uh...' Sheridan racked his brain, trying to think which of the multitude of faceless officers that had rushed on board when they'd been ordered to take off the man was.

'Wilkins, sir.'

'Right. Thank you, Wilkins.'

Sheridan moved to the captain's chair and picked up the radio.

'Cygnet, this is Volcano, do you read?'

The radio crackled for a moment then a woman's voice came over the speaker set into his chair.

'Volcano, this is Cygnet, I read you.'

'We're opening fire, keep your people clear.'

'Understood. Be advised that the enemy are already closing.'

'Don't worry, Cygnet, we'll shoot straight. Volcano, out.'

He turned the dial on the radio to switch to the intercom frequency. 'All crews, fire as your guns bear.'

Another artillery round impacted on the armour of the tank with no effect beyond rocking it gently and the commander laughed.

'Keep wasting your ammunition, Berty, old chap!' he crowed. 'Maybe after a hundred more shots you'll have better luck!'

His crew laughed. Their "Pathfinder" tank had been specially designed to be the vanguard of an invasion force. It was encased in incredibly thick armour and had just enough weapons to punch its way through a defensive force, but not so many that it would provide that enemy with weak points to exploit. It was slow and not very manoeuvrable as a result, but it didn't need speed or manoeuvrability, it just needed to keep going. And there was nothing the British had that could stop it. Nothing that they could have moved into place at short notice, anyway.

He bent to peer through the tiny slits in the turret, checking to make sure he was keeping position with the other twenty Pathfinders in his division and was just in time to see the one next to his peel apart like an orange and become engulfed in a hot red fireball as its fuel exploded.

'What was that?' Another explosion came from the other side of the tank and he swung about to look. 'Where is that coming from? Friedrich!' he shouted down to the driver. 'Can you see anything?'

'No!' the call came back.

'Take evasive action!'

The tank began to swing to the side, but it was so slow that it had barely shifted from its course before the high-calibre armour-piercing explosive round struck from almost directly above, killing its crew before they knew they'd been hit, or even where the enemy fire was coming from.

'Come on, Ellie, let's go!' Rob said as he ran from the room.

Ellie took one last look at the door that led out to Airfield Lane, then turned and raced after him.

Tanya had called in. She had made it safely to shore and the army had said they would make sure she got back to London, but, over an hour later, there was still no sign of her.

She sprinted through the hangar and across the apron to Heron and jumped up onto the wing. The Misfits had been called to scramble immediately and there was no time for the niceties of pre-flight checks and she barely had time to strap in and plug in the heater and radio before the others were powering away.

She waved to Sergeant Tonbridge, who gave her the all-clear, then pushed the throttle forwards.

'Four, are you with us?' Abby's voice come over the comms.

'Roger, Leader.'

'Good. Seeing as there's no sign of Tanya yet, you'll move onto Chastity's wing. Sort yourselves out once we're in the air.'

'Understood, Leader.' Chastity acknowledged.

'Roger that, Leader.' Ellie said, frowning slightly and peering back over her shoulder, still hopeful that Tanya would still appear.

Abby had gotten hold of a few spare aircraft for them - two Harridans and two Spitsteams, so that anyone who lost their aircraft would have their pick and be able to get straight back up and Ellie had been fully prepared to hand Heron over to the Muscovite when she arrived and take one of the Spits, despite how much she loved having her own aircraft. Now, though, she was going to have to fly on the wing of someone she barely knew, who barely knew her, and who probably fly very differently to how she was used to. She couldn't say that she was particularly looking forward to the experience.

The first of the Misfit aircraft, Abby and Penny, reached the end of the airstrip and swung around in a wide arc. They didn't slow or stop, but just accelerated immediately, buffeting Ellie and the others in passing. The rest took off in quick succession and Abby turned them to the south-east.

Ellie slotted in behind Chastity's wing in B flight and looked across, but the woman didn't even glance at her, she just continued searching the sky.

'Control, this is Badger Leader, I hear you have business for us?'

'Roger, Badger Leader. We have one hundred plus bandits approaching from the south-east at sea level. Vector one five five at angels five to intercept. Make haste, please.'

'Roger, Control.'

The black haze in the sky had thickened considerably and now covered almost the entire south coast and was visible almost from London. They hadn't been given any update on how the fight was going and they flew in silence towards it at full unwind, wondering what they would find.

They joined up with a couple of other squadrons on the way, one of Spitsteams and one of Harridans. They were both well under strength, though, and together they numbered only two dozen aircraft.

'Oh my stars...' Ellie gasped as the beach finally came into sight.

The situation had changed drastically in only a couple of hours. The Prussians were no longer confined to their ships, they had managed to land. Sinister dark grey boxes were rolling forwards, advancing inexorably on the rows of concrete bunkers protecting the British defenders, while behind them thousands of men were pouring out of dark grey tubes that extended out into the water for hundreds of yards. Ships were docked at the far end of those tubes and feeding them more men, while dozens of others waited their turn, yet others were already steaming away, supposedly to get more men. On both sides guns fired - the big Prussian battle ships in the water pounding the British lines, while the British guns did their utmost to hold back the dark grey advance. Sand and earth flew up into the air everywhere, but the Prussian men and tanks kept coming, just as the ships had, with apparent disregard for their casualties.

The Misfits weren't there to try to turn back the tide, though, and they flew past it, racing to intercept the dark cloud approaching from the south before it could rain fire on the British defence.

'We've just detected a second force of aircraft.' Di Fisher said, hobbling over from the radios. 'They're on a bearing for Dunwich, moving too fast to be bomber escorts and climbing hard.'

Pewtall nodded. 'Warn Volcano, please.'

'Yes, sir. Should we divert some of our fighters to help?'

'No. No need.' Pewtall grinned. 'It's the Fleas who should be asking for help.'

'Here they come.' Sheridan Hawking said.

'That's nice, dear,' his wife answered. 'It's no excuse to bite your nails, though.'

Sheridan pulled his finger from his mouth and stared at it in puzzlement for a moment, as if unsure how it could possibly have gotten there. He shook his head and grinned. 'Of course it isn't, darling. Shall we go and watch?'

He looked around the bridge at the various RAC officers stationed at the multitude of controls, gauges and other things essential to the smooth running of an airship. The only one whose name he could actually remember was the one at the chart and it wasn't as if he had anything to do since they weren't going anywhere at the moment, so he could be spared.

'Uh, Wilkins? Would you mind taking the controls for a while?'

'Sir?' The man looked at him with wide eyes, then nervously eyed the chair Harriet Hawking currently occupied, with its multitude of knobs and levers.

'Oh, don't worry,' Sheridan said, 'it's a doddle.'

'Very well, sir,' the man still looked worried, but the way he strode across the bridge to them betrayed his eagerness.

'Good man!' Sheridan offered his arm to his wife. 'Shall we?'

She linked her arm with his and together they strolled to the observation windows closest to where the attack would be coming from.

'There!' Harriet exclaimed after a moment, pointing slightly upwards and to the side. 'Looks like a few dozen at least.'

Sheridan's eyes weren't as good as his wife's and it took him a few seconds to find the black dots in the sky and even then it was only because they had grown considerably larger in that time. Almost at the same time as he spotted them, he felt a slight vibration through the deck as the air defence batteries fired and the first streaks of light reached out.

'Aren't they firing a bit early?' Harriet asked with a frown.

'We don't have three oh threes or point seven-nines like on a fighter, or even the fifties that bombers carry - we have the same anti-aircraft guns that ground batteries have, with a range of thousands of yards.'

Harriet shrugged. 'I was too busy with the wiring to take any notice of that kind of thing - the guns were your department.'

Sheridan laughed. 'They were my department only in that I asked Wendy to send us her biggest guns. I didn't see them or get to play with them at all, I just saw the specs.'

'Disappointed, Sherry?'

He grinned. 'Maybe just a little - look! There goes the first one! And another.'

The guns were quickly finding their mark, the stable platform of the huge airship making it easy for the gunners.

'And another,' Harriet said, 'look, another!'

There was some return fire from the aircraft now, but it was in desperation and they could see the tracer rounds losing velocity and dropping well short. Several more of the aircraft lost pieces or just fell apart completely and then suddenly they were turning, diving away, unable to face the storm raging around them.

'Well, I'd say the anti-aircraft guns work rather well.' Sheridan said.

'Yes,' Harriet agreed. 'Shame about most of the rest of the ship.'

The deck began to tilt beneath them and she sighed. 'Speaking of...' she turned and ran back to the controls as Wilkins began to cry out in panic.

Sheridan watched for a moment, but then looked back out of the window. They had decided not to fly nearly as high as the airship was designed to, both because they hadn't had a chance to test it, or even turn on most of the systems, but also because the gunners would be more accurate at closer range. However, even from only twenty thousand feet, he could see four Prussian invasion fleets. The attack on Dunwich that they were covering was the northernmost one, but there was another fairly close by, only half a dozen or so miles away to the south and there were two more a bit further away down the coast, on the other side of Felixstowe. While both of the furthest fleets seemed to have been stopped before they'd gotten to shore, it looked like the defenders were having a very bad time of it at the closest one - it was Sizewell or Thorpeness, he wasn't sure which - with the Prussian advance almost at their entrenched positions.

'Get me Sir Douglas on the line!' he called out, turning from the window. 'Tell him we're done here and moving to the next target.'

It's not Chastity, it's me... *no, that just sounds like I'm breaking up with her or something.* I don't think I'm the right fit... *Maybe.* I just don't have the same feeling with Chastity as I do with Tanya. *That's better, but talking about feelings? What is this? Primary school.*

Ellie groaned. She had no idea how to tell Abby that she didn't want to fly on the wing of one of her best pilots.

She was going to have to come up with something soon, though, because they were on final approach to Hyde and, if they were turned around as quickly as they'd been so far that day, she only had about half an hour to say something and for Abby to reorganise the squadron.

The Misfits had taken to landing in flight formations, just as they had the first time they'd arrived, both to save time and to give the best impression they could to the men and women working at the airstrip, and Ellie found herself on the far left of the finger four. That meant she had the best view of their hangar and the woman standing in front of it, looking extremely grumpy, with her arms crossed and a thunderous expression on her face.

Oh, thank the light!

Ellie's position in the formation also meant that she was one of the first to park up in front of the hangar and she handed Heron over to her fitters as quickly as she could, then ran to Tanya. She barrelled into her at near full speed and had the wind knocked out of her when she hit the brick wall that was the Muscovite, but didn't care, she just wrapped her arms around her and held on.

'Hey! That's my job!'

Ellie lifted her head from Tanya's shoulder to find Drake standing nearby, eyebrow raised and smirk firmly in place. She stepped back hurriedly, blushing.

'Sorry!'

He waved for her to continue. 'No, please, it looks like you need her more than I do.' He looked at Tanya. 'See you inside.

He started to walk past them, but Tanya reached out to grab his arm. She pulled him close and looked deep into his eyes. 'Sandwiches. Get me sandwiches.'

Drake lifted his free hand to cup her cheek and smiled. 'You're so romantic, darling.'

He winked and started away, but before he went even a single step, Tanya had pounced on him, spun him around and planted her lips on his. When she finally pulled back, Drake wavered slightly on his feet, then smiled happily and staggered away unsteadily, helped along by a not very gentle kick to his backside from Tanya.

The Muscovite laughed as he skipped away rubbing his behind, but then turned and looked at Ellie thoughtfully, screwing up her eyes and pursing her lips. 'Let me guess. Abby put you with Chastity.'

Ellie blinked at her. 'Yes! How did you know?'

'Because you look like I would if I'd been stuck with her.'

Tanya put her arm around Ellie's shoulder and guided her onto the apron, out of the way of the aircraft being pushed into the hangar.

'Tell me about it,' she said.

Ellie looked around to make sure nobody was within earshot, but still spoke fairly quietly. 'Chastity is a good pilot, great, in fact, but she's so... I don't know...'

'She's boring.'

'No!' Ellie protested, but then grimaced. 'Well... yes. Yes, she is.' She shook her head. 'She's stiff and does everything by the book. It's so different from how we usually fly. There's no freedom...'

'No fun.'

Ellie nodded. 'Exactly! And it just feels so bad.'

'I understand.' Tanya said. 'Chastity is a technical pilot. More like a machine than a person. It works for her because she can make decisions so quickly and carry them out instantly, but we rely more on our instincts to anticipate and on our understanding of our aircraft to beat our enemies.' She put her arm around Ellie again and started walking towards the back of the hangar. 'I will speak to Abby and sort this out, don't worry.'

'Thank you,' Ellie said, relieved. 'I'm sorry about Wolf, by the way.'

Tanya shrugged with her free shoulder. 'She was my second. There will be a third. I'm sure of it.'

'Abby brought in some Harridans and Spitsteams.' Ellie said, pointing her chin at the aircraft lined up at the side of the hangar. 'Would you like to take Heron and I'll fly one of them?'

Tanya shook her head. 'No, I'll take a Harridan,' she grinned at Ellie. 'It'll bring back memories and, besides, having a better aircraft is the only way you're going to score more kills than me.'

CHAPTER 16

Schmidt looked up from the map as the door at the far end of the theatre opened, letting daylight in from the lobby.

'*Weissman!*' he bellowed at the man in the light blue uniform leading the small group that had just arrived down the slight slope towards the stage, 'Get over here! NOW!'

The portly commander of the Fliegertruppe hurried over, his eyes wide in alarm. He huffed and puffed as he climbed the stairs at the side of the stage and was out of breath when he reached Schmidt's desk.

'Yes, Herr...'

'What in heaven's name are your pilots doing?' Schmidt shouted at him, not caring that he sprayed the man with spittle.

'Sir?'

'Against that airship of the British!'

'They were forced to retreat, sir, they couldn't...'

'I don't care how many of them get shot down, send them back! In fact, send everyone!'

Weissman frowned. 'Sir? What do you mean, "everyone"?'

'*Everyone!*' Schmidt bellowed again, making the man reel back.

'But what about our coverage of the invasion forces?'

Schmidt surged out of his chair and confronted the man face to face. 'They can take care of themselves! I want that airship destroyed! I don't care how you do it, just do it!'

'Yes, sir.'

Weissman staggered back a couple of steps, sketched a hasty salute, then waddled away at a run.

Schmidt glared at his back for a moment, then stalked to the front of the stage and gave the map below the same treatment.

The British airship was a complete and utter surprise. None of their spies had known about it and it hadn't shown up in any of the reports sent over by Cummerbund or his associates. It was a surprise that they hadn't planned for and had no answer to. One of the invasion forces had already been as good as destroyed by it, a second was now threatened by it and would likely go the same way as the first, and if the three remaining forces along the south coast couldn't close with the British or find somewhere to dig in and protect themselves, then they would be next.

The invasion might well fail in its first day.

Unless the fools in the Fliegertruppe did their job for once.

'What's happening?' Sir Douglas asked, standing to get a better look at the map. 'Di! Is this correct?'

'One moment, sir!'

Di Fisher was at the radios, scribbling furiously in her notepad, as the operators took call after call from the radar stations. He rushed over to her, but knew better than to interrupt her at work; she would say something when she knew something.

'Call Sheepish,' she instructed one of the operators, 'get him to corroborate.'

'I already have him,' another of the operators said, 'he confirms - the Prussians have turned around.'

Fisher turned to Pewtall, but continued to mutter to herself as she looked at the numbers on her pad. 'It's confirmed, sir,' she said eventually. 'Every single raid has turned back for home.'

Pewtall frowned. 'What does that mean? They can't possibly be giving up, can they?' He thought quickly. 'Get on to the army, find out if their troops are in retreat.'

'Yes, sir.'

Pewtall left her to it and walked back to his desk. He stared down at the map board again. Why would the Prussians turn their raids around? Some of them had been only a couple of miles from their targets. Even if they were retreating from British soil, there would be no reason not to carry out the attacks; it would only serve to better cover their soldiers. There had to be something else...

His eyes strayed to the east, where the large marker for the Hephaestus sat.

Surely not...

The Misfits watched from the armchairs in the middle of the room as Abby spoke to someone in the control office, trying to find out why they'd been ordered back to base. They waited patiently while she yessed and ahah'd and of coursed, but when she slowly put the phone down and started staring into space that patience ran out.

'Uh, Abby, darling!' Penny called out, drawing her attention. 'Would you care to share with the room?'

Abby looked at her, but then immediately turned to Gwen.

'Your parents are apparently swanning about in some giant airship called the Hephaestus, terrorising the Prussians.'

'Hephaestus? Is that what they called it?' She chuckled, shaking her head. 'I bet that was my mother's idea.'

'You knew about it, then?'

Gwen shrugged. 'Not really.'

'Excuse me,' Drake drawled, interrupting them, 'would you mind terribly going back to the whole airship thing and let the rest of us in on the joke?'

'Yes, of course,' Abby walked over and sat on the arm of a sofa, 'The Hawkings showed up over Dunwich beach in a gigantic airship just over an hour ago and in the course of about five minutes managed to completely rout the Prussian forces there. They're currently doing the same to the invasion force on the beach near Thorpeness.'

Abby finished her matter of fact statement quickly and in a rather off-hand manner, then immediately turned back to Gwen. 'You said you didn't really know about the airship. What does that mean?'

'When we were in America I met with Nikola Tesla and he showed me an electrical system he'd designed for my parents that was obviously for some kind of airship. I had no idea they'd be able to incorporate it this quickly.'

'Does this mean we're getting our own Bertha?' Drake asked, sitting forward. 'Because I'm not sure how I would feel about that.'

Gwen shook her head. 'I don't think so. Electricity isn't my thing, but I'm fairly sure there weren't any hangar doors or facilities for aircraft on the wiring design.'

'Good.' Drake said, relaxing back again and reaching out to squeeze Tanya's hand.

'How did they keep something like that secret?' Penny asked.

'Mac.' Abby said quietly. 'I remember Mac going off to speak with them when we had that party at Bagshot, right before going to Muscovy. I'm fairly sure the king was with them. They probably asked if they could use his place up in Scotland.' She smiled sadly. 'I think he would have loved that - having something so completely and utterly, well, *mad*, built there would have tickled him pink.'

There were smiles and chuckles from the Misfits who had known Mac.

'But what has all that got to do with why we got turned around?' Penny asked.

'We got turned around because the Prussians aborted their attacks.' Abby said. 'Sir Douglas believes that they might be planning a raid on the Hephaestus and he wants us to be ready.'

Sheridan stepped back from the spotting scope and smiled at the observation officer. 'Your people are getting the hang of this. Jolly well done!'

'Thank you, sir!'

Sheridan nodded. 'I think we're about ready to move on, aren't we?'

The officer bent to his own scope and looked down. He pulled the magnification levers on the sides and swivelled the apparatus minutely.

'I'd like to put a couple more holes in those piers as we go, but yes, I believe we are, sir.'

'Good, I'll let Sir Douglas...'

'Mr Hawing, sir!' an airwoman came running over from the radios, 'message from Sir Douglas!'

Sheridan smiled at the observation officer. 'Speak of the devil!' he looked back at the airwoman. 'What did he say? If he wants us to move on to the next target, you can tell him we're already on our way.'

'He sent a warning, sir - he thinks there's another attack coming soon. A big one. He thinks the Fleas are going to throw everything but the kitchen sink at us.' She smiled. 'His words, sir.'

'Thank you.' Sheridan nodded at her and returned her smile, but then turned away to look out of the window. He stared into the distance as if he'd be able to see the enemy aircraft coming.

They'd seen off the previous attack quite handily, but there had only been a couple of dozen fighters and they'd come straight at them, not knowing the Hephaestus's capabilities. He doubted they would do that again, and besides, if they sent bombers...

He looked up. The bombers definitely wouldn't attack from the side, they'd go over.

He turned from the window and walked across the bridge to his wife. She was looking increasingly tired and harried as time went by; she had been scheduled to start training men and women to fly Hephaestus two days from now, but that had all gone out of the window when they'd had to launch prematurely - as had much of their labour force when the boarding ramp had stuck closed, actually. Consequently, she was the only one who could control the airship and it wasn't exactly plain sailing with all the problems cropping up.

'Harriet, darling,' he said gently, 'how would you feel about taking us higher?'

She tore her eyes from the instrument panel in front of the controls and looked up at him blankly. It took a moment for his question to register in her mind, further evidence of her exhaustion, but then she nodded.

'I think we can risk it. The batteries aren't charging properly because two of the windmills aren't working, so charge is down to sixty percent, but number three fan is alright now. One of the support struts had come loose, but Hamish has it welded into place.'

Sheridan groaned. 'Why did you say that?'

'Say what?'

'That number three fan is alright... You know you should never say something like that.'

She rolled her eyes and shook her head in exasperation as she turned back to the controls.

It wasn't as if he was superstitious, and she certainly wasn't, but he was a firm believer in not ever tempting fate if you didn't have to, which was why he held his breath as she pointed the fans downwards and gently pushed the throttles forward.

The gentle vibration through the floor increased slowly, becoming a buzz and Sheridan closed his eyes, waiting for something to go wrong.

It didn't, though, and he sighed in relief and smiled. 'Alright, take us to...'

A sudden screeching noise of tearing metal filled the world around them.

'Fan two is losing pressure!'

'Fan three is overloading!'

The shouts from two of the four engineers at the gauges and wheels on the bulkhead at the back of the bridge came simultaneously, making them almost unintelligible, but the message got across.

'Shut down fans two and three!' Harriet shouted, even as she pulled back the levers.

The screeching noise continued, but its pitch was slowly lowering as the fan decelerated, setting everyone's teeth on edge. It lasted for almost a minute before ceasing abruptly as the damaged machinery finally ground to a halt.

'Report.' Sheridan said, leaning over Harriet's chair.

'The two fans we've still got are in opposite corners so she's still relatively stable, but one puff of wind might topple us and we're not going to be gaining height any time soon - she's barely managing to hold on to what we have already.'

'We need to land and carry out repairs.' Sheridan said.

'Sir!' the man at the radio called out, waving to catch his attention.

'What now?' Sheridan muttered as he walked over. 'What is it?'

'It's control, sir. The raid is building and they're definitely coming for us.'

'Drat!' He'd almost forgotten that the whole reason they'd tried to push higher was because of the threat from the Fleas. Now they were going to be a sitting duck.

He ran his hand through his hair as he racked his brain for a plan of action, then grimaced and wiped it on the thigh of his coveralls, which didn't do very much to clean it. He couldn't remember the last time he'd slept, let alone had a shower or a change of clothes. The plan had been to see Hephaestus completed and fully crewed, then leave them and the engineers to do the shakedown cruise while he and Harriet had a couple of days off at the Dorchester so they could take the king up on his invitation and see Gwen.

London...

That was it. Going up wasn't the only way to get to safety.

'You! Uh, Wilkins!' he said, rushing to the map table. 'Set a course to London, I want to get us inside the protection of London's guns as quickly as possible.'

The man found the closest part of the ring of guns around London and drew a line to it before measuring the bearing.

'New course is three two eight, sir, but that's more than seventy miles! If there's a raid building now we'll never make it in time.'

'Not if we just cruise, no.' Sheridan smiled. 'Harriet! Put us on course...' he pointed at the man.

'Three two eight!' the man called out.

'As soon as we're there I want you to angle us down and trade height for speed. Let's see how fast this thing can go!'

They might not get within the protection of the concentric rings of anti-aircraft guns surrounding London before the Prussians arrived, but neither would they be where they were expected to be and that might buy them enough time to do so.

'Will you look at that thing!' Rob said, incredulously as they climbed towards the huge airship.

'She looks like someone sat on a sausage.' Penny remarked.

With only a pair of red lions on the huge vertical rudders at the back to relieve the monotony of its dull silvery-grey paint, the airship did indeed look like a squashed sausage.

'It's big,' Abby said, 'but nowhere near as big as Bertha. What do you reckon, Gwen? Half the length?'

'A bit less, I reckon. But she's flatter as well, and that gondola is a lot smaller. I'd say she has about a tenth of the displacement.'

'What was her name again?' Ellie asked. 'Heffer-something?'

'*Hephaestus*, the ancient Greek god of the forge.' Drake answered.

'Looks more like she should be called *Heffalump*,' Ellie said, thinking back to one of the last books she'd ever read at school.

There was a moment of silence, then everyone burst out laughing.

'Oh, that's a good one!' Abby said. 'I'm sure your father would love that!'

'Why not find out?' Gwen said and there was a click as she switched to an open frequency. 'Volcano, this is Badger Five, do you copy?'

'This is Volcano, we read you,' an unfamiliar and slightly puzzled man answered.

'Get Zeus and Hera on the blower will you?'

'Say again, please, Badger Five, I...'

The man was cut off suddenly and a new voice came on.

'Gwenevere! How are you? *Where* are you?'

'Look out your port side.'

The Misfits were almost level with the airship now and Gwen lifted slightly out of formation and waggled her wings when a face appeared in the windows.

'Good to see you! Excalibur's looking a bit worse for wear, though.'

'All our aircraft are a bit worse for wear, Dad, but we're still flying.'

'Good show! Well, must get back to it. Take care, Gwen. Take care, all of you. And if there's ever anything we can do...'

'Well, Dad, there was one thing...'

'Name it!'

'Badger Four thinks you should change the name of your airship to *Heffalump*.'

Sheridan laughed. 'We will take that under advisement, thank you Badger Four. Heffalump out.'

The Misfits were past the airship now, climbing hard while it dove away. There were several other British fighter squadrons climbing with them, scattered around the sky on every side, all converging on the spot where the Hephaestus had been. The first squadrons to arrive at the rendezvous point at Sizewell had to orbit while they waited for the others to arrive, but everything had been coordinated well and in less than five minutes they were all together and they turned en masse to face the dark cloud on the horizon.

'Where is it?' Reitsch shouted. 'Someone find me that airship!'

The Barons were leading the formation of Prussian fighters and bombers and she had been anticipating an easy victory, shepherding the bombers over the top of the airship and then taking the credit when it was wiped from the sky, but it seemed that the British had anticipated their attack somehow and moved it. It was too slow to have gone far, though.

'Star Five, this is Star *Leader*,' Gruber drawled, piling as much scorn into his voice as he could. 'Enemy airship eleven o'clock low. Range approximately sixty miles. There's the tiny matter of the British fighters in the way before we can attack it, though.'

Reitsch had transmitted over the open channel and Gruber had naturally replied on it, so every Prussian pilot, bomber and gunner in the air with them had heard them and the channel was briefly swamped by cruel chuckles and mocking laughter as some of the men expressed their displeasure with her.

Gruber was as popular as ever with the pilots and still seen as a hero by them. His successes during the early stages of the war greatly overshadowed the recent failures he'd been involved in, especially as those were mostly brushed off as been more due to bad decisions by his superiors than anything he'd done. Those who weren't close to him never got to see how unpleasant he was in private and any reports of it were dismissed as the normal behaviour of a Hollywoodland star and personal friend of the Kaiser. Reitsch, on the other hand, was already deeply disliked. Nobody cared that she had scored so many victories in such a short time, all they saw was what she was doing with the Barons. Even though she hadn't officially taken over the squadron from Gruber, everyone could see that she was intent on forcing him out and they didn't like it one bit.

'I don't care how far into Britain we have to go,' she said angrily over the private channel she shared just with Gruber, 'we're chasing that thing until we catch it. And if anyone dares to turn back before we hit the target I will have them shot. *You* tell them.'

'If you insist.'

Gruber switched back to the open channel and gave the orders, a broad smile on his face.

The RAC intercepted the Fleas ten miles out to sea at thirty thousand feet. With no time to climb above the attackers, the British were forced to make a head-on pass to open the engagement, but they used it to great effect to cull the bombers, taking more than twenty out of commission in that pass alone, either destroyed outright or forced to limp home. Those losses were a drop in the bucket for the Prussians, though, and there were more than three hundred bombers left to continue to Britain in pursuit of the airship. The British paid a heavy price for the tactic, losing almost a dozen of their one hundred and fifty fighters in just those first moments, but, determined to give the Hephaestus as much time to get to safety as possible, they continued to concentrate on the bombers, ignoring the attacks of the Prussian fighters as much as they could.

The Hephaestus, even though it was hurt and running on just two fans, was streamlined and fast. Under normal conditions it would have taken almost an hour for it to cover the seventy-odd miles and get to within the protection of London's guns, but in a steady dive it managed it in only forty, arriving minutes before the Prussian bombers appeared overhead.

The British fighters peeled away from the bombers just as the massive anti-aircraft guns defending the capital of the Kingdom of Great Britain opened fire, immediately taking a toll on the Prussians. They persevered, though, and dropped their payloads, filling the skies with screaming black metal. The only trouble was, everybody had been so occupied by the British fighters that nobody had thought to order the formation to descend to compensate for the fact that the Hephaestus was diving. As a consequence they found themselves not just ten thousand feet higher than the airship, but more than twenty-five thousand feet, which made accurate aiming against a fast-moving target an impossible task.

A grand total of two bombs hit Hephaestus and that was only because one of the bombers had had problems with its drop mechanism and released a few seconds late. The damage they did was negligible and, ultimately, unnecessary, as the damage the airship had done to itself was already enough to take it out of the battle for the foreseeable future, especially if it couldn't get back to the facility in Scotland on its own. The rest of the bombs, numbering in their thousands, fell to the ground and obliterated a couple of farms. Both farms exclusively grew potatoes and the newspapers that night dubbed the Prussian attack "The Mashed Potato Raid".

'They're not like normal bombs; they don't describe a ballistic trajectory. Instead they have fins that are designed to completely stop their forward motion so that they can fall vertically. That means you have to drop a bit... later!'

Wendy punctuated the last word in her explanation by stabbing the bomb release button on the console in front of her. She immediately pulled up and put Dreadnought on her wing so that they could watch the show. By the time the tank they'd targeted came back into view, the smoke from the small explosions had already cleared and gaping holes were starting to appear in the armour. They laughed as the hatches sprang open and the crew clambered out, knocking each other over in the sand in their hurry to get away before the acid reached the ammunition and it exploded.

'Alright, you try.' Wendy said. 'You have control.'

'I have control, ma'am!'

They grinned as they went through the instructor - student ritual; it wasn't necessary and it didn't really apply to their relationship because they were more like partners in the flying of the aircraft than anything else, but they found it funny to do it.

Wendy let go of the controls and turned sideways in the seat to lean comfortably against the side bulkhead, putting her feet up on top of the instrument panel and crossing her arms across her chest as she watched Lottie control Dreadnought.

When the war minister had been removed from office and the king had announced the reforming of Misfit squadron, Abby had come to her and asked her to come back. She'd said no, as had Owen; they had both been given incredibly important roles outside of the squadron that they didn't want to give up and they were also rather enjoying not have to keep worrying if the other was going to be killed. She had offered to give Dreadnought to the squadron, though, and Abby had readily accepted. The only problem was that there was nobody that could fly her because Wendy's previous copilot had gone to a bomber squadron when the Misfits had been disbanded and been shot down on a raid. She had agreed to train someone up to take her place, but on her own terms and outside of the squadron. Abby had agreed, the king had signed off, and Sir Douglas had told Wendy she could have the pick of whoever she wanted.

Wendy hadn't wanted someone who had already flown missions as a bomber pilot because Dreadnought didn't handle like a bomber and would be wasted if flown like one, neither would a fighter pilot be appropriate, as Dreadnought wasn't a one-person aircraft, but had a team that had to work together to get the best results. She had naturally, therefore, looked at the men and women still in the middle of their training - the ones that knew how to fly, but hadn't yet gotten stuck in their ways and weren't too set in either the fighter pilot or bomber pilot mentality.

She'd flown Dreadnought to RAC Gwynedd at lunch time and parked her in front of the ready room buildings. Aviator Lieutenant Pierce, the base adjutant, had then come on board with a list of students and they had sat back to watch, hidden from sight in the darkness of the hull.

Every single one of the student pilots had stopped to look at Dreadnought, as had the instructors, but that was only to be expected seeing as how the aircraft wasn't exactly supposed to be there and was also ridiculously famous. That wasn't what she'd been looking for, though, it was the expressions on their faces that Wendy had wanted to see.

Anyone that showed distaste in any shape or form was immediately crossed off the list. Anyone that showed puzzlement likewise. Anyone that was amazed at the aircraft being there and just acted as if she was something famous to be gawped at or pointed at also got crossed off the list.

It was those few pilots that looked at Dreadnought as if she were the most beautiful thing they'd ever seen that she was interested in.

Those pilots that were desperate to see more, that reached out to touch her as if to touch a lover. Those were the ones she wanted because Flying Dreadnought was a labour of love, something you had to be dedicated to in body and soul - you had to know every inch of her, ever foible, every capability, otherwise you wouldn't get the best out of her and you wouldn't keep your crew alive.

Three pilots had fulfilled those conditions, but two of them had walked away after drinking their fill of the sight. Only one had stayed. Only one had walked around her, forgetting that she had a class to go to. And she was now sitting in the copilot's chair.

She hadn't been able to believe it when Pierce had told her afterwards that Lottie been in the same intake as the three newest Misfits, Eleanor Perkins, Rob Sherborne and Benedict Wilberforce. It had seemed too implausible, too unbelievable, but sometimes these things happened. Never usually to the same extent, but it did happen.

That had been only a week ago and since then the girl had been insatiable in her quest to learn everything she could about Dreadnought and the people who served her. Not only did she already know the systems back to front, enough to build another one, probably, but she handled her as if she'd designed and built her herself. Possibly even better than her designer and builder in fact.

The turn as Lottie brought the massive aircraft back around was tight and precise, Dreadnought's wingtip passing only yards above the heads of the defending British men and women, most of whom looked up as they passed and cheered. She brought the aircraft level again well past the target she was obviously aiming for, but it wasn't a mistake, it was deliberate, designed to confuse the gunners targeting them from the ship still loitering offshore and the small arms fire from the men on the beach. It was another mark of how good a pilot Lottie was; a lesser pilot would have just lined up on the target, making their aircraft easier to pick off.

The tank Lottie was aiming for was stationary, one of those that had dug in and fortified their position in order to cover the men and equipment still coming from one of the Prussian mobile piers. It wasn't an easy target because so little of it was exposed, but it was certainly one of the most important because its elimination would make the job of bringing more material onto the beach that much less secure.

Only when they were seconds away from the tank did Lottie bring Dreadnought level and line up on the tank and Wendy sat up straight and peered over the nose, judging for herself the optimal moment to drop. Even as she twitched her finger, Lottie was pushing the bomb release button on the instrument panel between them and there was a minute vibration through the fuselage as the pods opened, releasing the meltbombs, a vibration that would have been imperceptible to anyone that wasn't so in tune to the aircraft as she was. And apparently as Lottie was, because there was a tiny nod of satisfaction from the big girl as she seemed to feel it too. It was fleeting, though, and then Lottie was pursing her lips as she threw Dreadnought into a sharp turn, coaxing a manoeuvre worthy of a fighter out of an aircraft that definitely wasn't one. There wasn't much return fire, though; this Prussian attack was on its last legs.

'Only three tanks left,' Lottie said, disappointment clear in her voice.

The Prussians had launched four separate attacks on the south coast. This one, at Bournemouth, had been hit hard as soon as it had gotten onto the beach and all but destroyed, but for some reason the last few Prussians left weren't giving up and pulling back. An all-out assault by the RAC to mop them up would have been a waste of resources that were desperately needed on other beaches where the Prussians were making inroads, so Wendy had suggested to Douglas Pewtall that Dreadnought could handle things on her own. He had laughed and told her to have fun and so Dreadnought had the run of the beach and the pick of the targets. It was an ideal situation for Wendy to give Lottie her final training session.

The big girl looked over at Wendy questioningly; usually this would be when she took back the controls. Today was different, though and she waved for the girl to continue.

'You keep her. Take down the last tanks then hit a few ships or something. Have some fun and make sure it looks really good so the boys and girls in the army have a story to tell when they get back to barracks. And don't forget our gunners deserve a bit of the fun too, so swing over their infantry a few times.'

'Yes, ma'am!'

Wendy sat back again and enjoyed the sight and feel of Lottie flying her aircraft. It had been clear from the first moment the big girl had gotten into Dreadnought that the two were made for each other and she couldn't be happier leaving her in her hands.

Lottie swiftly and efficiently used the remaining meltbombs on a couple of ships and did a few passes over the infantry, but ammunition was getting low after that for even the smallest guns and there was no point in staying around and risking being hit by a lucky shot.

'Alright, take us home.' Wendy ordered.

Lottie immediately banked away from the beach, giving orders to the crew to secure the weapons as she did so. She took the time to overfly the British forces again, though, and waggled her wings in salute before turning for home.

'Nicely done,' Wendy said, smiling and looking back at the cheering soldiers. 'Put us on course zero five five and take us up to a thousand feet.'

'Yes, ma'am.' Lottie did as she was told, but then frowned. 'That course will take us to London, ma'am, not to Bletchley.'

'We're not going back to Bletchley, Lottie; it's time you and Dreadnought took your place amongst the Misfits.'

'Yes, ma'am!' Lottie said, grinning wider than ever.

The Misfits were in their ready room when Dreadnought arrived, but she was not unexpected and they immediately came running out to greet her and her crew.

The hangar was easily big enough to accommodate Dreadnought and, after Wendy had told Hyde Control that she'd be sending her ground crew and moving in, the Misfit fitters had made space. Everyone pitched in to push the huge aircraft into place, pilots included, and then the ground crews took the gunners and engineers to the crew room to rest and eat while Lottie and Wendy were all but dragged to the ready room by the Misfits.

'We haven't seen you for a while, where have you been?' Ellie asked Lottie as soon as they were sitting with tea and sandwiches.

'We had to ground Dreadnought for repairs and only just got back into the air.'

'We heard you were hurt,' Rob said, frowning at the cuts on Lottie's face and the bandage that she'd revealed when she'd gingerly taken off her helmet. 'Are you alright?'

'This is nothing,' Lottie told him, gesturing to her face. She grinned. 'You should see the cut on my left boob.'

Rob looked down at her ample chest and she laughed. 'I'm not actually going to show you!'

Ellie smacked Rob on the shoulder and he lifted his eyes and grinned sheepishly.

'So,' Lottie said carefully, looking from one of her friends to the other. 'You two...?'

Ellie shook her head. 'Not yet.'

'Not yet? But...' Lottie asked with a half smile.

Ellie and Rob looked at each other.

'Let's just leave it at "not yet".' Rob said, smiling at Ellie.

The three of them concentrated on eating for a while, hurrying things along somewhat because they knew they wouldn't have long before they would be back in the air. It was only when they were finished and sitting back to finish their tea that Lottie spoke again.

'I was sorry to hear about Benedict,' she said quietly. 'He was a bit of a prat, but he didn't deserve to die and Sandra loved him.'

'No, he didn't.' Rob agreed.

'Does this mean you've changed your mind and you're coming back to us?' Abby asked Wendy as the big woman took an enormous bite of carrot cake to rival Tanya's usual mouthfuls.

While the three newest Misfits had sat at the dining table near the buffet, the rest had gathered around Wendy on the sofas and armchairs and began pestering her.

Wendy shook her head as she chewed. 'No,' she managed to get out. 'Sorry, but no.' She swallowed and took a sip of tea to wash it down before smiling. 'I love you all, but there is no way I'm coming back. I've got my feet firmly back on the ground now. Owen and I have only come back to train our replacements.' She gestured towards where Lottie was sitting with Ellie and Rob. 'We're handing our aircraft over to the next generation and concentrating on our work.'

'I suppose that's fair enough,' Abby said, nodding.

'What are you working on at the moment?' Penny asked.

Wendy grinned. 'Can't say! But if it works it'll make one heck of a big bang!'

'The Hawkings are down safely, but they say they won't be able to fly again until they've completed repairs.'

'How long will that take, did they say?'

'They said weeks, sir.'

Pewtall stared up at Di Fisher, momentarily lost for words, then sighed. 'That's a shame; we could have done with that thing of theirs on the south coast. Make sure Dot informs the king, please. And speaking of which - what's the latest from Whitehall?'

Di Fisher turned the page in her notebook. 'The army report that the invasion force at Bournemouth has been defeated. Dreadnought destroyed the last of the enemy armour and the remaining infantry have laid down their arms. The remaining ships are abandoning the beach and steaming down the coast. The navy thinks they're going to join up with the fleet at Bexhill like the Littlehampton fleet did.'

'Good, then we can cross Bournemouth off our list of targets for now.'

'It seems so, sir.' Fisher said. 'The attack at Bexhill has progressed off the beach, unfortunately, and the enemy have started to form a perimeter to protect further landings. Army spotters report that our most recent attack did a lot of damage to those preparations and inflicted severe casualties among the men, but that we did not have much effect on the armour.'

'Alright.' Pewtall nodded slowly. 'What about Deal?'

'Deal is not looking good. The enemy managed to quickly overrun the defenders and establish their perimeter. They've dug in well and are constantly landing more armour and mobile artillery. So far none of their heaviest armour has made it to shore, but it can only be a matter of time and then they will have sufficient force to put together a column and push inland.'

Pewtall grimaced. 'So, Deal is our main worry for now. What's being done, do you know?'

'Reinforcements, including armour, are being moved from the failed landing sites. They won't arrive before dark, though, and will have to settle for digging in and establishing a cordon around the invaders.'

Pewtall sat up straight at that. 'Am I to assume then, that the king is accepting the fact that the enemy will not be driven back from our shores today? That they will be allowed to remain?'

'Yes, sir.'

'Well,' he said, subsiding back in his chair, his exhaustion suddenly making itself felt, 'we shall have to see if we can make them pay a pretty price for their room and board.' He nodded his thanks to her, smiling wearily. 'Let me know when our girls and boys are ready to go back up, please.'

CHAPTER 17

The Misfits had time to fly one more mission that day. Wendy had been able to rustle up a load of meltrockets for them from somewhere and they took off with Dreadnought as Badger Ten and flew at low level, as fast as the huge aircraft could go, to the beach at Deal. A few Prussian raids were on their way, but they were still building over the continent and the rest of the RAC fighters were being held back to counter them, so they were the only ones in the air. On one hand that was good, because they would have the pick of the targets and wouldn't have to worry about collisions or stepping on other squadrons' toes, but on the other hand it was also extremely bad, because the Prussians had set up half a dozen or so large-calibre anti-aircraft guns on the beach and they were going to be the only targets the enemy had to worry about.

The flat terrain at Deal made it an ideal landing place for the Prussians. Not only could they surge straight up the beach without worrying about being funnelled into gaps in cliffs, like would have been at Dover, but there were little in the way of natural features for the British to use as defensive positions and it wasn't as if the four-hundred-year-old Deal Castle had been designed to provide much protection against modern weapons. As a consequence, the tanks that had formed the Prussian vanguard had met little in the way of resistance. A few of them had temporarily gotten caught up in tank traps or toppled into ditches, but most had pushed straight off the beach and overrun the British positions, forcing them to retreat. They had then spread out in a semicircle and pushed a few hundred yards further, often driving straight through houses and other buildings, that had thankfully been abandoned a few days before, to establish a perimeter. The infantry had immediately followed, streaming from the "iron piers" as they were now becoming known amongst the British, and they brought engineers with them who swiftly constructed concrete bunkers and other fortified positions for a second defensive perimeter, a couple of hundred yards back from the tank, this one comprising large artillery guns. In short order, the Prussians had managed to set up a ring around the landing site and then the real landing had begun. Ship after ship had nosed its way to the beach to unload more and more men and armour until the sand could barely be seen along an entire mile-long stretch because of how crowded it was.

Despite the chaos caused by the severe pounding the ships had taken crossing the channel, Prussian organisational skills were such that a column was well on its way to forming within two hours of the first of the second wave of armour touching the beach and they were almost ready to move out when the Misfits arrived.

'Darwin's beard,' Rob muttered as the beach came in sight, 'that's a lot of Prussians.'

He selected his strongest magnification lenses and panned along the sea front, taking in the thousands of infantrymen drawing up in lines and the various types of enemy armour in evidence. He gaped at the sight of an enormous walker pushing itself up, looking very much like a dog staggering to its feet, then stalking up the beach to join its twin.

'Not really, Eight,' Drake said, grinning across at him. 'There were a lot of them in Muscovy - this is barely a handful.'

'Alright,' Abby said after she'd had a moment to take in the situation. 'So, here's what we're going to do - A flight, we're going to break off and approach parallel to the sea. I want as many of those anti-aircraft guns out of commission as possible before Dreadnought gets there. Ten, you're going to take care of their outer ring of tanks. B flight, you'll go in with her, but I want you to take down those walkers. Once your targets are down, hit the rest of their armour and strafe targets of opportunity. Any questions?'

There weren't any, so after a few moments Abby came back on. 'Alright, then, happy hunting, Badgers. A flight, turn with me.'

Rob lifted his hand to wave to Ellie, but she was already accelerating away with Abby, Penny and Tanya and didn't see. They swiftly grew smaller as they raced of at a tangent and he considered slotting lenses in place to better follow their attack, but then a flash of light, as the anti-aircraft guns finally woke up to the incoming threat, drew his attention away from them. The guns weren't turned towards Dreadnought, though, but towards A flight as they began their run and he urged them on as their noses dipped and fire spouted from beneath their wings. The rockets flew too fast for him to follow, but the results were obvious as relatively small explosions enveloped gun after gun. There were a couple of huge explosions a few moments later as the nasty acid in Wendy's rockets found munitions stacks, sending men and equipment flying, but those were isolated cases, due to luck rather than anything else and the real measure of A flight's success was that the guns fell silent one after the other. They weren't able to knock all of them out in one pass, though, and at least half of them turned towards Dreadnought and B flight as they approached. Streams of tracer rounds reached out towards them and they began bobbing and weaving sharply to confuse the gunners, but Dreadnought was such a big target that she couldn't avoid the fire completely and pieces flew from her wing.

'Looks like this is where I leave you, Five,' Lottie said. 'See you on the other side.'

'Happy hunting, Ten.' Gwen answered.

Dreadnought suddenly dipped, diving for the floor, and Rob's breath hitched, thinking she'd been hit, but almost as soon as her nose went down it came back up again and she levelled off only a few dozen yards from the ground.

Rob shook his head in admiration for his friend's control of the surprisingly agile aircraft, but then turned his attention to the targets on the beach.

'Seven, Eight, get those two walkers that just landed. We've got the other two.'

'Roger, Five.' Drake answered. 'See them, Eight?'

'Yes, Seven.' Rob turned with Drake as they banked slightly, lining up on the machines that had just been unloaded onto the shoreline. There was black smoke streaming from grills in the back of them as their engines started to warm up, but there was not yet any sign that they were ready to extend their legs and move.

The two of them sideslipped as a couple of the anti-aircraft guns homed in on them, fooling them into thinking they were going one way while in reality they were going a slightly different way, but they couldn't fire like that, so when they got within range they straightened up and dropped their noses towards the first of the walkers. Rob released his rockets and saw a flash out of the corner of his eye as Drake did the same almost simultaneously and he adjusted his course to target the second machine, but before he could fire his aircraft was thrown up onto its wing and tossed skywards. Rob's head was flung sideways with the unexpected and abrupt movement and there was a sudden pain in his neck, but he had no time to worry about that, or even to really acknowledge it, because his aircraft was sliding back towards the ground, her nose already well below the horizon. He kicked a leg forward, applying rudder to stop the slip and put the stick over in an attempt to get back to level, but his aircraft was sluggish to reply and a quick glance out the side showed him why - almost half of his left wing was missing, including the aileron.

He was dangerously low, only a couple of dozen yards from the ground, when he eventually managed to get the nose back to the horizon and his wings level.

'You alright there, Eight?'

Drake pulled up onto his wing, but Rob barely spared him a glance; he was too busy fighting with the controls.

'Oh, I'm wonderful,' he said, his voice sounding weak in his own ears. 'I think I might have to wander on home, though.'

'Don't be silly. They've reopened Hawkinge. Go there; it's just down the coast a bit, only a few minutes away. Heading, uh, two four zero ish.'

'Roger that.'

'Got to leave you, Rob; I still have a job to do. Take care and don't forget to jettison those rockets as soon as possible; who knows what kind of damage they've taken and you don't want acid eating through any more of your bird - she's ventilated enough.'

Rob laughed, but then gritted his teeth and hissed as pain shot through his neck and shoulder - he must really have wrenched something when he'd gotten hit. He lifted a hand to Drake and watched as the luridly coloured aircraft banked sharply away, back towards the invasion fleet.

The impact had thrown him off the course he'd been on, but Rob didn't need to look at his compass to know which way he was going - the coastline at this point ran almost directly north to south - so he pushed the stick over to turn west. Once again, his aircraft was extremely reluctant to obey his commands and he found that he was as good as following the land as it gently bent around. That was reassuring, because it meant that he couldn't possibly get lost, Hawkinge being not too far from the coast, but it did bring with it new dangers, namely the white cliffs that were rising up in front of him and the blocky form of Dover Castle on top of them, quite a way above him.

He gingerly let the aircraft bank slightly away from the land, but almost lost control for a moment and had to wrench the stick back the other way to stop her from corkscrewing into the sea. It was just enough, though, and the chalk face zipped by only feet from his wing. He thought he saw faces gawking out at him from a hole in the cliff as he flashed by and got the vague impression that he recognised one of them, but he knew that was impossible and put it down to seeing things due to shock.

As soon as he was out of danger, he put Finch into a gentle climb that took him above the cliffs and when he was past the castle he once again persuaded his aircraft to turn. If his recall of the map was correct, Hawkinge was only half a dozen miles due west of Dover and it was time to give them a call.

'Uh...' he started, but stopped when he realised he couldn't remember the callsign for Hawkinge. 'Uh, Hawkinge Control?' he tried, 'this is Badger, uh, Badger.... Eight? Emergency.'

'Badger Eight, this is Lumba control. What is the nature of your emergency?'

'Lumba, that's it,' he muttered, 'darn silly name...' He winced when he realised he'd spoken aloud and had to bite his lip to stop himself giggling, 'uh... I'm a bit shot up. Just had a bit of a run in with the folks at Deal and going to be with you very shortly.'

'Understood, Badger Eight. We have you in sight. You are clear to land.'

'That's jolly nice of you, thank you.'

The airfield was in sight now, only a few miles away and Rob blinked rapidly, trying to focus on it. There was a smart looking line of fighters down the left side of the large field, in front of a few hangars, but the rest of it was nice and clear and looked extremely inviting.

Acting more on instinct than anything, Rob throttled back and put down his gear. Thankfully he still had flaps on both wings and a quick glance told him that they still worked, but he had no idea whether or not his gear was down. He assumed someone would say something if it wasn't, so he just kept descending.

He was starting to feel rather faint now and for some reason he was losing his connection with his hands and feet. His eyelids drooped and his head tilted forwards, but then pain was shooting through him as his neck protested and he giggled when he realised that he'd actually started to nod off - yes, he was more tired than he'd ever been in his life, but now wasn't exactly the time for a nap!

The pain had cleared his head somewhat, bringing the world back into focus and he guided his aircraft down the last few hundred feet. He pulled off a perfect three-point landing and smiled in satisfaction as he cut the throttle; Abby always said that they should make a good impression whenever they went anywhere. To keep up morale or something.

Rob was still smiling when he passed out from blood loss and slumped sideways in his seat. The excellent landing he'd made was spoiled somewhat as his aircraft, unchecked because he hadn't applied the brakes before falling unconscious, ran straight across the perimeter track and into the fence, which finally brought it to a halt with minimal damage and fuss.

Schmidt sat on the edge of his desk, his arms crossed over his chest, uncaring that he was creasing his uniform, and stared down at the map on the floor below, at what remained of his plan.

Twenty percent of the navy's vessels had been sunk. Another ten percent would need significant repairs before it would be useful again.

Fully thirty percent of the Fliegertruppe's aircraft destroyed and five percent more grounded, possibly permanently.

And he didn't want to think about what kind of casualties had been suffered among the men of the invasion force.

Of the nine invasion beaches he'd chosen, only six had been real attacks and he had fully expected at least a couple of them to fail, but not four. And now the last two were running into trouble.

He scrubbed his hands over his face. The day had been just one setback after another, one mistake by incompetents after another.

Helmuth von Moltke, a great Prussian strategist, had said that no plan survives contact with the enemy, but it had become quite clear that things had been falling apart even before the invasion fleet had gotten to grips with the enemy and that his plan had been deeply flawed to begin with. That was no fault of his own, though; his plan had relied on information that had turned out to be just so much propaganda and lies. Britain was supposed to have been already as good as a defeated nation, with morale at its lowest point due to the war minister's manipulation and the army barely able to fight as a consequence. However, not only was that not the case, but the Royal Aviator Corps had turned out to have far more aircraft than they were supposed to. On top of that, nobody had seen fit to tell him about the acid-filled weapons that the Misfits had used against his ships and tanks, even though half his men had apparently seen them in use before! And how in Goethe's name had nobody even caught a sniff of that stupid airship!

And then, to cap it all off, there had been the fiasco with the minefields. Heads would roll in the intelligence services for that, he would make sure of it.

He found he was panting and snarling, his hands clenching and clutching at his uniform jacket under his armpits and his teeth grinding painfully. He forced himself to relax, then pushed himself to his feet and went back around the desk and flopped down in his chair.

All was not lost yet, though. While the invasion would have been accomplished extremely easily if four or five of the invasion fleets had accomplished their objectives, two was more than enough. A single beachhead would be enough, in fact, to ensure victory and the conquest of the British Isles. However, if neither managed to hold overnight then the failure would be absolute. Blame would fall firmly on him, no matter who was really to blame, and it was extremely doubtful that he would get a chance to redeem himself.

It was of the utmost importance, therefore, that those beachheads were protected. Fortunately, plans were already in place to do just that, these ones not dependent on faulty intelligence, but on the daring and skill of the men directly involved.

'What's happening?' Sir Douglas asked, standing and moving around his desk to look down at the Prussian markers that had been pushed out onto the table, already almost half way across the channel. With the sun down and the light almost gone he'd thought that they were done for the day, but apparently the enemy had other ideas. 'Di! Why are we only seeing them now?'

'One moment, sir!' Di Fisher called out. As soon as the contacts had been reported she had rushed to the radios to get reports from the radar operators.

Pewtall watched the men and women down below rushing to add more markers as the raids, or whatever they were, spread out as they approached the south coast. Di Fisher was hurrying towards him, but he didn't need her to tell him what was happening, he already knew.

'Scramble fighters!' he ordered. 'But first get on to all the radar installations and tell them to get to the shelters! And order Sheepish Squadron into the air!'

Fisher didn't acknowledge beyond a nod, she just spun on her heel and started shouting orders at the radio operators.

He looked back down at the steadily advancing markers.

He knew what they were doing, but not why.

Why would they knock out the radar towers again if the invasion was already on British shores and the battle in the air was as good as irrelevant?

CHAPTER 18

29th August 1941

'Two minutes.' Scarlet said, peering at the luminescent dial of her chronograph. 'Everyone get ready. Remember - go on the first explosions, not on the sound of the aircraft.'

The agents listening to her transmission knew better than to reply and she didn't need them to do so to know that they'd be in position and hadn't needed her warning. She'd done it because she knew that, at moments like these, just before diving face first into mortal danger, nobody liked to feel alone and she'd thought a gentle reminder that they weren't would be a good idea.

She also rather liked the sound of her own voice giving commands and didn't get to give them nearly enough.

Two minutes was just enough time to complete her most important preparation and she unclipped the thigh pocket of her sneak suit and brought out a matte black oblong-shaped canister. She carefully unscrewed it, releasing pungent fumes from the liquid inside and, as soon as she heard the engines of the approaching RAC bombers, carrying out their second raid of the night at precisely the scheduled time of ten minutes past two, she put it to her mouth and tipped its base to the sky. She smacked her lips as she brought it back down and smiled up into the darkness.

'Give them what for!' she whispered, then screwed the top back on the flask, stowed it in her pocket, stifled a belch and, as soon as the first explosions sounded among the men and equipment on the beach, moved forward towards the Prussian lines.

It was the smell that brought Rob floating back from the darkness of oblivion - an irritating mix of antiseptic and willow bark that brought back the memory of the time he'd slipped from the roof of Tayler's house and woken up in the village sanatorium. The smell was irritating and he snorted, twitching his nose, trying to rid himself of it, but it persisted. He tried to lift his hand to swipe it across his nose, but his arm wouldn't move. However, the pain caused by the effort finished the job the smell had begun and brought him the rest of the way to wakefulness.

He moaned and opened his eyes, but he barely had time to focus on anything before a face appeared in his vision.

'Rob. How are you feeling?'

'Ellie?' He blinked up at her. 'What are you doing in my room? Did we...?' He stopped and peered around. 'Wait, this isn't my room. Where am I? What happened?' He frowned at the bottles with dark red liquid hanging over him. 'I thought I got down fine.'

'You're in the medical centre at Hawkinge. You were hurt when your aircraft got hit.'

'No.' Rob tried to shake his head, but found that it was being held in place. 'I can't move!' He tried to look out of the corner of his eyes to see what was wrong, but couldn't.

'Shh!' Ellie said, putting her hand on his chest. 'There's no need to worry, you're going to be fine. The doctors just had to immobilise you completely so that you couldn't undo their work, that's all.'

She carefully sat down on the bed next to him and he felt her take his hand.

'I don't remember getting hurt.' Rob said.

Ellie nodded. 'The doctors said that whatever cut you must have been extremely sharp and that you might actually not have noticed if you got banged around at the same time.'

Rob thought back. 'When I got hit I was thrown sideways. I thought I'd hurt the muscles in my neck. I guess it was a bit more than that. But if I just had a cut, then why am I like this? Why did I pass out?'

'It was a bad cut.' Ellie said. 'Not deep, but in a really bad place and you lost a lot of blood. They said the only thing that kept you alive was that your flightsuit was so tight, actually; it stopped you from losing the blood too quickly.'

'Thank you, Lord Drake!'

Ellie nodded. 'We owe him a lot.'

Rob smiled. 'Yes. Mine saves my life and yours gives me something to think about when I'm alone at night.'

Ellie blushed, but smiled back at him. 'I think you're feverish; you're talking nonsense.'

Rob squeezed her hand. 'You know I'm not, but anyway, what did I miss?'

'Not a lot.' Ellie shrugged. 'We destroyed a few tanks, melted a few guns, strafed a few hundred infantry. Same as always.'

'Sounds boring. I'm glad I missed it.'

Ellie laughed, but then she grimaced and looked down.

'What's wrong?' Rob asked.

'Nothing.' Ellie answered quickly, but then sighed. 'Well, everything, actually.' She looked at him. 'It's this whole situation.'

'The invasion?'

'Yes.'

'I think everybody's worried about that.'

Ellie nodded slowly. 'Yes, I know... but not everybody can do something about it like we can.'

'And we are.'

'Yes. But not enough. I've lost count of the number of aircraft I've shot down, the number of tanks I've destroyed, the number of men I've...' her voice caught and she coughed.

'Killed?' he asked softly.

She nodded. 'And it never seems enough. There are always ten more men, ten more tanks, ten more aircraft to replace whatever I do. Whatever *we* do. I don't know how we can beat that.'

'It can't last forever.' Rob said. 'The Prussians don't have unlimited men and machines, even though it seems they do. At some point they'll run out. We just have to keep fighting and not give up before they do.'

'I suppose. We managed to knock out all their walkers and enough of their tanks to keep them from getting off the beach at Deal. At least for today. So it's not as if it's impossible to beat them, it's just hard to see an end.' She grinned. 'And of course I'm not giving up! I've only just become a Misfit and I want to enjoy it for a while - I don't think the Prussians would let me if they took over the country.'

'They might let you become a Baron - they already have one woman, why not two?'

Ellie made a face. 'No thank you! Can you imagine having to take orders from Hans Gruber!'

'You don't think he's handsome, then?' Rob asked slyly.

'Urgh!' Ellie shuddered. 'Not at all! I saw a couple of his flyvies when I was young and always thought he was a bit slimy.'

'You prefer nice British boys, then?'

'Of course!'

'Like me?'

'Exactly!' Ellie said, then reddened when she realised what she had said. 'No! I mean... Yes, but...'

Rob laughed, silencing her. 'I'm just teasing. But, yes, I much prefer British girls over Prussian ones as well.'

They smiled at each other for a moment, but when the silence dragged on and started to become a bit awkward Rob changed the subject. 'So, how long was I unconscious for? And how come you're here and not at Hyde?'

'Abby gave me permission to land here rather than going back to London. I'll take off from here tomorrow and join up with the others in the air. And as for how long you were out...' Ellie checked her chronograph. 'It's coming up for three in the morning now, so...'

'Three!' Rob exclaimed. 'You shouldn't be prattling on with me, you should be asleep, resting, otherwise you'll get hurt tomorrow! I mean, today!'

Ellie shrugged. 'I'll be a little tired, yes, but better that than sick with worry about you, don't you think?' she gestured at something beside the bed that he couldn't see. 'Besides, I've got a reclining chair that's actually pretty comfortable and I'd been dozing for a few hours before you woke up.'

'Oh,' Rob said, somewhat mollified. 'That's alright then. But you need to go and get some proper sleep.' He found himself yawning at the thought. He tried to cover his mouth with his hand, but couldn't and grimaced. 'Sorry about that, my breath must be ghastly.'

'Yes. Yes, it is.' Ellie said, grinning widely. 'But I don't mind.' She reached out to stroke his cheek. 'They've already given me a room down the hall, I'll go there when you're asleep.'

'I don't think I'll...' he yawned again, stopping his protest in its tracks and he huffed. 'Alright, I guess I will be able to...'

He was cut off by shouts and the sound of someone in heavy boots clomping down the hall outside and Ellie jolted as the door slammed open and a young airman burst in.

'Ma'am! The base commander has ordered all pilots to evacuate their aircraft!'

'Right now? In the dark?'

'Yes, ma'am. The Prussians are coming. You have to get to your aircraft right away!'

The man turned to go, but Ellie called out to him. 'What about the injured?'

The man looked at her, then at Rob. 'I don't know, ma'am. Sorry.'

He ran away, obviously with more jobs to do, and Ellie looked down at Rob.

'I'm not leaving you.'

'Don't be silly,' Rob said. 'If you stay you'll be captured. If you go now you'll have a lovely night flight, but, more importantly, you'll still be able to fight.'

Ellie stared at him for a moment, torn between common sense and what her heart was telling her to do, but then nodded when she realised he was right. 'I'm sorry.' She bent down to kiss him, lingering a few seconds before pulling back. 'I love you.'

She stood, grabbed her things from the table by her chair, then ran, not looking back in case her determination failed.

Rob could just about see the door from his position and he stared after her. 'What was that?' he called after a few seconds, as loudly as he could, 'what did you say?'

He strained his ears, waiting for an answer, but Ellie was too far to hear and after a moment he gave up and just lay there, grinning at the ceiling.

Ellie ran to the end of the corridor, went through the blackout curtains and out into the night. Not wanting to run around an unfamiliar airfield blind, she stopped a couple of steps from the door and blinked rapidly to get her eyes accustomed to the dark.

'Ma'am?'

Ellie jolted, almost screaming as the voice came from right beside her. She peered into the black and eventually found a shadow that was deeper than the others.

'Yes?' she said, after taking a deep breath to calm her racing heart.

'I've come to take you to your aircraft, ma'am. This way.'

'What way? I can't see...'

'Got you covered, ma'am'

The man shone something down at the ground and a small pool of very faint red light appeared around his feet.

Ellie followed him at a jog along a path then around what she was fairly sure was the perimeter track. Her aircraft was parked at the end of a line of Spitsteams that were all being prepared to take off and her guide handed her off to a fitter.

'She's been rewound ma'am, but we haven't gotten around to rearming her yet, sorry.'

'No matter, er,' she looked at the stripes on the woman's arm, 'corporal. Thank you for taking care of her.'

'A pleasure, ma'am.' The woman saluted, then used another red torch to light Ellie's way up onto the wing and into the cockpit.

'Any idea what this is all about?' Ellie asked as she was strapping in.

'Not a clue, ma'am.' The fitter patted Ellie on the shoulder. 'Chocks are already gone, ma'am. You're on your own now.'

'Thank you!' Ellie called out, but the woman was already gone, jumping down from the wing and disappearing into the darkness.

Ellie had never flown at night time, or in the dark, so she barely knew what to expect. Her instrument panel had lit up faintly when she'd powered up the aircraft - something she hadn't actually known that it did - and she checked it quickly, then turned on her radio.

'Lumba control, this is Badger Four, requesting permission to taxi.'

'Badger Four, the airfield is empty, you are cleared for immediate takeoff. Hyde is expecting you. Vector three two five and contact them when close. Safe journey. Lumba out.'

'Thank you, Lumba. Badger Four taking off.'

Ellie peered out around Heron's nose, expecting a fitter to be there to guide her out and make sure she didn't hit anything, but the woman had told her she was on her own and true to her word there was nobody there. It was quite unnerving, but she couldn't dither around, worrying about it; she'd told Lumba she was going and she had to get clear before anyone else asked to use the airfield.

Cracking the throttle, she gingerly moved forward, judging when she would be clear of the other aircraft, then, picturing the layout of the base from memory, she turned slightly to point in what was her best guess for directly across the airfield. She took a deep breath, aimed a quick curse at the Prussians for putting her in such a ridiculously dangerous predicament, then pushed the throttle firmly forwards.

There was nothing to see outside and no reference to work from, so she kept her eyes on the instruments, using the compass to make sure that she kept going straight and watching the airspeed indicator needle climb. The moment it got high enough she brought the stick back and climbed hard. Only when she was a few hundred feet up and sure she was safe did she release the breath she'd been holding.

'Lumba control, Badger Four is clear. Thank you for your hospitality and good luck.'

Ellie wasn't expecting a reply and didn't get one; local control was far too busy to take much notice of her.

With the sky to herself she turned to heading three two five and settled in for the short flight to London, hoping that they were expecting her and that someone would remember to turn the lights on.

Moments later she cried out as blindingly bright white light filled the world around her. She screwed her eyes up and shaded them with her glove until she could see again, then stared, awestruck at the sight of hundreds of Prussian aircraft being picked out in the beams of dozens of searchlights. As she watched, dark clouds blossomed around them as the British guns opened up and a few fell, but the rest continued regardless and black dots began to tumble from them in droves.

'The last of the company commanders has reported in, sir,' an aide said, bringing over another slip of paper and placing it with the others on Schmidt's desk. 'They too have taken their objective.'

'Excellent!' Schmidt said, rubbing his hands together gleefully and gazed down at the new map table he'd had specially constructed for that night's operation. Showing only the south-east of England, it was at a very large scale so that the position of each company of the twenty-thousand elite glidewing troopers he had sent over the channel a few hours before could be displayed as accurately as possible. There were purple markers on it now, each signifying a squad of one hundred troopers, and he took a moment to admire the smart, perfectly-planned and plotted lines they formed. The line to the west was a rough semicircle, about ten miles in diameter, around the beach at Bexhill, while the other formed a line that completely sectioned off the entire south-eastern point of Britain, from just west of Dover to a small village called Birchington-on-sea, with Deal at its centre.

The British had been taken completely by surprise by that night's operation. There had been no effort to intercept the transport aircraft in the air and losses to anti-aircraft fire had been less than he'd expected. The troops had then been almost unmolested during their landing, had been all but unopposed during the short advance to their targets and had found few defenders when they arrived, with the sole exception of at Dover Castle, where the five companies had faced heavy resistance but overcome it rapidly and with minimal losses. In far less time than he'd expected, in even his most optimistic projections, they were now all exactly where he had planned for them to be and controlled every single one of the strategic objectives that he had given them.

The operation was an unprecedented success and with the glidewing troops in place the invasion could no longer be stopped. The routes that the invasion armies would take from the beaches were secured and there was no longer anywhere that they could be bottled up and delayed, exposed to air attacks, and the British soldiers that had been sent to defend the beaches would now be caught between the two forces and crushed.

Schmidt allowed himself one last, self-satisfied smile, then finally lifted his head from the map and signalled the stewards he'd had waiting. The men around him jumped at the sudden sound of corks popping and he laughed, feeling a little giddy with anticipation of the success to come.

'Gentlemen!' Schmidt called out as one of the white-jacketed stewards handed him a glass of champagne. 'The British have committed too many of their limited resources to surrounding the beaches and tomorrow morning, after they are crushed between the hammer of our invasion forces and the anvil of the glidewing troops, the Kingdom of Great Britain will be left completely exposed. Within the day we will move on London and I fully expect to be in Whitehall the morning of the day after!' He raised his glass. 'To victory!'

Schmidt drained his drink while his men roared their approval and he smiled at them avuncularly as the steward refilled it. He savoured the second glass while he watched Weissman, the fat Fliegertruppe commander talking animatedly to Weber, the foppish aristocrat commander of the Reichsflotte. He sneered, covered by the rim of the glass; neither of the incompetent fools could spoil things now, their mistakes and failures could no longer affect the outcome of the battle; neither of them had had any hand in the planning of this operation, it had been his and his alone. And now, with the overwhelming success of the glidewing troops - the ace that he'd been keeping up his sleeve the whole time - the invasion could no longer be stopped. In a single stroke he had single-handedly won the war.

He never thought to wonder why so little resistance had been met by the glidewing troops or, more importantly, why there wasn't even a whiff of a counter attack from the British reserves.

The RAC bombers attacked both beaches at half past four in the morning, their third such raid of the night. Once again, their simple objective of doing what damage they could to the men and machines and making sure that the invaders didn't get any rest was only secondary; the main purpose of the raid was, in fact, to provide cover for what was happening on the ground.

The members of the Tactical Air Squadron detonated the explosives they'd planted as the first bombs landed among the Prussian forces and the explosions that destroyed almost all of the remaining tanks and artillery forming the perimeter around the beach blended in perfectly with them. The tanks of the British army surged forwards before the debris had even come back to earth, sweeping away what few men and machines were left and had covered the distance to the beach before the Prussians there were any the wiser. Sunfire shells illuminated the night over the Prussians as the bombers retreated, further disorienting them, and casualties in just the first moments of the attack were high. A defence was organised, but by then it was too late and, when the British infantry poured in after their armour, the Prussians were left with only two choices - attempt to swim out to their ships, or surrender.

CHAPTER 19

When the Prussians had converted the theatre into Schmidt's command centre they had turned the main dressing room, directly behind the stage, into a place for him to rest, complete with a bed and small dining table. He had retired there soon after giving his toast and had eaten something, then went to bed, intending to snatch a couple of hours sleep before the assault began at first light. However, his head had barely touched the pillow when a messenger burst into the room and turned on the light before rushing across the room.

'Herr Generalfeldmarschall!'

Schmidt groaned, but sat up quickly, blinking in the sudden light. 'Is it time already?'

'No, Herr Generalfeldmarschall, you are needed for something else.'

Schmidt looked up at the man's face, noted the alarm and fear there, and pushed himself to the door.

'Report!' he bellowed as soon as he came out of the corridor and strode onto the stage.

Most of the officers had gone, including Weber and Weissman, back to their billets and quarters, and there was only his efficient night crew left. None of them said anything to him, though, they just stood at the edge of the stage, staring down at the main map table. Rather than insist that someone answer him, Schmidt thought it would be easier and quicker to do it himself, so he pushed his way through the men with a snarl and looked down at the map.

'Where did those come from?' he asked incredulously as he took in the multitude of green British army markers mixed in with the grey Prussian ones on and around the two beaches. 'Tell our troops...' he began, but then stopped as the men servicing the map swept every single one of the grey markers off the coast of Britain, leaving just the ships of the shore and the glidewing troopers still in their positions.

'Get me confirmation of this.' He said quietly. None of his men moved, though, they just continued to stare at the map. 'Now!' he shouted, grabbing the nearest man roughly by the collar and shoving him in the direction of the radios.

The man only just managed to catch himself before he fell and staggered to the side of the stage.

He came back moments later. 'It's confirmed, sir. We have separate reports from the captains of a few ships, corroborating the earlier reports from the commanders of the land forces.'

Schmidt stumbled to his chair and sat down heavily.

There were more troops on the ships. A lot of them. They had been prepared to disembark at first light, so that they could follow the advance, but they were mostly light infantry to consolidate positions, sappers to destroy enemy fortifications and engineers to rebuild them - more supporting forces than conquering forces. There was also armour, not the least of which were two dozen *Goethe* tanks and half a dozen more *All Terrain Armoured Walkers*, but there were none of the Pathfinder heavy tanks that had made the breech in the first place. There was nothing, therefore, that could replace what had just been lost and with the British now holding the beaches another landing in the same place would be almost impossible. Added to that was the fact that, as soon as it was light, his ships would start to come under concentrated attack once more from the land and air.

There was nothing else for it. Only one decision he could make. It was inescapable.

'General retreat.' Schmidt ordered softly. 'Bring everyone back. Get our fighters in the air to cover them and send the bombers to hit the British on the beaches.'

The man blinked at him. 'Yes, sir, but what about the glidewing troopers?'

Schmidt shrugged. 'There is nothing we can do for them. They will have to fend for themselves.'

Things had seemed crowded at twenty or thirty thousand feet, with hundreds of aircraft from both sides trying to occupy the same piece of sky, but at least they'd been able to go either up or down if they'd chosen. At less than one thousand feet, with the sea right below, it was another matter entirely, and things were downright claustrophobic. With bombers from both sides crossing past each other to hit targets adjacent to each other and the escorts of both fleets trying to stop them, the skies over Deal and Bexhill were utter chaos.

Dreadnought banked and swooped through the smoke and fire over Bexhill, raining destruction down on the Prussian ships while remaining untouched by the fire of the Prussian fighters that inevitably tried to take her down. Due, in large part, to her escort of Misfits, but also to the skill of her new pilot.

Wendy Llewellyn had been a more than capable pilot, but she had never had any formal training as a combat pilot. She had obtained her pilot's degree as a private citizen and after being recruited by Abby had gone straight into the Misfits with no further training, except on the job, so to speak. Her knowledge of the aircraft she had built had filled in the gaps in her abilities admirably, but Lottie had had an instinctive understanding of the aircraft since the first moment she'd flown it and, when combined with weeks of intense training as a combat pilot, it made her a much more than qualified replacement.

Lottie swiftly unloaded her cargo of meltbombs, causing almost as much destruction single-handedly with the specialist weapons as the entirety of the RAC's bomber force, however, even though she wasn't taking much damage, she didn't hang around to allow her gunners to continue their work, opting instead to return to base to rearm and return with another load. By that time, the bombers of both sides had also long since dropped their payloads and gone home, but the two fighter groups lingered, knowing full well that if one side left before the other it would leave their ground and sea forces open to strafing attacks.

As soon as Dreadnought was clear of the battlefield, the Misfits were free to join the other fighters. Abby had been searching the sky around them and as soon as Lottie was clear and out of danger she led the Misfits around the seaward edge of the sprawling aerial fight, climbing as they went. It would take them almost a minute to get where she wanted them to be, so, as they went, she made them report on their condition. Everyone was good for spring tension, but, unsurprisingly, nobody had more than half their ammunition left. Hopefully the enemy would be worse off than them in both regards, though.

'Leader, this is Three - Misfits! Approaching fast!'

There was fear in the man's voice and Gruber found that he didn't blame him; he didn't particularly feel like facing the Misfits either. Not under these circumstances, anyway. The Barons were not what they once were. Their aircraft had been replaced by MU9s - the last of the Blutsaugers had become unserviceable a couple of days ago - and the pilots... well, they'd gone through so many of them that elite pilots were a bit thin on the ground now and he couldn't trust any of them to have his wing or his six. Especially not Reitsch.

'Alright, disengage,' he ordered. 'We've done enough. Let's head for home.'

'I'm not sure you're going to be able to run away with your tail between your legs this time, Leader.'

Reitsch's voice was filled with scorn and, as always it grated on his nerves. He usually disregarded what she said because she never usually had anything important or relevant to say - it was always just a criticism of him. This time, something told him he shouldn't do that and instinct had him craning his neck to look back over his left shoulder, towards the sea.

The Misfits had come around the fight for some reason instead of directly at them and, not only were they between him and safety, but, because the fight was taking place at such a low level, there was no way he could dive away.

There was no other choice but to fight.

Reitsch watched the Misfits racing towards them out of the corner of her eye as she took her flight up and round and into a clear part of the sky.

The pilots of the Fliegertruppe thought that she was pushing Gruber out of the squadron, and, to a certain extent, they were right, but the reality was that he had never really been very interested in running it, beyond making sure that he got the best of everything and, consequently, remained as safe as possible. He fought back a little in public, making his displeasure known, but she was fairly sure that was more to keep up pretences than from any real desire to get the squadron back and in private he left her to run things while he drank and ate and did whatever he did in his room with the girls from the local towns he had brought in his personal autocar.

All of which meant that she had plenty of room to prepare the way for when she became the true leader of the squadron. It had been a simple matter to find the best pilots that were still available and place them in her own flight. Similarly, she had gotten them the latest model MU9s, weeks before the line squadrons would receive them - MU9s that were actually quite a bit better than the old Blutsaugers that Gruber had insisted on still using. And while Gruber had been off doing his own thing each fight for the last few days - mostly staying out of the way of any danger and picking on isolated targets - she had been training those new pilots. As a result, her flight was competent and efficient, true Crimson Barons, and she was confident that they could at least hold off the rest of the Misfits while she dealt with whoever came after her.

She smiled when the Misfits split into two groups to take on the two flights of Barons; the leader of the flight coming her way was flying a very distinctive aircraft indeed.

It looked like it might be time for a little reunion of Oxford University's aeronautical engineering class of 1938.

'Are those really MU9s?' Chastity asked over the flight channel. 'We're barely catching up to them.'

'They look like MU9s, Six,' Gwen said, 'but I agree - they're a lot faster than they should be.'

'Maybe it's the shiny red paint.' Drake chipped in.

'Maybe it's Reitsch's boot up their behind.' Kitty suggested, lifting her aircraft up slightly to look at him over the top of Excalibur's tail.

'Maybe they've eaten too much sauerkraut.' Drake returned, sniggering.

'I think we'd be able to smell that from here.' Kitty said.

'Maybe!'

'Or *maybe*,' Gwen interrupted dryly, 'they're just modified MU9s, like our Spits were modified.'

Drake tutted and rolled his eyes at her. 'I think our suggestions were more plausible, Five.'

'Yes, don't be such a spoilsport!' Kitty said.

Gwen blew a raspberry and the other Misfits laughed, but the joking around hadn't done much to ease the tension; Reitsch had killed one of their friends and put another in the hospital, they knew how good she was and how likely it was that they wouldn't all survive the coming flight. This new development of the improved MU9s certainly didn't help either.

Even though she was wisecracking with the others, Kitty was feeling anything but relaxed. It wasn't herself that she was concerned for, though, because she was fairly sure she'd be able to win a one on one fight against her opponent, even if they did have a shiny new MU9. No, it was Gwen.

She let her aircraft drift slightly forward so that she was almost level with Excalibur and glanced across, but Gwen didn't turn her head. She had her eyes fixed forward, on Reitsch, and she had that look on her face, the frowning half-grimace with her mouth twisted to the side that meant she was really worried.

There was something that Gwen hadn't told them about the Prussian woman, she could tell. Something beyond the fact that the woman had tried to steal her soon to be husband in university, something a lot more deadly.

Gwen had told Abby she could handle Reitsch, but she wasn't too sure. Yes, she'd flown with her many times when they'd been at university together and yes, she knew her well and had been able to describe the tactics that the woman had used back then, but she hadn't told them everything.

She and Reitsch had both joined the Oxford University Flying Club in Fresher's week when they'd first come up to Oxford and it quickly became apparent that they were among the better pilots, if not the best.

The club brought in RAC instructors who not only taught new students to fly, but also helped those pilots who already had their pilot's degree to hone their skills and one of the classes they offered to the more advanced students was in dogfighting. The classes were largely technical and they spent a lot of the time on the ground, learning the basics of what manoeuvres were used for what and in what kind of situation, but every so often they went up in aerobatic capable machines to practise what they'd learnt. These mock dogfights weren't supposed to be competitive, because it was deemed too dangerous for student pilots to take them too seriously, but that didn't stop the majority of pilots from being very competitive indeed.

The pilots were supposed to pair up with a different person each time so as to get used to different styles, but after only a couple of months nobody wanted to fly with Reitsch because, just as quickly as she had shown herself to be one of the best pilots, she had managed to turn everyone against her; she didn't lose very often, but she was a sore loser when she did and an even worse winner, rubbing her superiority in everyone's faces instead of helping them to improve like Gwen did. As one of the most junior members of the club, Gwen would often get stuck with her and they fought dozens, perhaps hundreds of times in the three years it had taken Gwen to get her aeronautical engineering degree, so she got to know her very well.

She had, of course, told all of that to the rest of the squadron. What she didn't tell them was that Reitsch had won about half of those battles.

Gwen had assured her that she could handle Reitsch, so Abby put her and the rest of B flight out of her mind and concentrated on her own target - Gruber.

What remained of the Prussian army and navy were broken and either running away as fast as they could or surrendering, but the Fliegertruppe were still a real threat. As long as they continued to put bombers into the sky no man, woman or child in the Kingdom of Great Britain would be safe. If the figures published in the nightly RAC reports were anything to go on, about half of the Fliegertruppe's total bomber fleet had been destroyed since the current offensive had started, but they still kept coming, so knocking a few dozen more out of the sky wouldn't stop them, however, destroying their morale might. And the best way she could think of to do that would be to wipe the Barons from the face of the earth once and for all. It would also be extremely satisfying, personally, but that was only a secondary consideration. At least, that was what she told herself as she bore down on Hölle.

Gruber and his flight had turned towards A flight and accelerated, setting themselves up for a head-on pass. It was extremely risky, but, as it essentially put the odds of success or failure at around fifty percent, it was probably their best hope for making a kill or two; judging by recent form, their pilots most likely wouldn't be good enough to stand up to the Misfits one on one, or two on two. Unfortunately for them, the Misfits knew quite a few tricks that would shift the odds in their favour when going up against such a tactic.

The four Misfits broke formation in the instant before the Barons got into range, each of them spinning, diving or banking in a different direction, splitting apart and ruining the aim of the incoming aircraft. The sudden and extreme manoeuvres did nothing to put off their own aim, though, and three of the four Barons spun away, ripped apart by the cannons of the Misfits. The fourth, Gruber, survived, but only because he had carried out his own manoeuvre at the same time - diving down beneath the line of fire. He didn't attempt to bring his guns back in line and shoot, though, he just continued diving, picking up speed and racing towards the French coast.

'Oh, Hans...' Abby said, sighing, as she performed a spilt S turn that put her firmly on his tail. She was disappointed, but not really surprised; he had been avoiding a proper dogfight with any of the Misfits for a long time. Ever since he'd realised that his aircraft was no longer superior to theirs.

Dragon was marginally faster than Hölle, so Abby was closing in on Gruber's tail and would be close enough to open fire in seconds. If he didn't want her to get a clear shot at him he would have to turn soon, otherwise there would be no escaping. She could see his wide, panicked eyes in the mirror above his cockpit, flicking back and forth from her to the slither of land ahead, could imagine what he was thinking. She knew the inescapable conclusion he would have to come to - that he wouldn't make it to France before she caught him - but would his fear overcome his sense? Or would he gather enough courage to fight?

The eyes in the mirror narrowed slightly and Abby smiled as an instant later Hölle pulled up, turning hard at it did so.

It seemed like she wasn't going to have to shoot him in the back after all.

He completed the turn towards her, but she had already guided Dragon to the side of him, denying him a head-on pass and instead initiating a turning battle. They put their aircraft on their sides and began describing a huge circle in the air, only yards above the sea. Gruber had the advantage initially because of how she had refused the head-on pass, but it very quickly became obvious that Dragon was the tighter turner of the two aircraft and she slowly began to claw her way around the circle towards him.

'Come on, show me something.' Abby muttered.

Gruber had killed her sister in France and countless other pilots since and she wanted nothing more than to kill him. However, she didn't want it to be too easy, didn't want it to be just an execution; She wanted the hatred she'd felt for him over the past year to have meant something, for him to be the worthy adversary that she had once considered him.

The glass canopy of the Baron's MU9 shattered and it lost an entire wing and spun away towards the sea, but Ellie didn't watch it go; she was already pulling hard towards the nearest group of fighters. She no longer needed to look to know that Tanya was back on her wing and watching out for enemies, so she was free to concentrate on assessing the melee ahead. Nearby, a flight of Harridans had gotten into a brawl with what looked like an entire squadron of HH190s, with a couple of MU10s mixed up with them, the bigger, less manoeuvrable fighters racing in and out of the ball of smaller aircraft. The wreckage of one Harridan was in the sea below them, along with three HH190s, which was a damn impressive tally, but it didn't look like they were going to last much longer; their flying had a desperate quality to it and they were no longer firing back, just doing whatever they could to survive. Indeed, even as she watched, one of the Harridans got clipped in the wing. It was only a glancing blow, not nearly enough to take it out of the fight, but the impact did cause it to slacken its turn momentarily and that was enough for one of the 190s to pounce and the Harridan broke into pieces and scattered into the sea. Ellie made sure that HH190 was the first she blew from the sky as she and Tanya blasted through the middle of the group.

Ellie had flown from Hawkinge in the pitch dark, constantly on edge because she had no idea how she was going to land and also because she was flying by dead reckoning, which had never been one of her strong points. In the end Hyde control had found her on radar, guided her in, and she had been able to land easily enough with the few dozen torches they'd set up, pointing at the ground so as not to provide a beacon for any enemy bombers that might have been in the area to navigate by. It had been pushing four when she'd gotten to her room in The Dorchester and she'd collapsed straight onto the bed without changing out of her flightsuit. She'd been unable to sleep, though, and had already been awake and moving around when the phone had rung with her wakeup call.

She'd been exhausted when she'd taken off and more than a little worried about Rob, but as soon as they'd come within range of the fight over the beach her tiredness had just disappeared, her focus narrowing to the ball of sky around her. And as for Rob, well, she figured that the best way she could keep him, all her friends, the people and her country safe would be to kill Prussians. To knock as many of them out of the sky as she could.

So that was what she did.

The three other Barons in Reitsch's flight had broken off and scattered across the sky, but Reitsch herself continued to climb away.

Gwen pushed the throttle to emergency unwind and climbed as hard as she could, spending some of the advantage in tension she had to have over the Prussian woman not to catch up, but to decrease the difference in height between them.

The Lion pattern aircraft might not be good climbers, but Excalibur, with her over-sized airscrew, certainly was, far better than Reitsch's aircraft as well, apparently, and she was overhauling her so quickly that it would only be a matter of a minute or so before she did so completely. However, even as she had the thought, Reitsch's aircraft was banking around and diving directly at her.

Gwen pushed Excalibur's nose forwards so sharply that she felt herself lift slightly from her seat and put her into a shallow dive, aiming at a point well below Reitsch's aircraft, forcing the Prussian to choose between overshooting her or steepening her own dive to keep her in her sights. Both of those things were good for Gwen; Reitsch's aircraft had already shown itself to be highly manoeuvrable, the equal of the Lion pattern aircraft, which were the most manoeuvrable aircraft the Misfits had, however it didn't seem to perform as well at high speeds, which was where Excalibur excelled.

It appeared Reitsch didn't want to play Gwen's game, though, because she instantly pulled her nose up and resumed her climb, this time heading directly out across the channel towards France.

Gwen frowned; if Reitsch had wanted to escape she could have easily just carried out the attack then continued to dive and raced across the channel - with how fast Excalibur was going now it would have taken a while to turn around and she would have had too much of a lead to catch. Mystified, she resumed her climb and banked towards the black aircraft, willing to play the Prussian woman's game. At least for a while.

Prussian ships carpeted the sea in front of them in thick swathes, but none of them seemed to care about what was happening in the air over them, they were all far too occupied with steaming as fast as they could for the ports in Belgium and northern France. Behind them the coast of Britain was almost completely obscured by black smoke, the flash of artillery fire and explosions continuing unabated as the British forces made the Prussian retreat as costly as they could.

The sight of the coastline receding behind her sparked a realisation and she glanced at her spring tension indicator and huffed.

'*That's* what she'd doing.'

Reitsch wasn't running away, she was levelling the playing field. The Prussian already needed to take into account how much spring tension she had left and how much she would need to get home and she was making it so that Gwen had to as well.

The Prussian kept flying out over the water and Gwen kept climbing behind her. She reached the same height as Reitsch when they were about half way between the two land masses and Gwen wasn't taken by surprise when the woman chose that moment to turn back toward her, but had already pushing her nose down to pick up speed.

Alright, then, Gwen thought, *let's see if you've learnt anything new in the last few years.*

He's good, Drake thought as his shots went wide again. *Damn good.*

When Reitsch's flight had turned towards them they had split up and gone in different directions, clearly challenging the Misfits to solo combat. The Misfits had readily accepted and each of them had chased after one of the enhanced MU9s, confident that they would be superior in a fair fight. Drake didn't know how any of the others were faring, but he had found himself with a bit of a struggle on his hands.

Lion was a better aircraft than the MU9 in most regards, faster and with a better turn rate, but the Prussian pilot appeared to know that and wasn't falling into any of the usual traps, instead he was putting the MU9s better roll rate to good use. Drake had been able to snatch a few potshots, but they had all been at high deflection and the enemy had turned or spun at the last moment every time, as if he'd known what he'd been about to do. It felt that the Prussian was baiting him into wasting his ammunition, in fact, toying with him, even. Although, why he would be doing that, Drake didn't know.

As the fight progressed, Drake could feel himself tiring. It had been a very long week, with long hours, and fatigue was becoming a real problem for all of them. Sweat covered him and was pouring down his face from under his helmet, threatening to get in his eyes and become a real problem. He flicked the switch on the heater, but fumbled with the dial and put it on hot instead of cold. A quick glance, taking less than half a second, was enough for him to correct his error, but when he lifted his eyes back up his opponent was no longer where he was expecting him to be and it took him another half a second to find him, off to the side. It was only one second, but one second is a long time in a dogfight and, even as Drake reacted and spun Lion onto her wing, the Prussian had completed his manoeuvre and was firing.

Two heavy cannon rounds impacted on Lion, shaking her roughly. Drake couldn't see where they had hit, but it became very obvious when the aircraft instantly lost power - the spring had been hit. It didn't break apart and rip through him and his aircraft, thanks to Rentley-Joyce's recently implemented solution to the deadly problem, but it wasn't working. Neither could he switch to the auxiliary spring, apparently, as the lever between his legs refused to move.

The sudden deceleration took both Drake and his opponent by surprise, but, while the only thing that happened to Drake was that he was thrown gently forward into his straps, it caused his opponent to miss the rest of his attack and overshoot.

Drake had a decision to make and only seconds to make it before the Prussian swung around for another run, so he pointed Lion towards Britain, dropped her nose to conserve speed and assessed his options. The coast of Britain was too far away for him to glide all the way back to land and the enemy fighter would never allow him to do that anyway, so he had only two choices - ditch in the water or jump and trust to Liz's wonderful new wings. Prussian ships filled the sea below him and he didn't exactly want to ditch and have one of them pick him up, so there was only one thing for it.

He opened the canopy, pointed Lion at one of the biggest remaining Prussian ships, then undid his straps and climbed up onto the seat.

'Bye, old girl,' he said, patting the side of the aircraft. 'Thanks for everything.'

He put his hand on the glidewing lever, then dived for the trailing edge of the wing.

No, no, no! This can't be happening! Gruber thought, staring up through his canopy at the yellow aircraft that had haunted him for more than a year.

It wasn't fair! He shouldn't even be in this situation! If that Reitsch bitch hadn't poisoned the Kaiser to him he would have been in Berlin still, celebrating his barony, or touring the estates that came with it, or being paid homage to by high society. Instead he was stuck here, with a scar on his face, flying with incompetents and without the resources he needed to wipe the damned Misfits off the map once and for all.

It was all that bitch's fault. She wanted his squadron? Well, she could have it. He'd decided - when he got back he'd resign his commission, or no, better, he'd convince the Kaiser that he'd do more good for the empire making films. The scar wouldn't matter, it would be a sign of the sacrifices he'd made for his country - he could make it work. Yes! That's what he would do. He'd let Reitsch have the squadron, he was done with it, and he'd go back to doing what he was truly good at. Maybe he would even get the Kaiser to let him go back to Hollywoodland - it would be good for the empire for the Americans to see him back in the flyvies. He could work on making them allies, get them to fully support the empire, not just do it in the shadows.

Yes, that's what he would do. He was done with all of this.

First, though, he had to get away from this woman. As he flung his aircraft around the sky, using every little trick he'd learnt during all those years of flying for the cameras as a stunt flyer, then as a lead actor, he looked around the sky, searching.

Why wasn't anyone coming to help him?

Didn't they know who he was?

Gwen and Reitsch banked and spun and dived around in their own little piece of the sky, just as they had so many times at university.

At university, the first to gain an advantage had invariably been the one to win; their aircraft had been identical and, more importantly, neither of them had been experienced enough to overcome a disadvantage. That was no longer the case, and the initiative passed back and forth between them as each used the differing capabilities of their aircraft as best they could. The stakes had changed drastically as well and were now considerably higher than the pennies that the flying club members had wagered on the outcomes of such, supposedly friendly, contests.

The fight went on, neither of them gaining a clear opportunity to do more than snatch a passing shot at the other, until eventually they found themselves circling, looking up through their canopies at each other across the hazy, smoke-filled sky.

They remained like that for long seconds, going too fast for Reitsch's aircraft to gain on Gwen's, too slow for Gwen's to gain on Reitsch's. It would be easy enough for either of them to break the fragile stalemate, but for some reason neither of them did, they just stared at each other, taking in the changes that the war had scrawled on each other's faces, even after such a short time. Gwen was sure that the pain and loss she had felt over the last couple of years was plain to see on her face, just as the encroaching madness was clear on Reitsch's.

Gwen loosened her fingers on the stick, easing the cramp caused by the tension, and took a deep breath, preparing to resume the battle, but before she could do anything Reitsch grinned. She lifted her hand and waved, wiggling her fingers, then inverted her aircraft and dived away towards the French coast.

Gwen inverted her own machine instinctively, but stopped before she actually followed the woman - she could dive after her and certainly catch up, but, even if she killed her opponent in a single pass, she had used so much spring tension in their fight that she would never make it home again.

With a frustrated growl she turned Excalibur towards Britain. She was going to have to settle for strafing a few Prussian ships on the way home.

Gruber was as good as he'd ever been, but that was the problem - while everyone else had improved, learning new techniques and gaining experience, he flew exactly the same way he always had. There was nothing new to his flying, no surprises or innovation in his tactics - she had seen it all from him before, analysed it to death with the other Misfits and she countered it easily.

Abby had long wondered what had happened to Gruber. He had been a wonderful pilot and had rightfully earned a place amongst the greats of the Hollywoodland flyvies, even though his status as a heartthrob was highly debatable, at least in her opinion. He had pioneered some of the most technically difficult and dangerous stunts and opening the eyes of millions to the wonder of flight and inspiring many of them to take to the air themselves. However, when the war had started he had stopped working on his craft for some reason, resting on his laurels, as if his early successes had gone to his head. He'd seemingly fallen victim to his own nation's propaganda and come to believe in his superiority, as if it was something that was owed to him as his due rather than something that he needed to keep reaffirming through actions. If he'd kept up with his training, kept pushing himself, she had no doubt he would have been able to make up for any shortfall in his aircraft's capabilities and given her a run for her money, if not beaten her, but he hadn't and those days were long gone. It was a shame, really; he could have been one of the greatest aviators of all time if first Hollywoodland, then the war hadn't made him into whatever it was he'd become.

It was still hard to believe that it could be possible, that this ineptitude wasn't some kind of trick and he wasn't building up to spring something on her, but she was forced to accept that he was exactly as he seemed when he suddenly broke away and raced towards France.

Disappointed in so many ways, Abby slotted in behind him, placed Hölle in her sights and gently squeezed the trigger.

The aircraft hit the sea and cartwheeled as it was ripped apart, but Abby didn't see it happen; she was already turning back to Britain.

CHAPTER 20

'What are you doing in here?' Lang asked, coming to a halt just inside Gruber's quarters at the sight of Reitsch lounging in Gruber's armchair with a glass of Gruber's schnapps in one hand and Gruber's private correspondence in the other.

'Haven't you heard?' Reitsch answered, smiling as she took another sip of schnapps. 'The great Baron Gruber is dead. One of the ships found the wreckage of his aircraft a few miles from the coast half an hour ago.'

Lang waved her words away. 'Yes, yes, of course I heard. I mean why are you in this room? Why are you rifling through his papers?'

'It's such a shame,' Reitsch said, ignoring his questions and going back to reading.

'Is it? I thought you hated him.'

'I did,' she said, looking directly at him. 'And I wanted to be the one to kill him.'

He stared back at her for a moment, but then smiled widely. 'So did I.' The smile disappeared just as quickly as it had come and he scowled at her. 'But that doesn't explain why you're in here.'

Reitsch opened her arms wide. 'I'm here because this is my quarters. I lead the Crimson Barons now.'

Lang gaped at her. 'What? No, that's not possible!'

'I have already been in touch with the Kaiser and he has confirmed my position.'

'But... but...' Lang sputtered. 'I am von Richthofen's cousin, his rightful heir - the squadron is mine by right and the Kaiser promised it to *me*!'

'He promised it to you on the understanding that you reported back to him and did everything you could to make sure Gruber didn't do anything stupid.' Reitsch shrugged. 'You failed. On numerous occasions.'

'Of course I failed!' Lang spat, moving to the sideboard. 'The Kaiser gave him free rein to do whatever he wanted! Nobody could control him or tell him what to do after that!'

He uncorked the schnapps bottle, then began to pour into one of the cut crystal glasses with his left hand while his right slowly opened the drawer under the bottles.

'Looking for this?'

He turned to find Reitsch standing two paces behind him, the pistol that he'd been expecting to find in the drawer in her hand and pointed at his chest.

'No, I was...' His eyes widened at the cold look on his face and he took an involuntary step away. Bottles clinked as he was stopped by the sideboard and he put his hands up to plead with her. 'Please, I...!'

The gun went off, silencing him. The glass that had still been in his hand bounced on the floor, but didn't break, the impact cushioned by the thick carpet that had muffled the sound of her approach.

Reitsch downed the remains of the drink she was still holding in her left hand, then stepped over Lang's body to pour another at the sideboard. She tipped her head back and drained the glass, then sneered down at the corpse.

'Your services are no longer required.'

The decision was made to allow the Prussians to retreat in relative peace once they were out of range of the guns on the shores, rather than harass them. It would have been a risk to send bombers after them over the sea with Prussian fighters available to intercept them and an even bigger one to pursue them with the few ships the Royal Navy had available. It was far more important to deal with the threats that were still present on the shores, like the remains of the landed forces and the glidewing troops.

The Misfits flew two more sorties that day, supporting attacks on the glidewing troops dug in at various positions around the south-east. At four o'clock, they were stood down and they left Hyde airstrip through the door in the wall and crossed the street towards The Dorchester.

A group of a dozen or so extremely drunk RAC officers, most of whom they recognised as being from the squadrons that had been assigned to Hyde after their airfields were bombed out, were coming out of the hotel as they climbed up the steps and they were blocked briefly as the group chanted, shouting to the skies.

'We fought them on the beaches! We fought them on the landing grounds! We fought them in the fields and we kicked their bloody arses!'

The Misfits laughed and lingered a moment to join in as the group chanted again, adding their own twist to a quote from the speech the king had given at midday, but when the men and women staggered off they declined the inevitable invitations to join them in a pub crawl and instead went in and up to their rooms, intending to sleep for as long as they were allowed.

'That's the last of them, sir,' the aide said. 'All our ships are home.'

Schmidt nodded. 'Thank you. Compile the lists of losses and have them transmitted to central command, please.'

'Yes, sir.'

The aide saluted solemnly and Schmidt gave him a nod before turning and walking to his room behind the stage.

He wasn't surprised to find someone waiting for him. He *was* mildly surprised to find it was Melitta Reitsch and hope sparked briefly in his heart, but it was quickly quashed when he saw the gun on his desk. There was an official document underneath it, stamped with the Kaiser's personal crest, and he didn't have to read it to know what it would contain. It wasn't unexpected.

'I didn't think the Kaiser would send you as his assassin,' he said moving across the room to the sideboard. 'But I'm not surprised; I saw what you were as soon as you entered the meeting. Even before you opened your mouth.'

'You did, did you? And what exactly am I?'

He finished pouring a drink, then turned to face her. He deliberately didn't offer her one.

'I think you are self aware enough that you don't need me to tell you.' He separated a finger from his glass and pointed at the gun. 'What happens if I refuse to use that? Are you going to do it yourself?'

Reitsch shook her head. 'I've done enough killing for today. There's a firing squad organised for,' she paused to check her chronograph, an extremely expensive Swiss-made one, he noted, 'just over an hour from now.' She smiled. 'Besides, doing it myself wouldn't be nearly public enough and wouldn't make the same kind of statement.'

He took a sip of his drink, then stared at her coldly. 'Get out.'

She nodded and sashayed towards the door, the smile still firmly in place.

'Make sure you never lose your usefulness,' he said, 'or your looks.'

He smiled at the slight hitch in her step, but she didn't answer and just left, closing the door firmly behind her.

He turned back to the sideboard and poured more of his schnapps into the glass, filling it almost to the brim.

He had an hour to do what he'd known he would have to do, one way or another, when he'd ordered the retreat. That was plenty of time to finish the bottle - he wouldn't leave something as good as that to the philistines working for him - while he wrote letters to his family.

Once they realised that there was nowhere to go and no help coming, the men that had been abandoned on the beaches surrendered. A few stubborn groups of glidewing troopers held out for a couple of hours, surrounded by the British army and strafed constantly by the RAC, but even they eventually realised that the situation was hopeless, that their successes on British soil were meaningless and that the foolproof plan that they had been sent to carry out had failed.

Silence fell across the south of England, the echoes of gunfire finally fading away.

The entirety of Britain celebrated that night and, for once, there were no Prussian bombing raids to interrupt them.

EPILOGUE

The king announced a three-day holiday to celebrate the "Victory in the Channel" as it was bring dubbed. Flags and bunting were hung in the streets and, even though rationing was now in full effect because of dwindling food supplies, enough was found to feed whole communities as they came together around long tables set up in every town, village and city. Everyone was well aware that the fight wasn't yet won, that the war wasn't finished and that Europe was still in the hands of an oppressor, but for just a moment they were able to revel in their first real and meaningful victory.

The remains of Prussian tanks and aircraft were sent by ship and train to the far reaches of the kingdom and put on display in town squares and museums for all to see, symbols of the fight that had been won by the combined efforts of all three branches of the British armed forces, but which would have been lost if it hadn't been for the efforts of the country as a whole over the past couple of years.

The Misfits were also given three days of leave and they went their separate ways. Penny went back to Bagshot, Chastity disappeared to a bed and breakfast just outside London with Freddy Featherstonehaugh and Drake and Tanya went to the Drake estate, but Abby remained in London with Dot Campbell, who was busy helping compile the hundreds of different reports on engagements with the enemy, building up a picture of what had and hadn't worked. In the evenings they went to visit Derek, who was still reluctant to see anyone, but in the end was persuaded by a couple of bottles of wine, and they slowly began the task of bringing him out of his depression.

Kitty and Gwen flew to Plymouth to meet a ship coming from Gibraltar. The ship was one of several small and fast vessels that made the run from Britain to Gibraltar, taking supplies to the besieged outpost. Usually it came back empty, or as good as empty, but this time it had brought a single passenger, Eulalia Balsells Carles, and her rather unique luggage - an aircraft that had been dismantled and packed up in crates. They in turn had brought her something - a letter from Abby offering her a place in the Misfits and a document from the king, granting her a commission as an Aerial Officer in the Royal Aviator Corps. Eulalia accepted both in a heartbeat and the three of them went to the local pub to celebrate and catch up while her aircraft, Llibertat, was unloaded and taken to the nearest RAC base for reassembling.

Ellie had planned on going down to Hawkinge to be with Rob, but he turned up the morning after the decisive battle, looking pale and weak, but moving under his own steam. The airfield had indeed come under attack by the glidewing troopers and had been taken by them, but after clearing the medical centre of combatants, they had left it alone and the doctors had been able to keep working. His injuries hadn't been too serious in the end and once the bleeding had been stopped and he'd been topped off with blood the doctors had said that all he needed to make a complete recovery was a few days of rest and had sent him off to London in an ambulance. Ellie put him to bed in his room, waited for him to fall asleep, then went to make a few calls.

When Rob woke up at midday they had lunch, but then Ellie had him pack his things and they went to the Misfits' hangar where one of Lord Henry's aircraft, a little two-seater, had been brought out of mothballs for them - with Lord Henry's permission of course.

Ellie flew them to the airfield near Rob's village and they spent the next couple of days with his family.

The news that their promotions to lieutenant had been confirmed reached them that evening and after a couple of days, when Rob had gotten his strength back, "not yet" became "now".

While the British celebrated, the Prussian people mourned. Not for the defeat on the beaches of Britain, because they had been told it had just been a preliminary probing of British defences and very few of them knew the true extent of the loss of lives and machinery, but for the loss of a national hero.

Berlin was absolutely silent, for perhaps the first time in its history, as the horse-drawn carriage made its way out of Tempelhof Airport. Hans Gruber had been lying in state there for the last two days, his coffin draped with the Prussian flag and stood over by his old aircraft, Flamme, brought from the Berlin state museum for the occasion. Thousands upon thousands of people had filed past the coffin in those days, none of them suspecting that it was filled with sand from the beaches of France, the body of Gruber having been lost, sunk into the depths of the British Channel. Now those people and thousands more stood silently by the side of the wide boulevard, watching as the carriage passed by, going to the magnificent recently-built cathedral where Gruber would be laid to rest. Flowers rained down on the coffin, spilling off of it onto the street to create a carpet that was far too bright and gay for the occasion and were crushed underfoot by the hundreds strong escort, led by the fifteen Barons and their new commander, Melitta Reitsch, who was fast becoming a favourite of the people.

The coffin was received at the cathedral by the Kaiser himself and was carried up the stone steps by eight of the Barons and into the darkness.

The funeral was a spectacle of devotion to country and a reaffirmation of Prussia's commitment to the war and the defeat of the British, who had dared to take Gruber's life. It was recorded by dozens of movie cameras from every angle and copies were sent around Prussia for the people who hadn't been able to make it to Berlin to see. More importantly, though, copies were also sent to the eastern and western fronts and, just as the Kaiser had said he would, Hans Gruber proved far more useful in death than he had been for quite some time in life by stoking the fires of vengeance in Prussia's valiant soldiers.

ABOUT THE AUTHOR

Simon Brading's interest in aviation began when he was very young and at thirteen he joined the RAF section of the Combined Cadet Forces of Dulwich College with the aim of becoming a pilot. However, when he was 18, had reached the rank of Flight Sergeant in the CCF and was trying to get into a University Air Squadron, he was told that his eyesight wasn't good enough to be a pilot, so he had to move onto plan B... something else.

He tried his hand at many things before it occurred to him that he might have a few stories to tell. He never lost his interest in flight, though, and hopes to add a PPL to his very basic and probably extremely expired glider license.

www.simonbrading.co.uk

For news of special offers, upcoming releases, exclusive content, competitions and events, please follow me on social media.

Instagram - @sibrading
Facebook - Simon Brading Author
Tiktok - @SimonBradingAuthor

In addition, souvenirs and merchandise, including T-shirts, badges, stickers and more, are available from the Misfit Squadron store on REDBUBBLE at -
https://www.redbubble.com/people/misfitsquadron/shop

ALSO BY SIMON BRADING

The "Displacers" series - a young adult time travel adventure series for all ages.
The Pirate's Heir
The Secret of the Ancients
The Whitechapel Plot
The Price of Greed
The Time for Vengeance

The "Misfit Squadron" Series - a Steampunk series set in an alternate World War 2.
The Battle Over Britain
The Russian Resistance
A Misfit Midwinter
The Lion and the Baron
The Maltese Defence
Tales from the Second Great War
The Siege of Gibraltar
The King's Mission
The Home Front
Taking to the Skies
The Invasion of Britain

The "Twin Ambitions" series - ballet books for children ages 7 and up.
Fight to Dance
Back to Basics

The "Ni Hon - The Two Books" Series - a young adult series set in a dystopian future Japan.
The Black Book

Others
Public Enemy
Empath
The Lifeboat at the End of the Universe